LIFE'S JOURNEY

A YOUNG ITALIAN PEASANT IN 1899 TRAVELS TO SOUTH PHILADELPHIA SEARCHING FOR A BETTER LIFE AND LOVE

JOSEPHINE B. PASQUARELLO

josephine b pasquarello @ gmail.com

DORRANCE
PUBLISHING CO
EST. 1920
PITTSBURGH, PENNSYLVANIA 15238

Dorrance Publishing Co
585 Alpha Drive
Pittsburgh, PA 15238
Visit our website at *www.dorrancebookstore.com*

ISBN: 978-1-6386-7265-4
eISBN: 978-1-6386-7616-4

To my Nonna, Geltrude Carmela DiLullo Pasquariello,
a strong determined woman who led the way.

AND

To my husband, Robert Delaney,
for walking through this journey with me.

TABLE OF CONTENTS

PROLOGUE

June 1, 1894

Today is my thirteenth birthday. The weather is warm this evening. My sister Christina decided we should celebrate my special day by sleeping under the moon and stars.

Christina lays the blanket on the dirt and tells me to bring out two pillows for our heads. We haven't had rain in three weeks, and the dirt is dry and extremely hard. When we lay down and I look up at the stars, my mind starts to wander. I turn to look at my older sister to ask her something that's been on my mind for some time now; but, I have been too nervous about telling anyone."

"Christina, I want you to answer me truthfully because I have a question and want your true feelings about this thought." I look at her and ask, "Do you think I am a selfish sister or daughter?"

She immediately shakes her head no. She smiles and says, "Geltrude, you have a heart of gold. What would make you feel this way about yourself?"

I take a deep breath to muster up the courage and say, "Well, Christina, to be honest with you I don't want to live here in the hills of Ateleta for the rest of my life. I don't want to work the farm with my hands always dirty. No matter how many times I clean under my fingernails, there is always dirt under them. This is our parents dream to have a farm; it's not mine."

"Well, Geltrude, what is your dream?" I can tell by her voice that Christina is surprised but not shocked. "If you aren't here with your family then where will you go?"

I realize I'm holding my breath, waiting for her reply. Her reaction gives me courage to continue.

"Please Christina, don't think of me as being foolish if I tell you my thoughts." But before she can respond, I hear myself saying out loud. "I want to be a girl who lives in a large city like Naples." I close my eyes and smile; it feels good to share my dream. "This to me would be an exciting life. To be around many people. To see people dressed in beautiful and exquisite clothes. There has to be more to life than living here in this small village."

I open my eyes and glance at Christina.

"I know my sweet sister that you have found love and happiness here with Giovanni."

Christina blushes and glances at me; I can see in her eyes that she is also ready to share her dream. Smiling at me, she says, "I will be with Giovanni wherever he is." Suddenly her eyes widen, and she says, "Maybe if you found someone here, you would stay with our family."

I look at Christina with confusion because she doesn't understand that I don't want to find love here. I look her in the eyes and say, "Christina I want to leave here as soon as I am old enough. Even if our parents get mad at me, I will leave here one day to find my love and happiness elsewhere!"

CHAPTER 1

My name is Geltrude Carmela DiLullo. It is 1899, and I live in a village in the hills called Ateleta, Italia. It is July, and I can feel the sweat dripping from my head to the pillow. I lay here numb, staring at the moon through my open shutters. The sweet smell of fresh hay mixed with a faint touch of mint surrounds me. These scents always put me to sleep, but not tonight. I can hear our chickens beginning to stir, and I know it won't be long before I can hear our sheep reminding us it is time to break our fast. I will miss these sounds so much!

My parents are sending me to America to marry someone I have never met. Somewhere they call "Philadelphia." I don't want to go! I have to marry someone that I don't love. Since I was a little girl, I always thought I would fall in love and have children and live happily ever after! It's just a dream now that I will never be able to live because I must do what my parents tell me to do.

I've never had a boyfriend. What do I do with a husband that I don't even know? The questions in my head are: *Is he handsome? Will he be nice to me? Will he be kind to me?* And most of all, will we both love and respect each other? I hope and pray he will like me!

How can they do this to me? They should send my older sister Christina to America. I should stay here with my parents; I still need them!

I hear Mother's footsteps across the tile floor. She is standing at the doorway to see if Christina and I are sleeping. I pretend to be asleep because I don't want to tell them how I feel. I think if I tell them how angry I am at them for doing this to me, I will go mad.

I'm so angry at Mother, Father, and Christina. I may never forgive the people I love the most in this world for throwing me away. I know what my solution should be: run away to Naples. They will never find me there. Naples is BIG, and there are so many people. I was there once with Father when I was about 10 years old. It was so exciting to see all the people and big, beautiful buildings. When I went home the next day and told Christina about Naples, we were laughing and so happy that there is a place that's so beautiful. Christina told me we must promise that when we get older, we will go there to live. We would go to the fancy restaurants and pretend to be rich. We hugged and kissed each other, and we promised that's where we would live, and nothing could separate us.

Now I cry because that will never be. I will never have the life I want to live. Yes, I will make a new plan fast because in August, they will put me on the ship to sail away forever! Now maybe I can get some sleep and dream about my escape from this nightmare! Let me pray to the Blessed Mother for guidance, and she will help me to get some rest. Goodnight for now!

CHAPTER 2

I wake up early in the morning. I had so many wild dreams last night. I am so confused about how I should accept my fate. I can't run away. I could never live my life knowing my family and I are separated forever at my doing. And that's what would happen if I ran away to Naples.

If I could only put my immaturity aside and do for the family what I must do, for the good of all of us. That way, I know in my heart my family and my thoughts will always be of love for my family. We will always be in each other's dreams and hearts. That's what I want for us: to not allow anything or anyone to separate our love for each other. I will go into my parents' room and wake them, tell them it's time we spoke from our hearts about my going to America. I have gotten some sleep and rest; maybe now I can be rational. Leaving my family and the life I know and cherish will definitely be heartbreaking for all of us, not just me! I have to stop thinking of only myself. My mind has settled down, but my heart hurts so badly. It's the only organ I can feel in my body because it feels so heavy.

Yes, I have made my decision that I will go to America and marry Raffaele Pasquariello. He is six years older than me and from Potenza, Italia. He has lived in America for 11 years. His entire family went to America in 1888. Raffaele and his parents and two brothers all live in South Philadelphia together. Not one of the three brothers are married. Raffaele will be the first to marry, and he is the oldest. I wonder if his two brothers will marry girls from Italia? That way, I won't be the only arranged marriage. They have a house with running water, a bathroom with a toilet in the house. Father told me they have a dining room that is large enough for 12 people to sit at the table to eat. I guess they are rich, because they told Father Ricci, our priest, they will take good care of me forever. Oh! How long is forever?

What is forever anyway? Shaking my head, I quietly laugh at myself; at least my parents will not have to worry about me since Mr. and Mrs. Pasquariello will watch over me. We will all live together. I don't know about that... Do I want to live with Raffaele's two brothers? I better start to straighten my thoughts in my head. I need to talk with my parents and Christina about how I feel. I can't carry all of this myself. If I don't get all of my questions answered, I will get all scrambled inside my head and my brain will start to hurt. My heart is hurting enough; I don't need my brain to explode on me as well.

I tell Christina to wake up and follow me to our parents' room. She gets out of bed and walks behind me—still asleep, but walking. I knock on our parents' bedroom door, and I hear myself saying, "I need to talk with you!"

My father yells back to me, "Is that you, Geltrude? Come in, we would like to see and talk with you, too."

My father always makes life more pleasurable for me by always forgiving me and my bad behaviors, never being upset with me. I open the door and walk in.

CHAPTER 3

I run into Father's arms. We both are crying. He is holding me so close to him and kissing my face. Before I can say anything to my parents, he looks into my sad watery eyes and says, "Geltrude, do you believe your family, especially me, would send you to America and not have our hearts broken? Ever since you were a baby and so sick with your lungs, you were my baby angel! I have always held you close to my heart because I didn't think you would ever live through your first winter, with the cold and snow here in the hills. At night, so you could sleep, I would hold you to my chest to keep you warm. For three months I did that every night so you could sleep and become strong. Sometimes your sister Christina would want me to lay you on her chest."

Now Mother has her arms around my waist. She is pulling me towards her. I am laughing at them because it's always been a tug-of-war between my parents. We have always had this between the three of us. Father lets me go, and Mother is crying and whispering in my ear, "We will never forget you...ever! There isn't anything that could take you from our hearts. We believe you will never have the life we wished for you in Ateleta. But you go to America and you will find much happiness in your new life. Go there with an open heart for happiness, and you will find and receive love."

Christina walks into the room and sits next to me on our parents' bed. She puts her arms around me and lays her head on my shoulder. We don't say a word, just the two of us frozen in time. This is the memory of her that I will carry with me for the rest of my life. Christina has taught me everything I know. She has a good heart.

There isn't anything Christina wouldn't do for me. She is everything to me. No one could ever take away our love for one another. No one could ever break our sisterhood, our bond, because it's always been the two of us.

All of a sudden, there is a funny thought racing through my head. I push Christina away from me, laughing. She looks at me with a frown. Her eyebrows are almost crossed across her forehead. I jump up from the bed, and the three of them are staring at me as if I have lost my mind. Father reaches out towards me. I turn to run out of the room and then quickly turn towards them with a big mischievous smile on my face—a look that all three of them should recognize because that is my nature; to always enjoy the situation with laughter. I shout as loud as I can, "Christina, if you love me so much, then you should marry Raffaele Pasquariello. Besides, you're closer to his age than I am. I want to marry someone young, like me. Someone 18 years old, not 24! He's too old for me!"

I run through the house to the back door and out to the chicken coop to collect some eggs for breakfast.

I don't know why I am lighthearted this morning. I don't want this feeling to leave me. Until the day I get on that ship to sail across the ocean, I will stay cheerful. Not only for me but for all of us.

Christina comes rushing into the chicken coop to help me collect the eggs. We put the eggs in a basket, and she throws an egg at my face. That's usually something I would have done to her, but this morning, she got me. It's so nice to be laughing again at our silliness. The egg is running down my forehead into my eyes. I can't see anything! We both are laughing at what she did to me.

This sweet happiness is what I will miss. So, until the day I leave, I will fill my memory box with many beautiful memories of the three most important people in the world: Father, Mother, and Christina.

CHAPTER 4

I can only tell Christina how I feel. She's the only one who really understands me. Even though she's one year older and she thinks she's the boss of me, I can always count on her to listen to my every word. When I cry, she cries, and when I hurt, she hurts with me. How am I supposed to live without her by my side?

Now, I pretend that I am no longer worried about sailing to America. Everyone in my village wants to know how I feel about leaving here. I just talk and smile at everyone like I won't be on a ship sailing to America tomorrow without my loved ones. I leave tomorrow for Naples. Father has one of the men from our village taking us by horse and cart. It will take all day and night to get there.

Tomorrow morning, I must say goodbye to Mother and Christina. I keep telling myself to look at their faces and not to forget how they look. I will look at Mother's face and remember her big brown almond-shaped eyes. You can see her beauty straight through them. You can see her gentle soul. Mother has always been gentle to me. She has held me many times and would rock me back and forth in her arms to comfort me. Now, who will comfort me when I am in need? Who will hold me and tell me, "Tomorrow you will be better than today"? I will need to hear those words again and again throughout my life.

When Christina and I go to sleep tonight, this will be the last time I will ever sleep with her. I don't remember ever not sleeping with her. Sometimes, when one of us would be sad, we would hold hands and sleep through the night. Like when one of our sheep gave birth to a stillborn lamb. Tonight, will be our last night to hold each other, because in the morning my parents will have to pry us apart. I am already crying for Christina. I don't want to live without her. I am going to try my hardest to pretend that this doesn't hurt my heart. So, in the morning I will try not to shed one tear and smile the entire time. Even when I say goodbye to my chickens.

Oh, who am I kidding? I am going to fall apart when I leave this house. I want to look at everything in my house. I must study every inch of every room. How the house smells from Mother's cooking. I have to remember my favorite smell of chicken cooking in her stone oven. Mother would always surround the chicken with potatoes, butter, and fresh rosemary. When I would help her cook, my hands would smell of rosemary all night. I want to remember where I lived and where I came from.

Christina walks into our bedroom. She laughs at me because of the way I am folding the two dresses Mother made me for the voyage. One for traveling and one for the day I get to America. It's very fancy and made from purple silk that Father bought when he last went down to Naples. Christina takes the dresses from my hands and pushes me aside.

"Let me do this right, or your dresses will be all wrinkled when you need them."

"Christina, will you also pack my small brown leather suitcase for me?" I ask.

She pushes me out of the way again and pulls everything out of the suitcase, saying jokingly, "You must fold everything neatly because you don't want your clothes to look sloppy. They will look like rags on you. You must look clean and neat. You're going to be an American! You know those Americans are fancy people. They are not like us. We are poor people, just farmers. We don't have a lot of money, clothes, or big houses. But what we do have here in Italia is love for our families. Like no one else in this big world. So, when you are around some of those fancy people, and they are getting on your nerves, just smack them just like you do me. That's how you treat me when I am bothering you. I know you, Geltrude. You won't let them push you around. Just pretend you are 'Queen Geltrude,' just like you do here, and you will be fine."

Now, we are laughing, just having some fun together. I tell Christina, "You always make me laugh. Oh, I wish you could come to America with me."

She walks over to me and kisses my forehead.

"Come on, Geltrude, it's time for us to go to sleep, your bag is packed, and you have a very long day of traveling tomorrow, then at least 10 days on the ship."

We get into bed and under the covers. We both reach for each other's hand at the same time. We squeeze tight, holding our hands together. We have never held on as tight as we are tonight. I never ever want to forget this night or holding our sisterly hands together.

Our dreams tonight will only be good and happy ones. I hear Christina whispering into my ear, as our Mother always says, "Tomorrow you will be better than today! Goodnight, Geltrude."

"Goodnight, Christina."

As we say our prayers together like we always do, Christina says one more thing before she falls asleep.

"May God keep you safe in your travels! Amen."

CHAPTER 5

I hear Mother say to me, "Wake up, my little daughter. Today is a very busy day for you. You have to travel many miles to Naples. You and Christina come into the kitchen, and we will all sit and eat together just as any other day. Your father is waiting for you at the table. You must move quickly, Geltrude, we don't have much time."

Christina touches my foot with hers. She smiles at me and says, "Let's go eat. Then we will come back, and you will wash yourself and get into your beautiful dress. It's a pretty dress for you to wear on the ship. You have to wear those black leather shoes Father got for you in Naples. You will look sophisticated. Geltrude, you will be the prettiest girl on that ship with your dark brown, curly hair hanging to your waist. If you like, I will wrap your hair on top of your head, so you won't sweat a lot. When you smile, I can see how perfect and straight your teeth are. As Father would say about his animals when they are strong, 'what a good breed.' That's you, Geltrude. You are beautiful and strong; someone we are proud to have in our family. I should pray that Raffaele feels the same about your beauty as I do. When he sees you getting off that ship, his eyes will fall out of his head because you are so beautiful."

I can't stop laughing at Christina. In her eyes, no one is as pretty as me. Then I question how she can compare me to one of our farm animals.

"Should I walk down the gangplank on all fours for him?"

"Oh yes, Geltrude, you definitely would look classy doing that. Poor Raffaele! He better turn and run as fast as he can to get away from you. I hope you don't smell like one of those animals when you arrive to America." Christina pushes me and says, "Let's go and eat our breakfast with our parents. They are waiting for us. We don't have much time for you to get ready. You know how I like to wash your hair and brush the curls down your back. Today, I will do this for you one more time."

I walk over to Christina and put my arms around her waist. I pull her tight to me. We are standing face to face, just staring into each other's eyes. She puts her arms around my waist. Not a word is spoken.

Then Christina yells, "Ready!" We both charge into the kitchen.

We four sit and have a lovely meal together. Laughing, talking, and teasing one another. Mother made my favorite breakfast: fried eggs with eggplant. I could eat it every day. Christina thinks it's disgusting, though she still ate some of it today, in honor of me! They sure do love to keep me happy. They will do anything for me. That's what I will miss the most about my loving family.

After breakfast, Christina brings me outside to the back of the house. She pours the water on my head and starts to massage my head with the bar of soap.

"When you are finished washing yourself, call me in our room, and I will help you get into your dress." Christina paused before leaving and said, "You have such a tender heart, Geltrude, I pray Raffaele keeps it safe."

As I walk through the house, I am thinking this place will never be the same without me. I am the one who is full of life. When Christina comes in our room, I am sitting on our bed. She tells me my face is the color of a tomato.

"You can't get your shoes on your feet because you need socks. Put your socks on, and your feet will glide straight in." I give one of my smart-aleck faces, and we both laugh. I put my socks on, and my feet go right in. I bend over to tie my laces, then stand up to straighten my dress. "Geltrude, you look so beautiful, and much older than you are. When you get to Naples and you are standing on the dock preparing to board the ship, all heads will turn to look at your beauty. When Raffaele sees you for the first time, he will fall in love immediately. You both will have a great lifetime together. I know this because I pray to the Blessed Mother. I ask her for help to please make this a happy union between Raffaele and Geltrude, and to bless them with many children."

"No, Christina, why are you asking the Blessed Mother to give us any children? No, don't ask that for me. After watching our animals give birth, I don't want to go through that—at least not that many times! Two is plenty for me."

"But when you get married, I will pray that you have 10 children. That will make you happy."

I hear Father calling out to me, "Come on, Geltrude, it's time to go. The driver is here. Mr. Donatelli says we should start our journey now. Come say your goodbyes to your mother and Christina. Some of our family and neighbors are here to wish you well. They are outside waiting for you."

My stomach does a complete turnaround, and I think I may need to vomit. Christina sees my anxiety, and she grabs my arm. We walk out of our bedroom and over to Mother standing at the front door. She smiles at me and says, "Everything will be good! Remember, before you react to anything, think first. Maybe sleep on it for a night, then respond to your problem. I will always pray for your happiness. I love you. Goodbye, my sweet girl."

She slides beautiful purple glass rosary beads into my hands and kisses my forehead. Many people are here to wish me the best because they know they will never see me again. Some of them are crying. Christina walks over to me. That's when I can't control myself at all. We both are crying. She pulls me towards the horse and cart, so no one can hear us. She tells me that when our parents die, she will come to America, "Because you know our parents will never leave their farm."

The pain in my heart is unbearable, I hold on to the thought of Christina coming to America, to give me the strength to climb into the cart. I haven't lost her forever like I have my parents. I put the rosary beads into my dress pocket. I need them because I will say the rosary every night before I go to sleep. As a Roman Catholic, I always show my devotion to God through my prayers. Father lifts me into the cart and then he sits up front with Mr. Donatelli. I take one last look at my house and farmland, with all the trees and grass. How beautiful it all looks to me. I never realized just what beauty is here. I wonder if Philadelphia has a lot of trees and grass.

I hear Mr. Donatelli telling the horse to go and pulling on the reins. His horse is moving slowly because of all the weight we have on him. I look back one more time to say goodbye to Mother and Christina. They are waving to me and blowing kisses. I close my eyes to remember this moment in time and to keep it in my mind forever. When I open my eyes, we are now so far away that I no longer see my house. My stomach is hurting because this is really happening to me. There is no turning back now. I am on my way to America!

CHAPTER 6

I have been in this cart for hours now. I am restless, tired, thirsty, and hungry. My legs and back are hurting me. The sun is strong, and I am miserable. I feel empty inside and already lost without my sister Christina here by my side. I have to start to think good thoughts and let go of my heartache. If Christina was by my side, she would be upset with me. She would smile her big, beautiful smile and call me her baby sister. She would say to me, "Geltrude, let your thoughts and brain work for you. Stop thinking so many bad thoughts about how you feel sorry for yourself. Everything will work out, and you will be happy. Give yourself time. Besides, that's all you have now, time. Use this time to help you be happy wherever you are and whomever you are with. I will always be with you, no matter how far we are from one another. I am in your heart, and you will always be in mine. Now, go do what you are meant to do and be what you are meant to be in your life because it's what God wants you to do. We will see each other again! Our God would never keep us apart forever. Keep this in your heart because that's how I'm handling my loss of you for now. One day, we will be together. Kissing, laughing, and holding each other just like always. Really, Geltrude, who could love us the way we do but us?"

Father calls my name, pulling me out of my thoughts. He looks at me and asks, "Would you like to stop and get something to eat? We could rest for a short amount of time. You look worried. Are you okay back there?"

Before I can answer, Mr. Donatelli says that his horse needs some water and could use some rest.

"If we don't stop soon, my horse will fall to the dirt and never get up!"

We are all laughing because Mr. Donatelli is laughing at himself. He goes on to say that if his horse goes down, we will never get to Naples, and that won't be good. I think to myself, *That sounds good to me.* That would bring lots of joy to my heart. We then go over a couple of bumps in the road, and he pulls his horse and cart over to a big tree, stops, and the three of us start to get out. Before I can climb out, Father tells me to get the basket with the food Mother prepared for our travel. Mr. Donatelli unhitches his horse, who he named "Uno" because that's his one and only horse.

Mr. Donatelli is Father's childhood friend. He is a good man and would do anything for Father. He is married and has seven children. He lives in Ateleta and is also a farmer. I know all of his children, and they all work on the family farm. His farm is larger than ours, and he has a lot more animals than we do. He and his wife make cheese to sell to the people in our village. He is always working hard because he has so many children. His wife is pregnant with their eighth.

Father gets a blanket and the water jug for us. We are all weary and hungry, but first we walk around because our legs are so stiff, taking small steps because we can't feel them. Then, we sit and enjoy our meal. I open the food basket, and inside there is some provolone cheese, green grapes, a loaf of brown bread, and some lemons to squeeze into the water. Mother prepared a good meal for us. Mr. Donatelli eats his lunch quickly. Then, he walks Uno over to the pond, so he can drink some water. Uno's long tail is batting at the flies that won't leave him alone. They are all over his back. The horse is beautiful, with a golden-blonde mane covering his eyes. I don't know how he can see where he is going!

We had our lunch outside a small village called Colli a Volturna. It's about the same size as my village. I think all the villages in our hills kind of all look the same. They all have big gorgeous green trees and wildflowers growing all around the hills in so many brilliant colors. We are halfway to Presenzano, where we are staying for the night. Mr. Donatelli's brother lives there with his family. We are staying there for the night and leaving early in the morning. We have to get to Naples before 6:00 PM, because that's when my ship leaves the port. We can't be late; the ship will leave the port with or without me. After we eat lunch and rest for a while, we need to get back on the road because we still have a long way to go. We are back on the road and should make it to Presenzano in time for dinner, then up early and off to Naples. This journey is long and hard. We are traveling through the hills and we have seen much beauty here. Some of the villages have been here for hundreds of years. The people are happy and content with life here in the mountains. Each village is more breathtaking than the last. Each one has its own uniqueness. I wonder, *Will America look like Italia?* I lie down, hoping to take a nap. I cover my left eye, so I can stare at the sky. It's so blue with large, white clouds. The sun rays are so strong, I can't see. I feel myself relaxing and slowing my thoughts down. I feel myself falling asleep and hope I will dream of Italia and all its beauty.

We are hitting some bumps in the road and my stomach hurts. I call out to Mr. Donatelli to please find me a big tree. He laughs and pulls Uno over to the side of the road. He tells me "Geltrude, look, I found you a big tree." I stand up and there down the road is my tree. I jump out of the cart and down the road I go. As I am walking up the road to them, I hear Mr. Donatelli yelling to me. "You better move quickly, one of those grey wolves might get you, they could eat you alive."

We get back on the road again. Father is saying that we will be in Presenzano before dark.

"Try not to sleep again, because you won't sleep tonight. We have a long trip tomorrow, and you will need your rest. Our day will be hectic when we get to Naples."

We finally reach Presenzano before dark. It's larger and more beautiful than my Ateleta. There are more people here; it is busier and noisier. We finally reach Mr. Donatelli's brother's house. Everyone comes from the house outside to greet us. They have seven children, and each one is more beautiful than the other. Domenic and Marie Donatelli are so gracious towards Father and me. They do all they can to make us comfortable. Marie brings me in the house and takes me into one of the bedrooms. She tells me that she has a bowl of water and a towel for me to wash my face and hands and that's where I will sleep tonight.

"When you're finished, come out because we all will sit and have supper. Then off to sleep because you have to leave at daybreak."

We sit and have the feast that Marie cooked for us, but I am not hungry. What I am looking forward to is getting some sleep and rest. I feel nauseated from the sun and being in the cart all day long. I tell Marie thank you for the lovely meal, but I believe it's time for me to get some rest. To bed, I go as fast as I can. Before I know it, I hear Marie telling me it's time to wake up.

"Hurry, get dressed, and wash because Mr. Donatelli is getting the horse and cart ready."

I thank Marie again for being so kind to me. She hugs me, and I start to cry. She tells me everything is going to be fine, that I will have a safe journey to America, and she will keep me in her prayers. She kisses my cheek and tells me how brave she thinks I am to be doing this all by myself. I smile and kiss her cheek. She said she made us lunch and gave us fresh water for our long ride in the sun. Domenic and Marie stood outside and watched us go down the road, wishing us all safe travels.

Today, time goes quickly. Before I know it, we are in Naples. This city is so big with people all around. They are walking so fast; I get dizzy watching them. It's a lot busier than I thought it would be. My head keeps bouncing back and forth from watching the crowds. You should see how they are dressed. The ladies in beautiful dresses, big colorful hats, and black leather ankle shoes. The men are in their Sunday suits and white shirts. I bet they know I'm from the hills. I don't look like them because I work on my family's farm. I wonder what all these people do? If only Christina could see the deep blue sea, she would love it here. The Mediterranean is so big. I wish I could run into the water and swim around. With the sun shining down on the water, it makes the water look like ice it's so crystal clear. But I have no time to play here; I must go to the dock and look for my ship. I will be saying my goodbyes and boarding soon for America.

Oh, Baby Jesus! I can't believe how enormous this ship is. You can fit my entire village inside this ship. We would have plenty of room to run around and play. It's quite scary to me. I've never seen anything this big, I'll get lost just roaming around. Father told me that there are bathrooms with toilets. You pull on the chain and water will flush down a hole. I can't wait to use this thing called a toilet. Father is teasing me, telling me to hold onto the wall, so I don't flush myself into the sea. We are laughing and having fun because really, deep down inside, we both know how frightened I am of not knowing what really lies ahead of me. Father is trying his best not to get me upset any more than I am. He doesn't like to see me cry. I am trying my best to act like a grown woman, but we both know I am still a young girl who wants her family by her side.

I hear Mr. Donatelli saying to Father, "We better get Geltrude in line, so she can board the ship."

The ship leaves at 6:00 PM. We have less than three hours before the Tartar Prince sets sail. Father takes my luggage from Mr. Donatelli's hand. He tells Mr. Donatelli that he will stand in line with me till I get on the ship. I smile at Mr. Donatelli and thank him for getting us here safely and on time. He hugs me and kisses me on both cheeks. Then he gives me one more hug and says, "Geltrude, you're welcome. May God protect you out on the sea, and take you to America without any problems." He tells Father he will be down on the dock with all the other people who are here to say goodbye to their loved ones. "When you are ready, you will find me there.

Stay as long as you must to take care of your daughter." He smiles at me and says goodbye again. I am thinking he is such a gentleman for helping Father and me.

I feel so sick to my stomach. I think I need to vomit, but I will hold everything down. I don't want to get sick in front of all these people; I would be so embarrassed. I'm sure I will have a really hard time letting go of Father. It will be a bear hug when we have to say farewell. I won't want to let go. There is so much commotion here because of all the people. They are crying and showing so much emotion towards one another. I see Mr. Domenico Napoleone and Antonio Sciullo is with him, both from my village. They are talking to Father. I wonder why they are here? Maybe to say goodbye to someone special, but who could that be? Antonio walks over to me, and I ask, "Why are you in Naples?"

He replies, "I am going to America to be with my sister in Philadelphia, and Mr. Napoleone is sailing to America to be with his nephew in Philadelphia."

I look at the both of them and say, "I can't believe you are both going to Philadelphia, that's where I'm going! So, we will be on this ship together all the way to Philadelphia."

I am already starting to feel better about sailing across the ocean. Thank you, Blessed Mother. I couldn't have planned this any better than you. You are answering my prayers. But my big prayer, I don't think you heard. I'm not going to complain because I love you and Baby Jesus, but I have asked that you stop my father from sending me to America. My father paid $30 for my third-class ticket. He gave me $4 in case I need to buy something on my journey.

Antonio turns to me and says, "I have $11, and Mr. Napoleone is rich, he has $100." Antonio is telling me not to worry because he and Mr. Napoleone will watch over me and take good care of me. He says he will protect me like his sister. I feel much better and ready to go. I'm full of excitement now. What could go wrong with my friends taking good care of me? I feel like a new me is being born right here on the docks of Naples. I will go with that feeling and reach out to my new life. But I will never ever forget where I came from. My beautiful family and land. How I love them! Now, I will step forward and live my life in America with hopefully much happiness.

Father and I walk to the beginning of the gangplank, and he lets go of my hand. My heart sinks to my stomach. I stop, and I look deep into his eyes. He is crying and puts his arms around my shoulders. I can feel his body shaking against me. I have never realized such feelings could come from him. I start to cry and whisper to him, "I will never forget you, Father. Your love and kindness will be with me forever. I hope I am gentle through my life as you have been through yours." People behind me in line are shouting at us to move up. I let go of Father and look at him one more time. I kiss him and say, "This is goodbye for now."

He tells me that I must embark on the ship. I feel my feet walking, but I don't know how I am moving at all. I am going up the ramp to board the ship, and I hear someone saying, "Stay in line." I can't see through my tears to see who is talking to me? I don't know where to walk, so I follow the people in front of me. I feel someone touch my shoulder. I turn to see who it is and it's Mr. Napoleone. He asks me if I am okay.

"Do you need to sit down for a few minutes?"

Antonio gets a chair, so I can sit and get myself together. He says to me, "Geltrude, sit down and allow the passengers to walk past us. When the ship starts to pull out of the harbor, we can wave to your Father one last time."

I feel the ship moving and hear the whistle blowing. The ship's horns are so loud, you can't hear your own thoughts because people on the ship and the people on the dock are all yelling back and forth to each other. There is so much going on. My thoughts are racing through my head. I can't see Father because of my tears. My head and heart are both pounding. This is just too much for me to handle. I must get to the front of the railing, so I can see Father one more time. Antonio sees how upset I am and takes my arm and says follow me as we both push our way up front. Looking down at all those people makes me dizzy. There are so many people there, and all you can see are the handkerchiefs and arms waving goodbye. My eyes are searching for Father. I can see his bright yellow handkerchief waving in the air. I wave to him one more time. He looks so small to me. As I stand there, frozen in time, I whisper to myself, "You are the best Father I could ever have." I blow him my last kiss as we lock eyes. Then he disappears into the crowd.

Mr. Napoleone takes my arm and says, "Follow me, Geltrude, we are in steerage. Come this way, down the stairs."

Steerage is the lower deck on the ship where the cargo is stored. There will be 1,000 of us down there, and only 45 first-class passengers. He says that's fine because we will all get to New York on the same day and time. I just smile at him and follow him and Antonio. I take Antonio's arm and bury my head on his shoulder. I weep as though my heart will break. Antonio is telling me, "Don't worry, we will be in America before you know it. Come on, Geltrude, give me your suitcase, and I will carry it down the narrow staircase."

It's dark down here, the only light we have is the light coming in from the portholes. Antonio is pointing out to me that I will stay in the section for women without male escorts. "Mr. Napoleone and I will be in the section for men traveling alone, and they also have a section for families. We will take you to your sleeping quarters, and if you need us, we will show you how to get to our quarters."

As we are walking through to get to my berth, I see the large compartments with the individual berths. They are iron framework containing a mattress a pillow and a blanket. The mattress and pillow are filled with straw and seaweed. It smells strange down here in steerage. It is worse than our animals on the farm. There are only a few women down here so far, so I get to choose which berth I want. I will go for the bottom to be close to the floor. Being down here is like being in a cave, and I have to stay down here for up to 14 days.

I guess there will be a lot of things I won't like, but like Antonio said to me, "We will be in America before we know it." I will pray to the Blessed Mother tonight that Antonio knows what he is talking about.

But for now, let me see what surprises Christina has packed in my suitcase for me. She told me I couldn't see what it was till I was on the ship. Let me hurry and unpack and see what she did for me. Knowing her, it will be something fun. She is always full of life and laughter.

CHAPTER 7

August 31, 1899

It's 7:00 PM, and it's my first night on this ship. My suitcase is bulging. Christina and I packed so many items in my bag. I had to tie a rope around the suitcase, so it wouldn't fly open and have everything come soaring out.

As I open the lid, I see a beautiful red scarf folded neatly. I take it into my hands and then touch my cheek with it because Christina made this for me. My mother and Christina both are great seamstresses, and I am not good at sewing. I hate it! They always make me my clothes, and my mother made me two beautiful dresses for my trip. I look so pretty in them, and my mother made them with love. They were my going to America gift. So every time I wear them, I will think of my mother. And when I wear my red scarf, I will always think of Christina.

I found some sweets also in my bag. Pizzelle cookies, which originally were made in Ortona in the Abruzzo region. I really like these pizzelles because this is my region of Italia. Pizzelles have been in this region for centuries. I must go to the women's lavatory to freshen up. My bladder feels like it will burst if I don't get to a toilet soon. There is a girl washing herself at the basin next to me. She asks me if I have hot water in my basin. I tell her no hot or warm water here. I only have cold sea salt water. We both laugh because the water is so cold, you can't rinse your hands. I ask her what is her name.

She replies, "I am Sofia, and I am 18 years old."

I introduce myself as Carmela because I like my middle name. I don't like Geltrude. It sounds like an old lady's name. I tell Sofia

I am also 18 years old, and I am on my way to Philadelphia to get married.

Sofia starts to laugh and says, "Me too. I am getting married to a man in Philadelphia, and his name is Matteo Pesci. And that is all I know about him." Sofia is laughing and tells me, "With my luck he will be fat, bald, old, and have no teeth. Nothing good ever happens to me. That's why my father sold me to him."

I am bewildered. What did Sofia just say to me? I hear myself say to her, "I don't understand what you are talking about, your father sold you to him?"

"No," Sofia says. "He didn't really sell me to him. Mr. Pesci gave my father some money for my passage and some extra money." Sofia looks at me strangely and says, "All right," and smiles at me. She asks, "Are you finished getting washed because there are so many ladies and children waiting for a basin?"

I smile back at Sofia and gather my towel, bag of salt, toothbrush, and soap. I tell her, "I am ready to go get vaccinated. Let's leave the lavatory and go find the women's room for the vaccine. But before we leave, I have to get in line for a toilet or I will pee in my under-wear!"

We both get in line and wait a long time for one. But it was unique to finally use a toilet. It was strange to pull on a chain and see the water flush everything down a hole. I never used one before, so I was intrigued on how it operated. Before we get in line to be vaccinated, Sofia sees my confusion and explains this is normal and will keep us safe from illness. Her reassuring voice calms my nerv-ousness. This is all so new to me. They separate the men and put them in one room, the women and children in another room. We go into the vaccine room where there are hundreds of females and children. We all must get vaccinated before the ship leaves the port. After we are vaccinated, an inspection card is stamped by US Con-sulate, certifying that we have been vaccinated to enter the United States. When we are finished, I ask Sofia "Would you like to stay near me? You could sleep in one of the berths near me. The berth next to my head is empty so you could stay there for the entire time we are on the ship."

She agrees that us being near each other would be great, for we would have each other for companionship. I have acquired a friend already. She comes from Roma. That's a large city here in Italia. She's dressed nicely and quite beautiful. I would enjoy having her friendship. She is dressed just like the ladies in Naples. Her dress and hat are brilliant red and tailored to her body. She has fair skin, blue eyes, and light brown hair. I don't look anything like her. I have dark olive skin, dark brown eyes, and dark hair. Sofia tells me we should go and get her belongings, which aren't many. We get to her berth, and she has a small bundle wrapped tightly with rope. I asked, "What did you carry on the ship with you? Will you have a clean dress for when we reach America?"

She smiles at me and says, "I have in my bundle a dress for when I get to America. Some personal items, like what I just used in the lavatory. A hairbrush, and my mother gave me a Bible. So I can pray every day for a safe journey. That's all I have, and $10 in cash. I will keep that in my waistband to my skirt, just in case someone tries to rob me; they won't get my $10. My mother put some stitches in my waistband so I could carry my money. Let's get over to your side and put my belongings away."

We get to the berth, and she has a mattress and blanket but no pillow. She tells me not to waste my time looking for one; she will use her bundle of items for her pillow. "Besides," she adds, "I don't really sleep with a pillow." Sofia looks at me and tells me, "This trip will be so much fun now that we are together. I am not frightened now because I have you."

I tell her that she will be my traveling sister to America.

There are so many people that we don't have any privacy to change from our clothes. We decided to keep our clothes, shoes, and shawls on while we sleep. It's so cold down here. And there are men watching us all the time. They walk through here like they are lost, but they aren't. The men just want to look at us. So Sofia and I decide to keep our clothes on like so many other women are doing and put the blankets on top of us. We both get in our berths and say our prayers to the Blessed Mother out loud. Before we know it, there are so many people saying prayers. And we all are saying the same prayer to the Blessed Mother, "Please, get us safely to America!"

Sofia whispers to me, "Carmela, can we be friends in Philadelphia? I want to be near you because we both are young. And we can grow old together as sisters."

I tell her that she and I will be sisters forever on this ship and in Philadelphia.

I fall asleep so quickly, totally exhausted from my two days in the cart having dirt and mud hitting me the entire time from the wheels of the cart. I really need rest and sleep tonight.

The next morning, Sofia is telling me to wake up because the breakfast bell just rung at 6:55 AM.

"I didn't sleep well last night," I am telling Sofia. "You could hear the women and their babies crying all night."

"We must hurry, the steward told me, the longer we wait the less food there will be for us. We can get washed after we eat," she says.

The steward at the back of the line is handing out eating utensils. We are furnished each with a working man's dinner pail, with a spoon and a fork. We keep these for the entire trip. They are ours to wash and take care of. Without these utensils, we can't eat. After we have a disgusting breakfast of oatmeal, bread, and coffee that tastes like dirt. We go up to the main deck, I introduce Sofia to Mr. Domenico Napoleone and Antonio Sciullo. We walk over to where they are sitting on a bench, talking to a group of men.

When Mr. Napoleone sees us, he yells to us, "Good morning, young ladies. Come sit here with us." After I introduce Sofia to Mr. Napoleone, and he introduces us to his new friends. They are all complaining about the food and how it smells down there in steerage. Which it is all the truth, but Mr. Napoleone says we must look at what is at the end of our journey. America! We must keep that in our minds. He tells me, "If there is anything you need or any help needed with anything, come look for me. If I am not down there, I will be up on deck for fresh air and sunshine."

Our first day on the ship is fun. A lot of us are all from the same villages. We met a lot of girls our age traveling on their own to meet family members or to get married to a stranger. There's a lot of us who are going to arranged marriages. Most of us are not thrilled about it, but what can we do? It's too late to turn back. Sofia and I are up on deck with the mothers and their children. We are singing and dancing with them. It's fun to be acting silly and having a good time. It's 11:55 AM, and the dinner bell just rang. We have to go down to steerage and get our pails and utensils, so we can sit and eat dinner. The sooner we get in line to eat, the more of a selection of food we will be given. If you wait 10 minutes after the meal bell, there may only be bread to eat. I hope our food is better than this morning. The ladies were telling us on deck that the food will be the same all the way to America.

They serve us meat, potatoes, and bread for dinner. I eat just enough to satisfy my appetite. Sofia and I hide our pails under the foot of our mattresses and that way no one will take them. l tell Sofia I am going to take a nap because the waves are making me dizzy and sick to my stomach. Maybe eating dinner wasn't a good idea for me. Sofia tells me she's going to take a nap also. We both sleep for a couple of hours. I feel somewhat better, but we both decide to go up on deck. Being up on deck is far better than down in the steerage with the nasty smells that make you sick to your stomach and create a bad headache.

We hear all the children laughing, some running around chasing each other. And then you have the children who are seasick laying on their mother's lap for comfort. Sofia and I are playing tag "You're it" with the children. We are chasing and running after the other players in an attempt to tag or touch them with our hands. They are so brave to be on the ship and sailing across the ocean. I think the children are braver than I am. When I get married to Raffaele, I wonder how many children I will have. That would make me extremely happy to have a husband, children and a home. What more could I ask for? I would be complete as a woman if God gave me healthy babies. That's happiness I could handle. I've been praying to God since I was a little girl for that kind of life.

Time goes fast on the deck with so many people to talk with. We are headed downstairs because the supper bell is going to ring soon. We want to get in front of the line to see if the food is better if you get there on time. We get our pail and head for the line, which isn't long; not yet anyway.

The supper bell rings at 6:55 PM. I hear the passengers on the deck hurrying to get down the stairs. There are so many people, if you are near last in line, you probably won't get much food because everyone in front of you has gotten more food than they should have. The steward wants to get rid of the food, and then he is finished serving us. His job is almost done for the day. Well, almost completed; he still has to ring four bells at 10:00 PM. Then everyone in steerage has to be in their berths; no exceptions! Supper was just as bad as dinner.

Sofia and I say goodnight to each other and to the ladies around us. We are all friends now. We have a bond because we will be on this ship for at least 14 days. We are a family looking after one another. Not one of us has a male companion, so we are all on our own. We will take care of each other. We will protect ourselves from danger, especially at night when we are in our berths sleeping. If anyone attacks you, scream as loud as you can and defend yourself whatever way you can.

Sofia whispers over to me, "Good night, Carmela. See you in the morning."

I whisper back to her, "Good night, Sofia."

It feels good to have someone to say goodnight to. Someone to wake up to and feel that they care about you. I feel more secure knowing I have a good friend here in Sofia.

The water is extremely rough during the night, so Sofia and I are seasick this morning. We aren't going to eat in fear we will vomit all day. It's so dreadful to feel this sick, but we aren't the only ones to feel this way. Many of the girls around us are sick. Not one of us wants to move out of our berths for fear we will vomit again and again. That's all you smell down here is vomit along with all the other dreadful smells. If you aren't sick, then the rotten smell of vomit will make you want to throw up. The only time I get out to walk around is when I need to get to a toilet. Other than that, I can't even lift my head. I feel so weak and drained that I can't function properly. Poor Sofia. She hasn't gone to use the toilet in hours. She tells me she can't move her head or she will get sick.

She tells me, "I will wait to the last minute when I know I will pee in my underwear and that there isn't a long line. Then I will make a mad dash to a toilet I hope I will make it in time."

I think today we should stay here in our berths and not eat any food till tomorrow. Maybe our stomachs will settle down with no food in them. It's just filthy conditions down here. No one seems to care if the vomit is cleaned off the floor or not. The ship's stewards, not one of them, would tend to this problem. They don't care if it's clean down here in steerage. They treat us like animals.

The one good thing about being seasick is that the men don't bother you because they don't want your vomit all over them. Or if the motion of the ship is violent, they have a hard time standing or walking. So they tend to stay in their berths and leave us females alone. Thank God. There is lack of privacy here on the ship. It makes it hard for us females to change our clothes. Since I've been on this ship, we ladies haven't had one moments' privacy. The men are always staring at us. We get followed, and they always try to touch you in some way. The men are disgusting human beings on this ship.

When women are traveling alone, they are prey to both crew and male passengers. The steerage officials are of no help to us. I feel sorry for the children who have to witness this sort of behavior from a stranger towards their mother. And yet no one cares unless you are with a male companion. They seem not to bother you then, in fear that they will get their heads bashed in. I wish I could talk with some of the men, just to see if they have anything inside their heads.

When the supper bell rings, Sofia and I still aren't feeling like ourselves. We decide not to join everyone for their meal this evening. We are hoping to sleep the night away and feel better in the morning.

CHAPTER 8

It's so quiet down here in steerage tonight. It seems like everyone is sleeping but me. My nerves won't let me settle into the deep, deep sleep that I need so badly. I feel like there is lightening shooting out from my fingernails and poison releasing from every one of my pores. My eyes can't and won't close. They just stare into the nothingness. It's so lonely, laying down here in the dark. You can't see your hand in front of your face. The stillness makes me uneasy. I know what I did was wrong. But if I didn't help, who would have? It was up to me and Sofia. We did what we had to do to take care of our own. If we do not stand up for ourselves, who will? Certainly not anyone on this ship. It would have been covered up, just like many times before. I pray to God that He will forgive me and cleanse my soul. I prayed for His help so He could understand that I had to do what was necessary.

The first time I heard one of the young girls scream in the middle of the night I thought she was having a bad dream. At breakfast the next morning, the ladies were all upset because Antonia, a 14-year-old girl, was attacked. Someone came to her berth, put his hand over her mouth and raped her. After he was finished, he told her she better not say a word, or he would come back to kill her and Grazia, her 10-year-old sister. The ladies asked Antonia if she knew who attacked her. She hesitated at first, but after some encouragement, said it was Jim, the steward who serves the food and walks with a limp.

"He smells like rotten food, that's how I know it was him," she said. Antonia said that he told her he would keep coming back every night until the ship reaches America, and there's nothing she can do to stop him.

Sofia and I went up on deck to tell the men what happened. They asked a lot of questions about Jim, then told us they needed time to talk among themselves and figure out what to do.

"All right, girls," said Mr. Angelo. "Go back down and tend to Antonia. We will talk to you later."

We went back down to steerage to look for Antonia and Grazia.

My heart breaks for them because they are all alone. They were sent to America by their mother to live with their aunt and her family. Sofia and I tried our best to console their little hearts. We told them that we would watch over them until we reach America, which seemed to calm them down. Then, we started to sing their favorite song, and smiles slowly flickered back to their faces, beautiful with big hazel eyes and dark curls. We all sang "O Sole Mio" and laughed with each other because not one of us had a good singing voice. The time flew by until the dinner bell rang. We went back up on deck to talk to the men. They told us they had an idea to settle the problem once and for all, but they needed our help, Sofia and I told them we would help do what was needed, and they told us the plan: "One of you will have to go into Antonia's berth tonight and pretend to be her. Do not worry, Jim will not have time to harm you in any way. When he comes over to you, we will grab him and take over from there."

Sofia immediately volunteered herself.

"After tonight, this will be over and we will never speak of this again to anyone," said Mr. Angelo. "What we're doing is against the law of the land, but we don't follow that law on the sea."

Sofia climbed into Antonia's berth that night. I was in Grazia's because we were not sure which one Jim would go after. We were both prepared for him. I do not know about Sofia, but I wanted him to come to my berth, so I could claw his eyes out of his head with my bare hands. How much I hate him for hurting those two helpless little girls! But not anymore. Not after tonight. Not a word was spoken between us. That night, we were prey.

After what felt like an eternity, I heard someone walking, one foot dragging on the ground. The sound froze me in my spot. I felt his hand go over my mouth and then he was on top of me. His body weight held me down, and I could not breathe. His other hand pulled my hair as he whispered, "Do not make a sound or I will choke you to death." My heart was pumping so fast, and I felt his hand go under my dress and pull on my petticoat.

Then, all of a sudden, he was lifted off me, struggling forcefully. For a moment, I felt the hot air from his nostrils hitting my face, and then he was gone. Sofia came to me, gently putting her hand over my mouth, so I'd be quiet.

"It is over," she told me. "You were so strong, stronger than I could have imagined." She kissed my cheek. I asked her where the men were, and she replied, "I do not know, and I do not care. Let them do whatever they want with him. Throw him overboard and feed him to the sharks."

We made a promise to each other that we will never speak of this again or ask the men what they did with Jim. The women will be able to sleep without having to worry about him. The only thing to do now is take care of Antonia and Grazia, our little sisters on this voyage. We women can and will take care of each other on our journey. We sail across the ocean, taking turns watching over each other as we sleep. There were no more incidents after that night. I think the men realized we wouldn't put up with them without a fight.

CHAPTER 9

Life has to go on for each and every one of us.

We are all on deck to practice the answers for the immigration officials. The 25 of us are having fun because it is hard enough to understand each other in Italian, let alone English! We all come from different places, so we don't speak the same dialects. As for me, I have a hard time pronouncing the strange-sounding words correctly. I am quick to laugh at myself. Sofia is much better at it; she hears the word once and repeats it perfectly. I tell her, "Good for you! When we reach America, you must stay in line with me because I will need your help!"

Sofia laughs at me.

"Do not worry, Carmela," she says. "I won't leave your side. We are Siamese twins, joined at the hip forever."

I can hear the heavy footsteps of Assunta coming towards us before I see her. Assunta is commissioned by the ship to help us with our English. She is a young woman from Italia who told us she has been working on the ship for four years, since the age of 21. Although I appreciate her help, she makes me feel uncomfortable with the way she glares at me when I answer something incorrectly. But today, I'm not afraid to make a mistake; our trip is almost over.

Assunta tells us, "Your ship's name is the SS Tartar Prince. We are sailing from Naples, Italia, to New York, America. We will reach America tomorrow on Wednesday, September 13, 1899."

Assunta gets frustrated because we are laughing and having fun. She wants us to be serious, like her. She does not understand that we are giddy at the thought of our voyage's end. There is not one of us who cannot wait to plant our feet on American soil, the land we will grow our food on and call home.

I will not miss getting sick every day, eating spoiled food, sleeping in a small dirty berth, not bathing, and my least favorite, the over-ripe odor down there in the hull. I can't wait to step into a tub of warm water with a bar of soap and scrub off the stink of this ship. That is one of the first things I will do when I reach Philadelphia.

Now, Assunta tells us she will ask each of us the questions individually. A lot of the ladies answering the questions say the English words perfectly. Then I hear my name.

"Carmela it is your turn." My stomach turns upside down. I do not want these ladies to think I am from some small, backwards village because I cannot pronounce these English words. I am just 18 years old, with no formal education or ability to read or write.

Despite my nerves, I stand up and tell Assunta I'm ready. She smiles reassuringly and asks the first question. After I complete the practice interview, Assunta tells me I said all the words correctly and not to worry; "After all, we have been working on these questions for about 10 days. You will be fine."

We all say a prayer to the Blessed Mother to let us safely enter America and live happy, fruitful lives. Together, we have an immeasurable amount of love and trust. We helped each other in our darkest hours on this ship. Standing there with this group of women who started as strangers, I feel so much warmth and love. I know in my heart I will never feel a bond like this again.

Before dinner time tomorrow, I will have to say goodbye to Sofia and all my friends. Once we get off the ship, I may never see them again. Sofia and I are both shaken by this thought. We will not know how far apart we are until I show Raffaele Sofia's address.

I start to feel overwhelmed at the thought of all that will happen tomorrow. It is a strange feeling I have never felt before. Then again, I have never been on a ship sailing across the ocean to a strange country and a stranger I will call husband before. Why can I not leave these feelings deep inside? I hope they go away, along with the anxiety that makes my stomach hurt.

The supper bell rings, signaling the last inedible meal we will have to choke down. The last meal we will spend together as a family. Time to say our goodbyes. In the morning, we will rise before dawn, have a small breakfast, gather our belongings, and prepare to depart the ship.

The most exciting part of tomorrow will be when we see what everyone talks about: The Statue of Liberty. They say Lady Liberty has been here since 1886 and stands over 150 feet tall. Around the world, people know her as the symbol of how great and free America is for immigrants like us. In America, we can make anything of ourselves by working hard and being good citizens, which is what I plan to do. I feel more confident, ready for my new life. I cannot wait to begin.

Everyone is talking about the how streets are paved with gold. And this is the land of opportunity for immigrants. This is what all of us believe in our hearts about us coming to our new country, America. Not that we are looking to get rich, we want to have a good happy life. Isn't that what everyone wants with their life?

CHAPTER 10

Sofia and I really didn't get a minute of sleep. We are excited about getting off this ship. We have so many plans in our heads, and we can't wait to live out our dreams. We are up and dressed, me in the beautiful dress my mother made me, ready to go along with all the other passengers. You can hear the trunks moving around on the wooden floor. People are putting their belongings in their suitcases. Everyone wants to get washed, so they won't smell dirty. We are all filled with happiness. Many people are going to have family members here to meet them. But not me and Sofia. We are here to meet our future husbands. Antonia and Grazia are up on deck with us. Everyone has clean clothes on, even if our bodies are dirty. We want to look nice for our families and friends here in America.

It's Wednesday, September 13, 1899, Sofia and I are on deck with Antonia and Grazia, it is a little past 7:00 AM, and the medical inspectors are boarding the ship. They are here to inspect first- and second-class cabin passengers. After they are inspected, those passengers are free to leave the ship.

The inspectors climbed down the ladders to their barge. The ship moves through the narrows leading to Upper New York Bay and into the harbor.

Slowly, the tip of Manhattan comes into view. That's when all on the ship see the most beautiful sight any of us have ever seen. With the sun beaming behind the top of her head. There she stood in front of us: The Statue of Liberty.

Most of us can't even speak because of her beauty. Sofia and I are holding hands and crying. I can't even express to her my thoughts. I am truly speechless. There is such beauty on Bedloe's Island, just a short way to Ellis Island; this beauty is the Statue of Liberty.

The ship has docked in Manhattan. First- and second-class passengers will be released. All of us from steerage pour across the pier to a waiting area. I take Antonia with me and Sofia takes Grazia with her. Each of us wear a name tag with the manifest number.

Then we are assembled and told to get aboard a barge, while our luggage is piled on the lower decks of the barge. Meanwhile, Sofia and I are still together, but we aren't crying. Our thoughts now are to remember the questions they will ask us. Now, we will meet our interpreters. We are nervous that if we don't answer the questions correctly, they will send us back to Italia. But Assunta told all of us that these men frequently saved many immigrants from deportation. I hope I can remember how to respond to him in English.

The interpreters are leading 30 of us through the main doorway to the Registry room. A doctor stands there, looking our group over to see if he notices any symptoms of a mental or physical deformity. We are keeping the girls with us the entire time, so they don't get frightened.

Each of us passes the doctor with an interpreter at our side. The doctor examines our face, hair, neck, and hands. The doctor holds a piece of chalk. If I fail or pass, the doctor will scrawl a large white letter on my chest that will indicate whether or not I am to be detained for further medical inspection. Mental defects are marked with a large X, meaning they will not be admitted.

Whole groups could be told to bathe with disinfectant solutions. The next group of doctors were the dreaded "eye men" looking for eye disease, "trachoma" which could cause blindness, even death. That was certain deportation, which meant you were sent back to your port of origin. Sick, too ill, feeble-minded to earn a living. They would be deported. Sick children age 12 or older were sent back to Europe. Under 12 years old had to be accompanied by a parent when deported.

Now on to the inspector, who is seated on a high stool with the ship's manifest in front of him and an interpreter at his side. He has two minutes to ask you questions from the 30 questions on the manifest. Thank God I answered everything correctly.

We were free to go after only a few hours. Sofia and I stayed with the girls as the inspector went over their manifest for Antonia and Grazia. The inspectors were gentle with the girls. And both were free to go. The girls answered the questions in better English than me. Next, those of us with landing cards pinned on their clothes are moved to the Money Exchange area.

One of the inspectors took the girls into the next room because that's where their aunt and uncle were waiting for them. We kissed and hugged each of them and said our farewells. For those of us traveling to cities or towns beyond New York City, the next stop was the railroad ticket office. We waited in areas marked for each independent railroad line in the ferry terminal. We were ferried in a barge to the train terminal.

Finally, with admittance cards, railroad and ferry passes, and box lunches in hand, our journey to and through Ellis Island is completed. I feel like there was a large sign hanging over my head saying, "Welcome to America." These were the only words going through my head.

Sofia and I arrived in New Jersey because we were taking the train to Philadelphia. It will take almost a day to reach Philadelphia, our final destination. Our journey is almost over. Once there, we will say our farewell to each other. We will finally get to meet our future husbands.

The excitement of being off the ship and answering all the questions correctly is slowing wearing away and being replaced with fear. My heart is pounding, and my stomach is twisted in knots.

What if Raffaele has changed his mind? What if he isn't there? What if I get off the train at Philadelphia and I am alone? What do I do? Where do I go? What if he sees me, and he's disappointed? What if I'm disappointed?

This is my forever! Despite the heat in the air, I am shaking.

CHAPTER 11

Pulling into Philadelphia, I hear the steel wheels moving against the steel tracks. We are slowly moving into the train station at Broad and Market Street. I see the conductor walking down the aisle here in the coach compartment. He is asking to see everyone's ticket before leaving the train, trying his best to be heard over the squeaking wheels. Luckily, the conductor speaks Italian. He tells us to gather our belongings and make sure to take everything with us.

When I show him my ticket, he smiles at me and nods.

"I hope America is all that you hoped it would be! – *Spero che L'America sia tutto quell oche speravi chef asse!*"

I turn to look at Sofia and see she has her hands over her face. I nudge her elbow and ask, "What is wrong?"

She looks at me with tears streaming down her face, trying to catch her breath. Voice cracking, Sofia takes my hands in hers and tells me she does not want to leave me.

"I will be lost without you Carmela. We have been together for two weeks, constantly by each other's side. I am scared to meet Matteo and whatever awaits me here."

I say to her, "Sofia, we have to get off this train soon. Until we walk outside to our future husbands, I will be with you. Please, be calm and breathe deeply. This is the time we have left with each other."

After some time, Sofia tells me she is ready.

"I want to be the first to step down off the train, but you must be behind me, Carmela."

As the train comes to a stop, I follow Sofia down the hallway, hoping to catch a glimpse of Raffaele through the windows. I feel myself starting to panic. I don't even know what he looks like! Trying to calm my anxious stomach, I take slow, deep breaths.

The conductor standing at the door takes Sofia's hand to help her step down onto the platform, then mine.

"*Benvenuto* in America," he whispers to us. I turn to the large crowd of people standing in front of us, waiting. An older gentleman and an extremely handsome young man are walking towards me. They both are dressed in suits, pressed white shirts, and silken black hats.

I find myself frozen in fear, unable to move. Could this be the man I have traveled so many miles for? The older man asks, "Would you be Geltrude Di Lullo?"

I muster up the courage to smile and tell him, "Yes, I am she."

He extends his hand to mine and introduces himself as Michele Pasquariello and the younger man as Raffaele. Raffaele smiles at me and takes my suitcase, his hand pressing into mine for a moment. His soul-penetrating eyes have me blushing from embarrassment. The two of us stand there for a moment, just looking at each other.

Raffaele has dark olive skin, smooth and unblemished. Thick, dark curls adorn his head. He is beautiful, this man I am to marry. I hope he thinks the same of me. We Italians do not believe in divorce, so I will be his wife forever. I hope the happiness I see in his eyes will be present in our future together.

"We are very happy you made it safely here to America," Mr. Pasquariello tells me. "And we are delighted to have you as part of our family."

As the three of us begin to walk to Market Street, Raffaele gently takes my arm and we begin our first journey together. I am suddenly self-conscious about my body odor. It has been two weeks since I have taken a bath and I am in dire need of clean clothes.

Raffaele says to me, "Geltrude, when we reach our house, I will show you to your bedroom and introduce you to my mother and brothers. The entire family is waiting to welcome you. I cannot wait to sit and talk with you. I have so many questions about your trip to America! It has been 11 years since I came here as a youngster, so I have forgotten much about it."

We walk across Broad Street, and it is so big, this city. Carts, wagons, and horses are bustling noisily down the streets. There are so many people I find myself looking from one side of the street to the other. Most are well-dressed men and women out enjoying themselves.

Mr. Pasquariello turns to us, making sure no one is running us over. As we walk up onto the stone walkway, I hear someone shout, "Mr. Pasquariello!" A man on his horse is waving at us, saying, "Come over here! I will take you back to 8th Street."

Raffaele and I climb in the back of the wagon while Mr. Pasquariello sits up front with the driver.

The driver asks me, "How was your journey? Were the seas rough? When I came over 10 years ago, it was brutal for me and my family. We were all seasick for days. Now, we are all happy to be here in America as Americans. I am sure you will be delighted with Philadelphia and the Pasquariellos. They are generous people."

Before I can respond, I hear a lady calling out to Mr. Pasquariello, asking to meet the young girl who just came in from Italia. The driver stops his horse and yells down to her, "Come see the beautiful young lady!"

She walks over and tells us she is so happy I got here safely.

"You will be happy with the Pasquariellos," she says.

Mr. Pasquariello tells her, "We must get Geltrude home, she must be tired and hungry for some good food."

I thank the lady for her kind words, and she leans into the wagon to kiss my cheek. "I will see you tomorrow at the celebration," she says.

I wave to her and say goodbye, thinking, *There will be a party for me tomorrow!*

Raffaele asks the driver to stay on Broad Street, "So Geltrude can see the magnificent features of our city." We pass what Raffaele tells me is City Hall—the tallest building in the world! At the top is a statue of the city's founder, William Penn. Raffaele says, "There are many beautiful buildings here, and now we Italians coming to America have many stonemasons to build churches and buildings with greatly detailed stonework."

We continue left on Washington Avenue as we get closer to the house. Raffaele looks at me and says, "We have so many things to do tomorrow! You will meet the rest of the Pasquariellos. They are filled with excitement to meet you. I hope you will come to love them like your own."

I can already see and feel that Raffaele is a gentle soul and a good man. He has much love and respect for his parents, brothers, and family. I am starting to feel safe and secure with him. Though we were many miles apart, we are meant for each other. This is what God has given me, and I will accept it in my heart.

The driver turns down a narrow street and in the middle of the block is a stone house. Mr. Pasquariello tells Raffaele to pass me my suitcase and help me out of the wagon. As we step down, I hear a lady speaking to Mr. Pasquariello and turn to see who it could be. The lady walks straight over and puts her arms around my shoulders.

"Welcome to your new home," she says. She tells me she is Raffaele's mother, Rosa. I see Raffaele's warmth in her face.

Rosa calls two young men over and introduces them as Giovanni and Orazio, my future brothers-in-law.

"I only have three sons, but now we have you!" she says. "Please, come see your new home."

As I walk from the street to the house, I notice the many houses on this street, so different from Ateleta. I have seen many new sights since the beginning of my trip, but all of these people here on one street start to overwhelm me. Today has been full of new things to learn and see, an overload of information. Stepping into my new home, the first thing I see is a gorgeous vestibule. Next is the parlor, possibly even more beautiful, with wallpaper. Then, into the dining room. Oh, the furniture is a beautiful dark brown wood, and the tabletop has such a shine to it. We did not have any of this in Ateleta. It must be true; everyone in America is rich.

Rosa comes over to me and asks, "Are you tired, Geltrude? Maybe you should have something to eat first." I tell her I would like a bath and then some food. "Follow me," she says. "I will show you where everything is." She yells to Raffaele to take my suitcase to my room.

Rosa shows me the bathroom that has a sink, tub, and toilet! All the modern conveniences we never had back home. I guess I should stop comparing my new home to my old one. I'm beginning to think the Pasquariellos are very wealthy. Rosa tells me she will draw a bath and leave new clothes in the bedroom for me.

"Please leave your underwear in here, then pick out what you would like to wear when you finish bathing. We will all be downstairs waiting for you. I will have supper ready, and then you can relax and enjoy yourself. If there is anything we can do for you, please do not be reluctant to ask. You are one of us, Geltrude." My heart warms at her words.

Finally, stepping into the warm bath water is a wonderful feeling. There is shampoo and soap on the lip of the tub, and toothpaste and a toothbrush on the sink. I cannot wait to use everything. I lean back against the tub and close my eyes, grateful for a chance to slow my racing thoughts.

Rosa knocks on the bathroom door, asking if I fell asleep. She says I have been in the bath for over an hour. I realize I dozed off and did not even wash myself. I apologize, hoping I have not ruined everyone's supper. Rosa tells me she understands.

"We will wait for you so we can all eat together." I quickly scrub myself clean and wash my hair with the castile soap, the smell is very sweet, so I rub the bubbles over my skin hoping it absorbs the sweet smell. I get out of the tub and into my new bedroom. Combing my hair, I think of my sister, she always combed my hair and made it look pretty. I miss her so much! I don't want to go downstairs with tears streaming down my face, so I quickly turn my focus on the new clothes that Rosa bought me. For the first time in two weeks, I feel pretty.

CHAPTER 12

I quickly get into my dress. I brush my long, curly hair one more time and I am ready for dinner. I make my way downstairs to join the family. Everyone is waiting for me in the dining room. All four men stand up when I enter the room. I look at Raffaele and he smiles and says, "Geltrude come sit next to me."

Mr. Pasquariello sits at the head of the table, and Giovanni and Orazio sit across from us. The end of the table closest to the kitchen is where Rosa sits. The table setting with the fine china, flatware, and the green wine glasses is beautiful. Rosa has a special way to make everything look so grand. I express how lovely everything looks, and the aroma in the room is pleasant and familiar. How happy I am to be in their home with such a good family.

Mr. Pasquariello stands up and starts pouring wine into each of our glasses. He says to me, "Geltrude, you will enjoy this wine because Raffaele and his brothers made it. I had each of the boys stomping the grapes. Before we drink any of it, Raffaele will give a toast in honor of you."

Rosa brings a large platter with meat including meatballs, sausages and pork and puts it on the table. She looks over at me, smiles, and says, "Geltrude, I hope you are hungry because, for your first night here in America, I have made a feast for you." I smile back at her and off she is back to the kitchen for more food. There is salad with fresh, juicy tomatoes. The pork is falling off the bone, and my mouth is waiting for the spaghetti alla puttanesco. You can smell the garlic and anchovies all mixed together. She hands the bowl to me and says, "Geltrude, you start to fill your plate."

Rosa finally sits down. She turns to Raffaele and says to him, "Please stand and give Geltrude a warm reception with your words." After we thank God for our food, Raffaele stands up. He first looks at me and touches my shoulder. I feel the excitement going through my entire body. He definitely has my full attention. I sit straight up and put my hands in my lap. He says, "Geltrude, first I must express my amazement at your strength to come across the ocean by yourself at the age of 18. When my entire family came across in 1888, we were together. We had each other for strength. You on the other hand had no one. I believe you have an enormous amount of qualities that I look forward to seeing. I, and also my parents and brothers, would like to express our gratitude to you for you for your willingness to come to America and marry me."

"Carmela?" I find myself begging them to never call me Geltrude because I don't know anyone with that name my age. "Could everyone call me Carmela?"

Rosa says, "Sure, Carmela, that's not a problem." She goes on to ask if that was my mother's or grandmother's name. I tell her no, "It's just a name my mother liked. I know you hear Gertrude all the time, but it's an English form of Geltrude. But not to worry because I would never name my child Geltrude, maybe Carmela." Everyone at the table is laughing at what I just said.

Rosa says to me, "Well, Carmela, don't worry, you don't have to name your daughter after me. You name your future children whatever Raffaele and you decide. As long as they are healthy, that's all that matters."

Rosa's spaghetti alla puttanesco is the best I ever tasted. The wine is relaxing me, and I feel myself become sleepy. After we finish our meal, everyone gets up to help clear the table. We bring everything back to the kitchen. Rosa puts on a pot of coffee and hands Raffaele the bottle of Grappa to put on the table. Rosa tells Giovanna and Orazio to start washing the dishes.

Giovanni, who is 20 years old. stands up and says, "I am too old to wash dishes! Orazio is 14 years old, and Carmela is 18; this should be their job. Raffaele hasn't washed dishes in years. It's been Orazio and me. I am now a man with a job. So, I am giving up doing women's work in the house."

Rosa turns to me and says, "I think Giovanni could give the dish-washing to you two. How do you feel about that?"

I say, "I am good washing dishes, that was my job every evening at home. So, I can do that here. I don't mind at all."

Rosa tells me, "Carmela, we will all get along fine in this house. You're such a joy to me."

We all go back to the dining room for fruit, coffee and Grappa. The house is full of laughter. I don't know if it's from the wine or Grappa, but I think we are all feeling fine this beautiful night. It's a warm night here in Philadelphia on Thursday, September 14, 1899. Giovanni is telling us stories about his parents. He is saying that his father married his mother when she was 16 years old, and he was 32. And it took them 20 years before they had their first son, Raffaele. Everyone is laughing, and Mr. Pasquariello says it wasn't from not trying.

I am having a wonderful time here in their home. But with this Grappa, I feel so tired now I could close my eyes and have no prob-lem sleeping here in my chair. Rosa must have noticed my exhaustion; I hear her tell Raffaele to bring me upstairs to get washed and go to bed.

Rosa says, "Tomorrow will be an extremely busy day for all of us, but mainly Carmela, since she will be meeting the family, friends, and neighbors."

He takes my hand and walks me upstairs. He tells me, "When you are finished in the bathroom, call downstairs, so Orazio can get washed."

I wash quickly and call down to Orazio to come up and get ready for bed. I hear laughter from the end bedroom. He and Raffaele walk out of the bedroom and Orazio says, "Now you will be first in the bathroom because you are the special person in our family." He walks over to me as we stand in the hallway, he has light brown eyes that almost look gold; a small dark curl hangs over his eye, and his lips always appear to be in a smile. He approaches me and gently puts his arms around me to give me a hug. He pulls back and looks me right in the eye and says, "Carmela, I am so happy you finally got here safely. We are all so happy about your living here with us. We can always use another female in the house to help our mother. But I can tell my mother already likes you. And that is very special to all of us."

Orazio kisses me on my cheek and says goodnight and goes into the bathroom. I've already decided to love Orazio like the little brother I never had. Raffaele approaches me and says, "Carmela, it's time for bed." He leads me to my bedroom. He lowers his head and kisses me tenderly on my lips. He says to me, "Good night my beautiful bride-to-be."

I almost faint and quickly rush through the doorway. Closing the door behind me, I lean against it and said, "Oh my God. I am so happy. I know I have met the man of my dreams."

This is the first time I have been kissed by a man. I never knew how good a kiss could be. It must be Raffaele that made it so tender and sweet for me. I know I will have pleasant dreams about Raffaele tonight.

CHAPTER 13

What is all the banging going on outside this morning? It takes me a couple of moments to realize where I am; yesterday felt like a dream. The bed is so comfortable, I don't want to get up. If it wasn't for all this noise, I would still be sleeping.

I sit up slowly and stretch. As much as I don't want to get out of bed, my curiosity has gotten the best of me. I go over to the window and look down; the street is covered with people rushing around, putting tables and chairs out. With all of this rushing around, I start to feel the excitement in the air because today is my welcoming party. I am ready to meet everyone. I hope it's all happiness and love for me, that everyone treats me with kindness and generosity, because I love to be the center of everyone's attention. But today, I must share this with Raffaele and learn that from now on, it will be the two of us together. I am not the main attraction any longer.

I go downstairs into the kitchen, and there is Rosa. She looks at me and tells me after the men set all the tables and chairs out, the women will start to bring out the food. She smiles and says, "Get yourself some coffee, and I will cook some eggs for you. After breakfast, see how you can help Raffaele bring out dishes, glasses, and flatware. We are really busy with setting this celebration up in the street. After it all comes together, I have a special dress for you to wear today. With your brown skin, the colors gold and ivory will look especially beautiful on you."

I walk over to Rosa and thank her for caring for me like my mother would.

Rosa takes my hand and says, "You and Raffaele, get busy now!"

We start to carry out wine glasses, and Raffaele tells me not to drop any glasses because his mother will be upset.

"The wine glasses came with us from Italia and not one broke on our voyage here."

I tell him not to worry. "No matter what I do, your mother will never be mad at me. You know why that is, Raffaele?"

He looks at me with astonishment and asks, "What makes you think that about my mother?" I rush past him on the front steps and down to the pavement. He calls out to me, "What makes you think that?"

I smile back at him and say, "Because I am the daughter-in-law that will make your mother a grandmother. Just for that, she loves me like I am her daughter, which I appreciate her feeling that way about me. Because I feel only love for her."

We both work real hard carrying out everything we will need. Giovanni and Mr. Pasquariello are helping with all the tables and chairs with their neighbors. People are coming over to me and introducing themselves, shaking my hand, kissing my face, and giving a lot of hugs. They are gathering around me in a large circle. I am feeling overcome with all of these people. I start to panic, and fear is overcoming me.

Then I hear Raffaele behind saying, "Let me take you out of this circle. Here, sit on the chair. Carmela, you look upset, and you're shivering. Calm down and breathe. Everyone is happy to see you. I don't think they realize it's so overpowering for you. Do you feel better, or should I take you back in the house?"

I tell Raffaele I should go in the house and get dressed for the party and I will feel better: "I just need some quiet time with my thoughts." Raffaele looks concerned, so I continue, "It was just so many people talking to me at once. I didn't know who to answer with all of their questions. I couldn't get my mind to stop racing until I heard your voice, which made me instantly feel better knowing you were there."

He smiles and gently touches my face; we make eye contact, and I can feel chills going down my spine. I go inside the house and upstairs to my room. It's so calm in here. My bed has pretty pink sheets on it with a white bedspread with pink flowers sewn on. Rosa decorated my bedroom just the way I would have but even nicer to the eye. My carpet is burgundy with white colored squares. I will lay down for a few minutes to catch my thoughts on this cozy bed.

I hear Orazio in the hallway calling out my name.

"Carmela, you have to get ready. Come downstairs. Soon people will be gathering outside for the festivities."

I call out to him, "I am up and have a few things to do before I can come outside. I will be there shortly."

I tell myself that I will have to keep myself together and not let my anxiety overwhelm me, no matter how many people there are. I must tell Raffaele to stay by my side so, he can help talk with everyone when it's just too much for me to handle.

I hear Orazio out in the hallway again. He is waiting to escort me downstairs and out to the crowd. When I open my bedroom door, there he is standing in a navy-blue suit and a stiff white shirt. I can't keep from smiling at him. He is such a handsome young man. I already have an attachment to Orazio and to his kind and caring personality. He and I will always be brother and sister to each other, even though we didn't come from the same parents.

Orazio says, "Come Carmela, they are all waiting for you and Raffaele."

I ask him, "Where is Raffaele now"?

He replies, "He is in the living room waiting for you."

As we are walking down the stairs, I see Raffaele, and I already feel safe. Raffaele takes my hand and whispers to me, "Get ready because there are many, many people outside waiting for us."

I feel a rush of emotions coming from my stomach to my head. I tell myself that everything will be fine; just stay with Raffaele, and he will watch over me. I tell him and Orazio that I am ready to go and meet everyone but to please stay by my side.

As we get to the front door, I take in a deep breath of air. I exhale and tell them I am ready to walk outside. Orazio opens the door, and Raffaele, looking dashing in his black suit with his handsome face, walks out still holding my hand. I follow him and when I reach the top step, I look out into the street. *Oh my God!* my mind screams. There are a couple hundred people. It's so noisy with everyone talking. Then suddenly it's quiet, and everyone is staring at us. I feel Raffaele squeezing my hand tightly. For a moment, I feel as though I should turn and run back into the house.

We walk down the steps and everyone now is cheering. They are yelling things, "Welcome to America!"

And, "We hope you had a good journey!"

"You're an Italian beauty!"

I can't help but feel happiness at how kind everyone is to me. I didn't expect such a heart-warming experience like this. It's unbelievable!

They have all opened their hearts to me. They have the most amazing decorations on the tables. Red, white, and blue tablecloth covers on every table. They have an American flag on a short flagpole, flying in the wind in the middle of the street. You could see the Italian immigrants are so happy to have America as their new land.

On the tables are large platters and bowls filled with eggplant, salad, macaroni, meats and as always bread. Lots of bread. The men are putting out bottles of red wine. Raffaele is saying that every man on the street has their own wine on the table. We will drink and eat all day. This is beyond happiness to me. For a moment, I get sad. I need my father, mother, and Christina here with me. I focus on my new family and friends to push past the sad feelings I have.

We walk over to Raffaele's father's table with six other men and their wives. They all stand for me. I giggle out of embarrassment because they, one at a time, kiss me and tell me that I am welcome here. The women are as kind and warm to me as their husbands. Raffaele is telling me, "There is an accordionist and a violinist coming later today. We have an opera singer who sounds like Enrico Caruso, the operatic tenor. You will hear familiar instruments and singing happening here today. We will all be dancing the tarantella, our southern Italian folk dance. We hope this will make you feel at peace here with us."

Raffaele puts his arms around me and tells me, "I will take very good care of you. I am the man of our house, and whatever you desire, I will make it happen. Carmela, I know I will always be proud of you. I hope you will feel the same towards me."

Rosa walks over to us and says for us to follow her. She looks at Raffaele and tells him, "You go sit with your friends and neighbors. I'll take Carmela around and introduce her to everyone."

I sigh quietly to myself because I don't want to go with Rosa. I would like to get to know Raffaele. My feelings for him are growing, and I would like to know if he has a temper because when he sees my temper for the first time, I am afraid he will run as fast as he can. What can I say? I do have an Italian temper and a head full of Italian marble. People say Italian marble is full of charm, and certainly, that is me.

CHAPTER 14

The party is wonderful. People are eating and drinking wine, but now they have bottles of grappa and anisette. Everyone is laughing, talking, or dancing. We are having so much fun. Coffee pots are put on the tables. There are all sorts of cookies and cakes. But of course, my favorite—pizzelles—are the one dessert I can't say no to. Especially when they have anise seeds in them. I have eaten and drank so much today. They sure did put on an enjoyable occasion for Raffaele and me.

As I am winding down and sitting with Rosa, I hear someone calling my name. I instantly think I can hear my sister Christina calling out to me. I get a chilling feeling that I am in Italia. It is the strangest cold chill I ever had in my body. I miss my sister, but I can't cry now. I look at the lady walking towards me and calling my name again.

"Carmela. Carmela, it's me, Sofia!" I jump to my feet, and we embrace. Sofia is telling me that Raffaele and Matteo are friends and that Matteo and his parents are from the same village, Marsico Nuova, Potenza, Italia, as Raffaele's parents. "It's a small world for us, isn't it Carmela?"

I smile and say, "I can't believe you are here with me, Sofia. The Blessed Mother has truly watched over us to have put us in the same place."

Sofia says, "But the last of it is the best, Carmela. We live only two streets away from here on Ellsworth Street. It's just a couple of minutes away from here. So we can see each other frequently. We will remain good friends. Besides, we told each other we would be sisters here in America. I would like to keep our bond forever. Do you still feel the same, Carmela?"

"You make me smile with much happiness, Sofia. Yes, I am a person of my word. I will always be your sister. We will look after each other. We both will go through life together, being by each other's side. Oh, Sofia, I am so happy knowing I have you in my life." We hug and kiss each other's cheeks.

Matteo walks over with a glass of wine for Sofia. He introduces himself to me and expresses how fortunate it is that us girls have each other now. He seems to be a gentleman in his manners and his appearance. He tells me that Raffaele invited them to the party. He dresses as all the Italian men with a starched, white shirt, suit, and nice leather, black shoes. I enjoy seeing well-dressed men and women, how stylish they are. Everyone is up to date with today's fashions here in Philadelphia. Sofia asks if she can go into the Pasquariellos house. She would like to see how Rosa decorated the house because everyone in the neighborhood says her house is beautiful. I take her up the front steps, tell her to open the front door and walk into the foyer.

Then she opens the living room door, and you hear her saying, "Oh my, this house is beautiful. The Pesci's house isn't anything like here. I guess we aren't as wealthy as your family." Sofia says, "Both families came from poor villages in Southern Italia."

So I tell Sofia, "Who cares who has more or less. We can do our best to make our lives here better. Isn't that why we came here?"

Sofia says, "You are correct, Carmela. I guess I am surprised how lucky you are. Your future husband is not only handsome, has a good job as a laborer, but also Matteo told me everyone looks up to Raffaele's father and family. If there are problems with any Italians here in South Philly, they go to Mr. Pasquariello for guidance because he has the ability to make the issue go away."

"Sofia, I have no idea about what you are telling me. If that is the case, then what you have to say about my future family does not disappoint me at all. If Mr. Pasquariello helps people, then I say, God bless him for helping. And if your family ever needs his help, please allow him to give your family guidance. After all, Sofia, you said he has the ability to solve problems. Now, let's go back outside and enjoy the party."

I am feeling angry at Sofia with her foolish talk.

When we get to the table where Raffaele and Matteo are sitting, I see discomfort in Raffaele's eyes. He motions his head to keep walking. So, I take Sofia over to Rosa's table. We sit and join the ladies there. Hearing the music, watching them doing the Tarantella folk dance and singing is comforting to my soul. We all are enjoying ourselves this evening, and I don't believe I will ever forget tonight.

But I don't like how Sofia spoke about Mr. Pasquariello. She showed him no respect. Raffaele would not be happy about that. I see Orazio. He is helping everyone with the tables and chairs. He walks by me and stops and bends down, hugs me and kisses me. Walks away with not a word to me. Orazio is such a good and like-able kid. I am thinking he can be my little brother; someone I can watch over and make sure he stays out of trouble. Though at the moment, I feel like he's watching out for me, to make sure I don't need his help.

Rosa says, "We must get moving on your wedding plans. I would like to help the two of you with your wedding. So, whenever you are ready, I am here. I know of a store that has the most elegant wedding dresses. When you and I go, we won't tell the men. It will be a surprise for them when they see you dressed in white on your day." I think to myself Rosa sure is not letting any grass grow under her feet. She wants me married to her son as quickly as possible.

As we say our goodbyes to the guests, I see Raffaele and Matteo talking. No one else is with them, and they seem to be arguing loudly. Mr. Pasquariello walks over to them, and I hear him saying, "Raffaele enough. You two with your loud voices could wake the dead." Matteo walks over to Mr. Pasquariello, and they shake hands.

Raffaele tells Matteo, "You're not getting off that easy. So you better be prepared for my actions. Now, get out of here, and don't let me see you until I want to talk with you again."

Matteo is speaking softly. I can't hear him. But I surely hear Raffaele's voice; it is strong and directed at Matteo. I don't think Raffaele likes Matteo much. I hope Matteo is going to be a good husband to Sofia. Matteo walks over to me and kisses my cheek and tells me, "It was a pleasure meeting you. I hope you and Sofia remain friends through your lifetime."

I giggle at what he is saying to me. I reply to him, "The friendship between me and Sofia is going to be for many years to come. And I know Sofia and I are looking forward to this with much happiness." But I am thinking as we say goodnight that if Raffaele and Matteo don't like each other, how will this affect Sofia and me?

I rush over to Sofia and we embrace and wish each other goodnight. We promise each other to say a special "Hail Mary" for our future husbands, who I say definitely need the Blessed Mother's help. Sofia is yelling at me as Matteo is leading her away that she will see me soon. No matter who likes it or not. We both blow each other a kiss goodnight. Their silhouettes are fading away as they get to the end of the block. Now, they are totally out of my sight, and I don't feel good about Matteo. My intuition tells me that Matteo may be trouble to Raffaele, and I don't like this feeling, and I surely don't want Raffaele to get hurt.

I am saying my goodbyes to everyone and thanking them for coming to meet me. Orazio tells me it's time to go in and prepare ourselves for bed. We will clean the street tomorrow in the daylight. But for now, everyone has gone home, and the celebration is over.

I go over to Raffaele and his father to wish them a goodnight in hopes that Raffaele would give me insight as to what happened between, he and Matteo. But he leans over to me, kisses me on the cheek, and tells Orazio to take me in the house. I say my goodnights, and off I go with Orazio.

Orazio offers me his arm in an exaggerated gentlemanly gesture, smiles at me, and walks me to the house. When we step inside, he asks, "Did you have fun?"

I smile and nod. My curiosity gets the best of me, so I quietly ask, "Raffaele doesn't seem to care for Matteo, does he?"

Orazio glances sideways at me and says, "Nope!"

I sigh and say, "You're not going to say anything else, are you?"

His smile widens and he repeats, "Nope."

His expression makes me giggle, I lean over and kiss his cheek goodnight.

I feel exhausted from all the activities and a very long day. But in the same instance I felt so much love today like being in Italia; eating, laughing and dancing, everyone sharing their love with one another.

I hear a knock at the door. I open it and there stands Raffaele. He says, "I want to explain what went on between Matteo and me." His face is very serious, he waits for me to nod, and continues, "Matteo has been demanding money from the local shopkeepers. I want him to stop taking money from our fellow Italians. But he doesn't want to listen to me. I told Matteo to stop and now we will see if he listens." Raffaele kisses me on my cheek and closes the door.

I wash and get into my nightgown that Rosa has bought for me. She has filled the drawers to my bureau with many beautiful things. I have to thank God and the Blessed Mother for all of their help. They know I belong in this family, and that's why they have sent me here. I say the Our Father prayer for my father, mother, and Christina. I am telling them not to worry about my well-being and that I am happy here, because I am with a warm, caring, and loving family who will unquestionably take very good care of me.

CHAPTER 15

"Carmela, hurry downstairs to eat," Orazio is yelling to me.

When I reach the kitchen to eat breakfast, Rosa tells me that she is taking me around the corner to "The Italian Market" on 9th Street. Raffaele tells me, "South Philly was the favorite landing place of a large wave of Italian immigrants because of the availability of work, factories, farms, and other industries. Ships dock between South Street and Washington Avenue." He also tells me most merchants will be closed on Monday because after the big traditional family supper, no one needs food on Mondays because of the leftovers from Sunday. So, it became a "day of rest." We need to go to the market today.

Rosa says, "We Southern Italian immigrants started the market not too long ago. We can buy fresh fruits and vegetables from the hucksters with their wooden wheeled carts or sidewalk wooden stands. There are many shops with the purveyors selling meats, cheeses, breads, and pastries. Because we can't keep the food cold for long periods, it goes bad and rots quickly. I go there frequently to shop and enjoy all my ethnic foods. If you need anything for yourself, like personal items, we have many other shops on the street for you to visit.

"Orazio works at Mike's Fruit and Produce stand. All of my boys have worked on 9th Street at one time or another. We Italians all help each other. If it's a job, food, or even to find a wife. We stay in the same neighborhood to be around our people who speak the same language. The people here in America don't think much of us. When you go out, Carmela, you must always be with one of us until you get to know the area. You must stay within our boundaries, so no one hurts you. I am only telling you this to protect you. Because many of us found out the brutal way that we are looked upon as peasants. Let's go shopping, and stay close to me. This will be an enjoyable day for us to explore. I will show you how to shop here and bargain with the shopkeepers."

As we leave the house and get to the end of League Street, we turn left, and it's amazing to see so many people. The carts are all side-by-side all lined up like a parade of food. Rosa and I get to 9th Street, and the first cart she stops at is selling vegetables. They are colorful and good in size. I see the purple eggplant. My eyes are wide open. I touch one, and Rosa says, "Would you like eggplant for dinner"?

I quickly smile and respond, "Yes, I know we just ate this, but I could live on this and eat it every day."

She purchased tomatoes to make sauce and eggplant, green squash, and fruits. We stop at a cart and buy a small fig tree that Raffaele will plant in the backyard. After shopping at many carts, we have several bags of food. We stop at a storefront that sells meats and go inside. The floor is covered with sawdust and behind a large butcher block stands a man wearing a long white apron covered with blood. They have Italian sausage. It's so fresh, and the aroma in the air is so sweet.

Rosa asks, "Would you like sausage with the eggplant for supper tonight?"

I answer, "Yes," and ask, "could we get bread? That would make our meal complete for tonight?"

Next to the meat store is a bakery that sells different assortments of baked bread. Some long and thin with sesame seeds. Short, fat ones that are seedless. Rosa picks three loaves of bread. She starts to haggle with the shopkeeper over a few pennies. Her persistent bargaining with all the vendors gets her a bargain every time. She thanks the men and turns towards me and says, "That's how you do it," and laughs. We both are having a good time shopping, talking with everyone. Lots of the shoppers and vendors were at my party yesterday. It feels good to see familiar faces with smiles. They are happy to see me and Rosa. This reminds me so much of home in Ateleta.

On our walk back home, Rosa tells me that we should start to think about me and Raffaele getting married.

"Don't you think sooner would be better? Because Mr. Pasquariello and I would love to be grandparents. He is 71 years old, and I am 57 years old. We would like to see a baby in our house. A child we could love would be a happy feeling for us. We waited too long to start our family, but you are young enough to start soon. Hopefully Giovanni will find someone, but he doesn't want a girl from Italia. He told us when we were talking to Father Foglia about helping us find Raffaele a wife that he wasn't interested in Father finding him a wife. He has an Italian girl that was born in America in the neighborhood he is seeing. He told his father he is in love with her and would marry her when she turns 18 years old next year. We would like you two to marry before he does. We must get you and Raffaele to see Father Foglia at our church. You will love this church; we Italian immigrants built it last year. Our church is beautiful with its stained glass and many statues of our saints. It's called Our Lady of Good Counsel. It's at 816 Christian Street. Only a few blocks from here so very close to home for us. What do you feel Carmela? Would you like to marry soon?"

Rosa looks so sincere with her questions that I feel very comfortable being honest with her, "I do have reservations about rushing into marrying your son. I would like to get to know him for a little time. I want to feel comfortable around him." I see Rosa shaking her head, so I rush on to make her understand. "It's out of nervousness of not knowing him. What he likes? Does he enjoy being around me?"

Rosa puts her hand on my arm and asks, "Carmela, do you think you could fall in love with him after some time together? I married my husband when I was 16 years old because that's what my father said I should do. I never regretted marrying him. I didn't know him, and he was much older than me. I thought when I first saw him that he was an old man." She drops her hand and grins at me, "Don't tell him I said that; he likes to believe I fell in love with him at first site! The truth is, I met him, and two days later we were married. All our days together have not been happy ones. But I would never want anyone else but him as my husband."

We begin walking again, and she continues, "Look at all the blessings he has given me. First of all, my three sons. He has always taken good care of us. As I am sure Raffaele will do the same for you because he has witnessed his father being a good husband and father." Before I can respond to Rosa, she smiles and says, "You think about what I just said to you. We will, in the future, talk about your feelings. Then, we will decide what we will do with your wedding plans."

CHAPTER 16

As the days fly by, it seems as though time is quickly moving. The one true happiness I have here is Raffaele. I get excited every day at 5:30, knowing he will be walking through the front door from a hard day of working. He, too, sells fresh produce going from alley way to alley way and door to door, I call him my salesman, "Il mio venditori." When he comes home, I greet him with a kiss and a hug. I hope the way we greet each other will not change drastically when we marry. In the first few weeks, it was hard to be more open about my feelings with his parents and brothers here all the time; their presence was my salvation due to my shyness. But I am no longer feeling shy, I am self-confident being around the family and expressing openly my feelings towards Raffaele.

After supper on most nights, we have our family talks. It could consist of one or many topics. This evening, it's about Raffaele marrying me soon. Raffaele has chosen the beginning of February 1900, his parents both agree, and so do I. Rosa tells us she is taking me to the largest retail store in America; it's called John Wanamaker's located at 13th and Market Street. It is also called "Grand Depot." This is where she will buy my wedding dress and beautiful white satin shoes. I can't wait to try on wedding dresses with a veil sitting on top of my head. I want Raffaele to be proud of me when he sees me in my wedding dress and happy that I will be his wife.

Walking into Wanamaker's with Rosa is such a sight for me. I've never seen anything, other than my church, as beautiful as this store. It has electric lights and escalators going up and down. This store is one entire city block. That's how large it is. It has clothes on the first floor in one part of the store, dishes, pots and pans on the second floor. The third floor is women's fashions and bridal dresses from all over the world; Paris, London, Italy, and New York. I never felt so important as when the salesman asked if he could help us. Rosa introduces herself to the salesman and then introduces me as her soon to be daughter-in-law. How special and loved I feel from Rosa at this time.

Suddenly, I see the most beautiful painting, it covered the entire wall! The colors remind me of the hills in Ateleta in springtime. The salesman walks up behind me and says, "It is beautiful, isn't it? It's called a mural. Mr. Wanamaker commissioned an artist named, George Washington Nicholson, to paint this."

I feel like jumping in the painting and walking through the hills, it is so lifelike.

Rosa smiles at me and tells me to tell the gentleman what I am looking for in my dress.

"Please, Carmela don't worry about the price."

Mr. Elkins, the salesman, introduces himself to me and suggests I look around and select a few dresses that I like. I tell Mr. Elkins I want everything in white. He says, "We surely can do that. Then we should try a few dresses on to see which dress makes you feel the most beautiful."

My eyes see a white dress with half sleeves and pearls around the trim of the sleeves. It has a high collar. The bodice will fit close to my small chest; this way, I will look like I have breasts. Then it drops at my tiny waist with layers and layers of satin with pearls coming across the front of my stomach in a V shape. The material is so soft to the touch. Rosa comes into the dressing room with a pair of satin wedding shoes for me to try on with the dress and a veil for my head. She starts to show her emotions to me with a few tears in her eyes. She looks me up, and down a couple of times and says, "Oh, Carmela, you look just how I would want my daughter, if I had one, to look like on her wedding day."

As I slide my feet into the shoes, I become two inches taller. I sure do like being over five feet tall. I look at myself in the mirror and feel like a princess. I am astonished at how much older I look and feel since I arrived here in America. I have grown so much without my family. I now realize how much I was treated as a child not as a young woman. Tears come to my eyes, and now we both have misty eyes.

Mr. Elkins calls in to me, "Carmela, do you like the dress?" I open the door and step out towards him. He smiles broadly and says, "You could go across the street to City Hall and marry your fiancé now. You look beautiful!"

I tell him this dress was made for me. I hear Rosa from the dressing room area say, "Come in here, Carmela. We are going to buy you a dress, shoes, a pair of gloves and a veil today. You must wear a wedding veil as symbol of purity." My first response towards Rosa is to put my arms around her and hold on tightly. She giggles and says, "Now is the time to prepare for you and Raffaele to start your life together as husband and wife. I for one am so happy for you both, and I hope you have much happiness in your life together." She kisses me and helps me get out of my wedding dress. "Now Carmela, let's get you and Raffaele to set the exact date of your wedding, so we can prepare for your special occasion. Your ceremony will be first, then your celebration!" She puts her hand under my chin, looks me straight in the eye and says, "I am so happy to have you as my daughter." She turns and begins walking down the aisle.

I can feel the heat in my face from embarrassment at Rosa's kind words to me. We both stop in the middle of the aisle surrounded by many wedding dresses. I have mixed emotions arising inside of me towards her. I look deep into her beautiful, dark brown eyes. I can see love for me in them. I express my sadness at leaving my family in Italia to her.

"How heartbroken I was to hear I was coming to America without my family! But, in a very short time, Rosa, you have made me feel like I am your family. I have much love and respect for you and Mr. Pasquariello for giving me this life. How will I ever repay you?"

As Mr. Elkins is wrapping my dress in cloth so it won't wrinkle, Rosa tells me, "I will do the alterations on your wedding dress. You owe me not a thing. It is I who owes you, for uprooting you from your family and having you travel here to America. We will put all of this to rest. We will always remember where we came from and our love for our Mother country and family left behind. Now we will move forward with love and respect for our new country and family."

I reply, "Yes Rosa, that's what I will do. Move forward, and never, ever forget."

Rosa smiles at me and says, "Speaking of never forgetting, Carmela, today is a great day for all of us Italians. Not only here in America, but also in Italia. Today we celebrate that on October 12, 1492, Cristosoro Colombo discovered America. This is a great day for us to be proud to be Italian, but also, we are Americans. We celebrate his accomplishment every year, this holiday began in New York in 1866 and then in San Francisco in 1869, followed by the rest of the country every year."

I look at Rosa and before I knew what I was saying, I heard myself say, "Oh now I know why Raffaele is always telling me history stories about us Italians! He not only has your wisdom, but he also has your love for history, not only for Italia, but for America as well."

CHAPTER 17

Raffaele and I have settled on Monday, February 12, 1900, for our wedding day. I am so excited that I soon will be Mrs. Raffaele Pasquariello, though am somewhat nervous about our wedding night. With all the excitement of the celebration and festivities on our day and all the people attending our wedding, I will be very flustered. However, the thoughts of our wedding night are taking a greater toll on me.

So, I went to talk to Father Foglia. I told him I am a virgin, and I don't know what to expect on my wedding night. He sat and talked with me for what seemed like hours. Who am I kidding? It was two hours of him lecturing me. The only thing I remember is him repeating, "Never go to bed angry at one another."

I decide to go to Sofia for some information about sex because she is no longer a virgin. I also go to her because I don't have my sister Christina or my mother to talk to. So, her input will be a great help to me. I am not embarrassed to talk with her. As I sit and ask Sofia many questions, she laughs at me most of the time. She keeps saying to me, "It will all be fine. Raffaele won't hurt you, and he knows you never had sex before. Trust him with your body. You already trust him with your heart. He is affectionate towards you and grateful to have you in his life. You can see how he feels about you by his eyes and his actions. He is loving towards you and gentle."

Sofia takes my hand and looks in my eyes, "I will tell you about my father and mother and their marriage. My mother never enjoyed sex, so my father began to hate her. So, whatever you do, Carmela, always say yes to your husband. Because if you don't, Raffaele may do what my father did. He found someone else to have sex with and started another family."

I look at Sofia and see how distressed she is that her father did that to the family. I will always be kind and understanding to Raffaele because I know he will always be a true gentleman to me. After my talk with Sofia, I feel much better and look forward to my first night with Raffaele. Now that I have this issue settled in my head, I will move on with my plans for my wedding day.

Today, November 23, we celebrate a new holiday for me, my first Thanksgiving! I have never seen so much food served at one time, and it is delicious. The men laugh and play cards while the women work in the kitchen. Well, it really isn't work; we laugh as I clumsily try to follow Rosa's lead in preparing the meal. Rosa laughs with me, not at me, which makes the cooking lesson so much fun. Though she is pleasantly surprised that I can make the porchetta all'abruzzese without help. My father loves pork, so we made this dish often at home.

Besides the porchetta all'abruzzese, supper consists of turkey stuffed with Italian sausage, mashed potatoes, baked squash, and of course, a pan of Rosa's baked lasagna with meat, all served with homemade red wine. My favorite part is the Italian lasagna and porchetta. For dessert, scrippelle filled with nuts and dates, and pizzelles. After desert, we have coffee, anisette, and grappa. For Thanksgiving, we Italians love our new country and want to celebrate our new lives here in America by combining foods from Italia and America.

Much of the dinner conversation is about Christmas decorations and shopping. Rosa's whole face lights up when she speaks of the beautiful Christmas trees and holly decorations. She also tells me that some Americans are against Christmas trees since they are a German tradition. But Rosa thinks they are beautiful, and I cannot wait to see one. I am excited to see the silver and gold bows and crystal stars that decorate the stores and windows.

Six days after Thanksgiving, Raffaele and I are in the kitchen talking, and a loud commotion begins outside. The sounds of loud whistles, yelling, and people running in the streets cause panic throughout the house. Raffaele tells Rosa and I to stay in the house while he goes to see what is happening.

It seems like hours have passed, Orazio comes in and tells us there is a large fire on Market Street; many businesses are burning to the ground. The fire started in a store called Partridge & Richardson and spread to at least seven other stores, including Strawbridge & Clothier, one of Rosa's favorite stores.

After the fires are out, we learn eight firemen were injured and over 2,000 people have been put out of work. This is devastating news; families will be without food and can lose their homes or apartments. Raffaele spends the next couple weeks gathering names of people who lost their jobs in our neighborhood, so we can help them however we can. We begin gathering everything from food baskets, to clothes, and a toy for each child affected for the holiday. The smiles of appreciation make me feel so good and blessed that I am a part of a family that cares so much.

Raffaele is so busy helping people affected by the fire that I don't get to spend much time with him and miss talking to him. But I would never be that selfish to demand time when people need his help just to eat.

Before I know it, it is Christmas Eve. Our Christmas Eve meal is one of our favorites: it's called the meal of seven fishes. Rosa and I go on 9th street today and purchase scallops, shrimp, flounder, oysters, clams, calamari, and smelts for Christmas Eve supper. The center of the table is decorated with an advent wreath with five candles. It is so busy in the house with everyone sharing the duties of getting the table and meal prepared for our supper. The table is set with roses, beautiful fine china, crystal stemware, and silver flatware. I begin to feel overwhelmed with emotions. I feel so loved from everyone here. At times, it's not at all what I expected, I am very grateful for my family here in America. It is only us tonight for dinner, and I'm looking forward to the quiet time with Raffaele and the family.

At 6:00 PM, we are all ready for our feast to begin. Rosa is absolutely the finest cook. The pleasant and familiar aromas going through the house make me feel at home. The scent of the fish, garlic oil, and red sauce are warming my mouth and senses, I am having a strong craving for our traditional foods.

On Christmas morning, Raffaele has a beautiful box wrapped in green and red paper. It has a large, red bow and ribbon on it. He hands the box to me and wishes me happiness on our first Christmas together. He asks me to unwrap the box in front of everyone because they also will be happy with what is inside the box. The weight of the box feels like there isn't anything inside. So, I hurry to take the wrapping off, and to my surprise, inside is a smaller box. It also is wrapped. Everyone is laughing, and Orazio is saying, "Carmela, hurry and open the box. I can't wait to see what is inside."

I again unwrap the next box and to my surprise inside it is a ring box, "mahogany wood." I am frozen in my seat, and I can't speak or even look at Raffaele. My hands are shaking so much that I can't open the box to see what is waiting for me inside. As I finally get the lid open, my dream comes true in the form of a ring. It's a platinum diamond solitaire engagement ring.

Orazio jumps up and cheers me on by saying, "It's about time you become my sister."

Then I look at Raffaele, and we finally kiss a warm, long lips-to-lips kiss. Oh, how sweet he is to me. He takes the ring out of the box and slides it on my ring finger.

"It's a perfect fit," he says to me.

"It's beautiful," I tell him. I am so happy at this precious moment between Raffaele and myself that we soon will be married, start a family, and always be happy together as we are now.

Everyone in the house is so excited for us. They all are expressing their happiness for us to wed. The entire family is a blessing to me. Now to get the wedding plans together for our big day.

Christmas is celebrated with lots of gifts. Here in America, they sure have many holidays for celebrating with food, alcohol, wine, and lots of family. The Pasquariellos are many. We are going from one home to another, visiting relatives and even some friends. After I marry Raffaele, I will have many new relatives in America, the place I now call home. I couldn't be any happier with life than I am now.

The week following Christmas was quiet and cold. Though we don't have any snow, it feels very cold. During this quiet time, I begin to think of and miss my family back in Italia. Sofia helps me put a letter together to send them, so they will know how happy I am and not worry.

It's New Year's Eve, and tomorrow will be a big day for celebrating. It's the turn and beginning of a new century. It will be the twentieth century with so much to look forward to for me and Raffaele.

But before that day to celebrate, we will start with tonight. Raffaele is taking me out for supper with some of his friends. This evening, I will tell him of my New Year's resolution for 1900. We will take the trolley car into town to meet his friends near City Hall. It's an Italian restaurant that his friend owns, and all the patrons are Italians from Italia. Raffaele only has Italian friends. Except at his part-time job at a bar, where the two other bartenders are Irish. Raffaele tells me that they have his back whenever one of the Irish patrons start a fight with him because he is Italian. He likes being a bartender much more so than selling fruit and vegetables. He likes talking to the patrons, and he makes more money.

He tells me many interesting and funny stories about the bar with lots of characters, coming in and out every day. Raffaele says, "Carmela, look across the street. You see the sign that reads 'Cosimo's Ristorante'? That's where we will meet my friends."

When we reach the front door of the restaurant, the door swings open, and a man comes rushing out to Raffaele. You can see he is drunk. He is so loud and staggering all over the sidewalk. I think to myself, *Before he can get to Raffaele, he will fall flat on his face.*

Raffaele is holding him up, and he quickly turns towards me. I back up about two feet, so he doesn't grab me because I can't support or hold him up. Raffaele grabs him again and holds him steady on his feet. Here come two more men out the front door to help Raffaele. They bring him inside the restaurant and tell the waiter to bring back coffee for Carmen. The waiter is telling them that if Carmen gets loud one more time, they will put him out onto the street. He finally settles down by falling asleep. Raffaele and his two friends take him into a back room and lay him down on the floor, so he can sleep off being drunk. I ask them who that man was, and Raffaele tells me, "He is a customer at my bar."

When they return, Raffaele introduces me to them. First, he says to them, "This is my future wife, Carmela." I blush at the thought of him saying I am his future bride.

Both men extend their hands out to shake my hand, but I say, "I am from Italia. I would prefer a hug from a *paisan* of my future husband."

They both laugh, and we hug and kiss each other. Raffaele introduces them to me as Pasquale and Vincenzo Mozella. They are brothers that own this restaurant with their mother and sister.

Pasquale says, "I am delighted to meet you. Please follow me. I have a special table set up for you two. And we have prepared several special dishes for you to try. Come sit and enjoy the food and wine. It's time to enjoy yourself and bring in the New Year, 1900, with us."

This is my real first date with Raffaele. And a wonderful one at that. There is a small band with a violinist, celloist, and an accordionist with a clarinet player. I've never had so much fun and laughter, watching everyone dance. They sure are enjoying themselves. But me, I am too shy to dance in front of Raffaele. And he doesn't dance at all. It's great meeting his friends and especially getting to be with only him at the supper table. We can finally be by ourselves and talk. Then they come out with the limoncello and grappa. I have three glasses of grappa, and on the trolley ride home, I have to get off to vomit. The trolley conductor waits for me to get back on. The only thing I remember is telling Raffaele I don't want to vomit on my new dress, so he had to make sure I didn't, or I would be mad at him.

The next morning is a killer for my head. When Rosa sees my condition, she's upset with Raffaele. She blames him for my getting sick. Rosa must say to him at least a dozen times, "You should know better than to give her so much grappa to drink. Look at her."

Orazio can't stop laughing at me. He gets me so upset that I tell him I will take him out back and tie him to the clothesline post.

"Oh Carmela, you are a mean drunk, and you would never hurt me," he says as he is still laughing. I look over at Rosa and tell her I am going upstairs to try and rest. But before I leave the kitchen, Raffaele says, "Why don't you tell everyone your New Year's resolution. I am sure they would love to hear this."

I must look puzzled because I say, "I didn't tell you my resolution for the New Year."

Raffaele says, "Come on Carmela. You told me your resolution on the trolley car."

Mr. and Mrs. Pasquariello, Giovanni, Orazio and Raffaele are all looking at me. So I feel the heat, and it's extremely hot where I am sitting.

Mr. Pasquariello laughingly says, "Come on Carmela, we are family now. Tell us your New Year's resolution."

"Raffaele, could you help me because I don't remember saying anything about that. I knew I wanted to tell you, but I never had the opportunity to express myself to you. What did I say to you, Raffaele?"

"Remember when you got sick on the trolley ride home?"

"Yes, I remember that."

"Well, Carmela, you told me that after we get married that I would only listen to you because your smarter than I am. Not only will you run the household, but you will tell me how many babies we will have."

I must still be a little drunk because of the way I respond to Raffaele in front of his family. I don't know where the courage came from, but it came flying out of my mouth in front of Raffaele's parents. I don't want them to think I am being disrespectful towards them. After all they have been so kind and loving to me from the moment we met.

"Who doesn't know that the female keeps the house clean expected to fulfill the roles of matrimony and motherhood? As mom and I know that Italian women are encouraged to be confident and courageous from a young age that family always comes first, but most importantly, that we should never dishonor our husband or embarrass our family, an Italian female can make a meal from a bag of beans, she can raise 10 children without anyone helping her, and will make a home for her family, wherever they live, even if it's in a two-room house.

"Well, Raffaele, if that's what I said then that's what I mean."

The entire room lit up with laughter. That is except me and Mom. I look at her and without saying one word, she stands up and says, "It's about time that a woman ruled the home. Because she's the one who takes care of the house and the children. So, Carmela, I am with you. And if you boys think you can handle everything, please, cook supper tonight and clean the kitchen from breakfast. I will come back and inspect the kitchen after you clean it." Rosa walks over to me and says, "Come on Carmela, it's time for you to take a nap." We walked out of the kitchen with our heads held high holding hands. As soon as we reached the staircase, we were laughing and enjoying every moment that we finally told them who was the boss of the house. They didn't clean the kitchen or cook supper that night. But it was fascinating how great Rosa and I felt to finally tell them how we feel. Rosa told me, "You do not have to get drunk to speak your thoughts." I knew right then and there that I would always have Rosa on my side. After her living all those years with four males, it had to feel good with finally having another female in the house.

As a result of my overindulgence the night before, we do not get to attend the "Mummer's Parade" that day, but at least I got to speak my mind for the first time with the family. I promise myself that next year I will attend the Mummer's Parade.

Tomorrow is the sixth of January, "the Epiphany" An Italian Christian festival, commemorating the manifestation of Christ to the gentiles in the persons of the Magi, or three wise men, it is known as the Twelfth Day of Christmas. This is one of my favorite holidays! Italian children everywhere are expecting an overnight visit from La Befana. La Befana is the Italian Christmas Witch who will fly on her broomstick to all of the children's' houses, go down the chimney, and leave the good boys and girls a gift and sweets in their stockings. For naughty ones, a piece of coal or garlic. She does-n't miss one house where there is a child. When we were children, Christina and I would try and fall asleep fast, so we did not see her, but we would wake up early to check our stockings. I am proud to say that we never received anything other than sweets.

CHAPTER 18

Today, January 7, 1900 is a day I will never forget. It starts out the usual way.

We are all at the breakfast table eating; the smell of coffee and toast fills the air. Suddenly Raffaele's father grabs his chest with both hands and falls to the floor. We all jump to our feet in disbelief. Raffaele quickly gets on his knees and tries to cradle his father in his arms, yelling, "Padre don't die, please don't die."

Rosa stands next to Raffaele with this strange look on her face, her mouth wide opened, unable to move. Her lips are turning blue because she neither is breathing nor making any sounds. Orazio rushes over to his mother and gently puts her in a chair. He is telling her to breathe.

"Madre take air into your lungs and then exhale. You need to breathe now because your face is turning blue!"

She takes air into her lungs, but when she exhales, a sound comes out of her that I had never heard before. This sound goes through me like a knife and causes my body to shake. I sit down before I fall to the floor. My mind becomes numb, and I feel like I am in a bad dream that I cannot wake up from, Rosa is on her knees next to her husband praying to God to save him. She is screaming, "Please don't take him from me. What will I do without him?"

Raffaele looks over at Giovanni and says to him, "Go and get our next-door neighbor, Philip. He will help us get father to the hospital."

Giovanni says, "He is gone. We can't save him." Rosa has Mr. Pasquariello's head in her lap. She is rocking back and forth. She kisses his lips and tells him, "I will see you again. *Ci vediamo presto.*"

I am vaguely aware that Philip comes into the kitchen, I see his mouth move, but the ringing in my ears is louder than his voice, I watch him speak to us and point to the other room. He is now talking to Giovanni. I hear the words, but they have no meaning to me, I'm still shaking uncontrollably. I feel Orazio's hand on my shoulder and slowly his words penetrate my brain, his voice was starting to crack, "Come Carmela."

I turn my head and look at Orazio, he suddenly looks so young. I realize that I need to be strong for my new family and walk over to Rosa to help guide her into the next room. We both sit, and I cradle her in my arms, I can think of no words to say, so I slowly rock her back and forth while she sobs. This strong woman who walked the streets of Philadelphia like she owned them, suddenly feels so fragile.

On Wednesday, January 10, 1900, three days after Mr. Pasquariello died, we bury him at Holy Cross Cemetery. We had three nights of a viewing and then his burial with his family and friends. Rosa gave him a traditional Italian wake and funeral. And now she will wear black for two years in mourning, and the boys will wear a black arm band on the left arm, the one closest to their heart.

Raffaele and I have decided to wait for our wedding day. We feel it should be in the summertime, but Rosa feels we should marry in May, putting our plans on hold for four months is a sufficient amount of time. Besides, Rosa told us that Raffaele's father would want us to carry on with life. Our new date for our wedding will be on Monday, May 14, 1900. Raffaele and I believe if his mother feels that this is an adequate amount of time, we will follow her wishes.

After the funeral, many people come to our home. An old lady comes into the kitchen and hands Rosa an envelope. Rosa smiles at this lady and asks her to sit and have a cup of coffee with her. They both sit down at the table and Rosa gives Giovanni the envelope and says to him, "You know where to put this." Giovanni takes it from her and walks towards the living room and up the stairs. Though I can hear the stairs creaking, I'm not sure exactly where he takes the envelope, or for that matter, how much money is in the envelope. This is all mind boggling to me; what exactly is happening here?

During the wake, many people came to our home with Mass Cards and envelopes. Or they handed Raffaele cash. They would shake his hand and put the money in his palm. Raffaele said most of the men all said the same thing, "I loved and respected your father..." then they would kiss Raffaele. Tell him they owed his father the money they had borrowed from him for one reason or another.

"My father had such a positive impact on all of these people," Raffaele is saying to me. I feel so emotionally drained, but I feel Raffaele is totally lost. He is putting on a brave appearance for everyone, especially for his mother. Rosa told Raffaele that after they bury his father, he will be the man of the house. All responsibilities will be on his shoulders to keep the family strong and the business in the street running smoothly. She quietly but firmly states, "It is your line of work now Raffaele. You must keep it going."

I am puzzled.

"Raffaele, what do you mean business in the street? What is your mother saying to you?"

Raffaele looks at me with an overwhelmed look and says, "Carmela, there are things that are better you know nothing about."

I give a puzzled look to Raffaele and think to myself; I won't say anything to him about what this all means now. But after things settle down in our home, I will speak to him about what is truly going on. I will let all things rest, but I will remember.

After four very long, heart-wrenching days, I say my prayers before bedtime and have a conversation with the Blessed Mother. I always start my prayers to her with much gratitude for her love for me. But tonight, my prayers to her are not about Raffaele's father, but about my father:

Dear Blessed Mother, the grieving I am experiencing to-night is the worst I could ever imagine. For when my father dies, I won't be by his side to hold his hand, or to tell him how very important he is to me; how he always cared and protected me with his love.

I feel my last farewell to my father was when he was waving to me when the ship was departing the dock. He was standing there, moving his arms up and down with his yellow handkerchief. This will be engraved in my memory forever. Tonight, I come to realize that this was our last goodbye to each other.

"I will always love you Father."

CHAPTER 19

Tomorrow, May 14, 1900, is Raffaele and my special day. We will finally be married. Tonight will also be special for us because this is the night that Raffaele will serenade me. I've dreamed of being serenaded by my future husband since I was little. I am so glad that many of our old traditions have followed us to America. I will keep as many of these traditions alive as I can.

There is a large crowd of people on our street this evening. People from all over South Philadelphia are here to listen to Raffaele sing to me. He will sing about his love and devotion for me. I can feel the enthusiasm in the air. People are speaking loudly, laughing and enjoying themselves. The men come to drink and to be with their *paesani*, but the women want to feel the love in the air. They all want to remember the night that their husbands serenaded them. That's what we females want to feel, the intense enjoyment of love in our lives.

I hear an accordion and violin playing out front of the house. I am waiting for Raffaele to call out to me to come outside. I can't stop giggling at all the excitement out there on League Street.

I hear Raffaele calling out my name.

"Carmela, come to the window. I want to sing to you. I want all of my family and friends to hear of my love for you."

I look down from the bedroom window. There are hundreds of people waiting for me to join them. They are yelling, "Carmela, come outside. Raffaele is waiting for you." My heart starts to beat quickly when I see Raffaele's face in the crowd.

I hurried downstairs to the front door. After I open the door, I walk down the front steps and stop at the last step. The crowd opens up, and there stands Raffaele. I can't express the happiness I have in my heart. Rosa walks over to me and hands me a glass of wine.

She kisses my cheek and says, "Enjoy the love Raffaele is expressing to you." She smiles and turns to walk away. She turns back to me and says, "I am proud to have you as my daughter." Rosa turns back to the people and tells everyone, "Let the festivities begin, because Raffaele is wooing Carmela's heart tonight."

Raffaele walks towards me, and he is singing in his beautiful baritone voice. His words are coming from his heart. I never heard these words before in a song. He is telling me how beautiful and dainty he thinks I am. When he first saw me, he knew instantly he wanted me to be his wife. I can't stop smiling at him for all his beautiful words about me. Everyone is having fun and drinking. They are all singing and dancing. Men with men and women with women. It's all wonderful. Here I stand on American soil to start a loving life with Raffaele. What else could I ask from the Blessed Mother? Not a thing!

Now he is singing a song all us Italians know, "O Sole Mio" or in English, "My Sunshine," "My Sun." He continues to sing the last verse:

I stay below your window. When night comes and the sun has gone down.

After Raffaele sings this verse about 10 times, that's when I realize that he has had too much to drink. I conclude that the celebrating has to end, or Raffaele might not make it to the church tomorrow.

I thank everyone for coming and sharing our joy but explain Raffaele and I must get some rest for a busy day tomorrow, "our wedding." As I blow kisses to everyone and say good night, I am yelling on top of everyone else's voices and say, "I hope to see you tomorrow at the church." I say my good night to everyone and notice Rosa pulling Raffaele aside. She hands him something small, and I see Raffaele straighten up looking surprised. He slowly bends over and kisses his mother on the head. I smile to myself. This family is so loving; I can't help but wonder what she gave him.

I am having a restless night. I close my eyes, but they have springs on them. They just pop open. Anxiety has taken over me. I feel so exhausted, but I can't settle my mind down. It feels like my brain can't stop from spinning. I should have had a few glasses of wine. As I think about the wine and the smiling faces, my mind starts to relax, and I stop worrying about tomorrow. I think how nice it will be to eat, drink, and dance with Raffaele. I picture my head on his shoulder as we sway back and forth in a slow, romantic dance, and I'm drifting to sleep with a smile on my face. Why was I so anxious? After all, this time tomorrow, it will all be over, and Raffaele and I will be...OH MY...the wedding night! And now I'm back to worrying! Forget the wine; I should have had grappa, that would have made me relax and hopefully sleep. Oh well!

Daylight has lit up my bedroom, and the sun is full blown in my room. I can't and won't get any rest now. I need some coffee to help me get moving. But I know coffee will only make me jittery.

Orazio is knocking on my bedroom door and asking if I am awake.

"If you are, Carmela, come downstairs. We are all in the kitchen having breakfast."

I call out to Orazio and tell him I need a couple of minutes, and I will join them. I share with Orazio that it felt strange not having Raffaele in the house last night. That's the first night we didn't sleep under the same roof since I've been here for nine months. But we will be together tonight. I ask Orazio if Raffaele went to his cousin Antonio's house to sleep last night. He tells me that Raffaele went over there after I went in the house, right after I said goodnight to everyone.

"He didn't want to talk or see you again until you are walking up the church aisle towards him."

At the breakfast table, Orazio tells me that I should use the bathroom first since it's my wedding day, and I have so much to do. He walks over to me and gives me a tight hug. He always makes me laugh at his silliness and his tender love towards me. Rosa yells at Orazio to not be a pain today.

"Your brother and Carmela are getting married. Now, let her go. After Carmela is finished in the bathroom, you go and get washed and dressed. Go over to the church, and see if Father Foglia needs you to help with the flowers for the altar."

As I am getting washed, Rosa knocks on the bathroom door and tells me she is waiting in my bedroom for me. She wishes to talk with me and has something very special to give to me. And she also would like to help me get into my wedding dress. When I go into my bedroom, she is sitting on my bed. In her hands, she has a small metal box. She tells me that, she and Mr. Pasquariello, before his death, went into Center City to Bailey, Banks and Biddle on jeweler's row, and, "We both thought you would look beautiful in these on your wedding day."

I open the lid and, in this box, lined with red velvet was a pair of pearl earrings in platinum. Rosa starts to cry and tells me that she and Michele always wanted a girl, but it just wasn't meant to be.

"We have three good sons, but a girl in the house would have brought me even more joy. She could have helped in the kitchen and helped around the house. Her children would have been my children because mothers and daughters are close. Boys, they have a tendency to go to the wife's family. You have been a joy for us. God gave us you, and we couldn't be happier. It's sad that Michele didn't live long enough to see today."

I take Rosa's hands and look her in the eye just for a brief second. I couldn't look any longer because I knew I would fall apart.

"Rosa, you will always be welcome in our lives. And our children will always be yours to love and cherish because Raffaele and I will always be by your side. We will never leave you." I smile and tell her, "It's time for you to button all those 20 buttons on the back of my dress." We now are laughing and having fun in my getting ready.

To my surprise, Sofia walks into the bedroom. She is here to help with my hair. Rosa tells Sofia to take over for her with my dress, so Rosa can get ready for church. She reminds me not to look into the mirror after I am dressed. I smile; I almost forgot it is bad luck to look in the mirror while in my wedding dress until after the wedding. If I do, I have to take one of my shoes off until we say our vows. I don't want to hop down the aisle, so I turn my back on the mirror.

I am having a hard time getting my shoes on. Sofia is helping me. She asks me, "Why did you get a smaller size than you are? You know you have big feet, and we will never get them on unless I tell Giovanni to get me some grease from the kitchen. Maybe that will help get your feet to slide into your wedding shoes. Or maybe you could look in the mirror; that way we only have to get one shoe on."

"Please, Sofia could you be nice to me today? I have a long day ahead of me."

She bends her head close to my ear and says, "Oh, but wait for tonight!"

I look at her as if my eyes were knives. And if it was up to me, those knives would stick her to my bedroom wall.

"Oh Sofia, could you not? Please don't. I have so much going on in my head, and you are not helping me. Just for now be kind and gentle because I want to scream at someone because my nerves are so bad. So, help me today, and keep your remarks to yourself." We both laugh and hug.

After Rosa and I are dressed, we go outside to meet the carriage, which will take us to the church. When we arrive at Our Lady of Good Counsel Church, I have a hard time breathing. Giovanni is waiting for us at the top of the church steps. He must see the panic on my face because he runs down the steps straight to me and reaches into the carriage for my hands. He touches them gently and smiles broadly at me. He says to me, "Carmela, step on this step-down, and I will hold you till your feet touch the sidewalk."

I smile at Giovanni; he can tell how nervous I am and is helping me. Before we go into the church, Orazio hands Giovanni a beautiful bouquet of flowers, Giovanni turns and tells me that Raffaele bought these for me. I hold them to my face and breath in the beautiful smell. Orazio rushes on and tells Giovanni to hurry up and give me their father's ring that mother gave Raffaele last night. Giovanni reaches for my hand and puts their father's ring in my hand, it is so beautiful; a large ruby is nestled between two diamonds. The band is heavy and gold, I can feel Raffaele's father's presence in this moment. I close my hand around the ring and put it to my heart to think of him for a moment. I am so happy to be able to put this ring on Raffaele's finger to symbolize our marriage. I take a deep breath as I realize, I am marrying the man who will take care of me. I will honor him and do whatever is necessary to keep him happy.

Now, it's all happening. I am here to marry Raffaele. My thought is, *I can't wait for Raffaele to see me in my wedding dress. I hope he thinks I am beautiful because I feel just as I thought I always would.*

It's a warm and sunny spring day in Philadelphia. A wonderful 72 degrees. Many people are on the sidewalk waiting for me. You hear some of the ladies saying, "Carmela, you are a beautiful bride. Oh, wait till Raffaele sees you in your wedding dress."

As I walk up the church steps, I stop at the entrance just for a moment for me to gather my thoughts for this day.

Giovanni says to me, "It's time to walk up the aisle to Raffaele."

My heart jumps at the thought of seeing him. As Giovanni walks me to Raffaele holding my arm, I feel my legs are weak. I have so much happiness going through my body at this time. I see Raffaele at the end of the aisle. Raffaele looks handsome in his vest, striped trousers, suspenders, wing tip collar shirt, bow tie, and black shoes. He looks so handsome in a tuxedo. As I approach him, he takes my hand, and we walk to the altar. We kneel down, and Father Foglia starts with thanking everyone for attending Geltrude Carmela and Raffaele's wedding.

He begins with his prayers, then Mass and Communion. Everyone in church all received Holy Communion. Our Mass is over an hour long because of all the guests. It is a beautiful ceremony. There are flowers of all colors in the aisle. The beautiful statues of our saints make the church look like a castle. During the ceremony, I walked over to Our Blessed Mother's altar and laid a bouquet of yellow roses at the foot of the Virgin Mary. Our family, friends and neighbors are here to celebrate with us.

We are walking out of the church, and everyone is throwing Italian coins and rice at us. With all the rice that's thrown, we will have lots of babies. That's what we Italians believe anyway. I am thinking, *I sure hope not!* Though the coins are to bring riches to us, and I admit, I wouldn't mind that at all.

We walk down the steps to the carriage. We are on our way in town for our wedding reception. Raffaele helps me to get in the carriage and turns to me and kisses me on the lips in front of everyone standing outside the church. He laughs and says out loud, "Now no one can say anything about us because we are married."

Everyone is cheering us on as we are leaving. He kisses me again and tells me that today is the happiest he has ever been. I tell him that's exactly how I feel at this moment also. I couldn't be happier now that I am Mrs. Raffaele Pasquariello, a married woman.

Raffaele touches my hand, and I hold onto his for a moment; I cannot move. He leans in real close to my face and stares into my eyes, kisses me and says, "Carmela, I will always love and cherish you forever.

CHAPTER 20

We ride directly to Cosimo's Restaurant for our wedding reception. Raffaele and I are the first to get there. There is a photographer behind his camera taking photographs of us. He keeps saying to us, "Smile! You two look like you're angry at each other."

I reply, "No, we are just tired."

I smile at him, and he tells me his flat folding Kodak Camera can take 48 pictures. I have never seen anything like this. He only has about 20 plates because he used the other 28 at the house and church. So, he wants me and Raffaele to smile more because the pictures will look like we are having a good time at our wedding reception.

After he takes a couple pictures, I excuse myself. I tell Raffaele I should go to the bathroom to freshen up before all the guests get here. When I reach the bathroom door, I lock it behind me. I feel an enormous amount of emotions running through my body. I can no longer hold them in, so I just let everything out. These emotions release with such a force that the tears are coming out of my eyes like a flood. I can't stop crying, and there is a sharp pain in my heart that is deeply felt on my wedding day. I can't help thinking of my family today who are all in Italia. I say my prayer to the Blessed Mother and ask her to watch over each and every one of them. Oh, how I miss their love.

I hear Rosa, my new mother, and Sofia, my best friend, knocking on the bathroom door calling on me to open the door. I open the door, and Rosa says, "Carmela, your guests are arriving." Then Sofia pushes me back into the bathroom and pushes Rosa into the hallway, Sofia closes and locks the door. Rosa is saying, "Carmela, please come and greet everyone." Now, I am laughing because Sofia always says Rosa has to control everyone and everything.

I tell Rosa to just give me two minutes, and I will be right there. Sofia gives me a big, warm smile. I laugh even harder at Sofia and tell her that her beautiful smile always calms me down. And it surely has worked this time. She puts her arms around me and says, "Everything is fine. Take a deep breath and just hold yourself together a little while longer. I know you're upset that your family isn't here, but now the Pasquariellos are your family. Let's clean your face and straighten you up. Go out there with a smile, and enjoy yourself."

After I brushed my hair and wiped my tears away, off we went.

We go into the dining room and straight over to Raffaele. He takes my arm and gently pulls me closer to him. Sofia wishes us happiness in our life together, kisses me, then Raffaele and turns and walks away. Raffaele asks me if I am fine. I smile and nod. He puts his arm around my waist and gently pulls me to him to assure me that he is by my side now and forever. Standing next to him is exactly where I want to be.

Raffaele and I happily greet our guests. They are kissing and hugging us. The men are giving Raffaele envelopes, and some are giving him cash for a wedding gift. He has bulges in his tuxedo jacket pockets from all of the cash.

We go to sit down and enjoy our food. There is antipasto, ravioli, manicotti, braciola, roasted chicken with rosemary, and plates full of cold meats, cheese, and hard crusted breads of all sizes. There is a bartender pouring beer, wine, and other liquor for all of our guests. There is so much food, but before we start to eat, Giovanni stands up and asks everyone if they could be silent for a minute. The room became quiet and Giovanni thanks everyone for being here to celebrate Raffaele and my happy day. He says, "I don't have too long of a speech. Everyone here knows I am a quiet person." He lifts up his wine glass and says, "I am so honored to be here for my brother and his beautiful bride. All of us Pasquariellos are so happy, Carmela, for you to join our family." Giovanni holds up his glass of wine and says, "May God bless you both, Raffaele and Carmela. *Salute!*"

Many joined in by holding up their glasses and echoing, "*Salute!*"

Once the voices quieted down, a small child's voice can be heard saying, "Can we eat now? I'm hungry!"

And with that, the party started.

During the dinner, Raffaele takes my hand and leads me to the center of the room. My dream has come true; Raffaele and I are dancing.

After dinner, we have a three-tier wedding cake from Termini's Bakery in South Philadelphia along with pizzelles and biscotti with almonds. We had wine, Anisette, Sambuca and beer. Everyone is having so much fun. Then we decide to cut the cake. Raffaele gives me my first bite, and then I fed him his. Everyone is applauding with such happiness for us. The music is playing, and lots of people are doing the Tarantella dance, an Italian wedding tradition; even Giovanni is dancing! I'm dancing with Sofia, and I feel just like a little girl filled with much laughter and happiness dancing in my wedding dress.

Finally, we say our farewells and off we go to the Lorraine Hotel on North Broad Street. It's just a few blocks from here. This hotel is luxurious and 10 stories high. It has many new features like electricity and an elevator. It also has some apartments that are for some of Philadelphia's wealthy residents that live there. As we walk into the hotel, the doorman holds the door for us.

We reach the reception desk, and the bellhop is bringing in our luggage. I can't believe how splendid the furniture and carpet look. Most of the walls are covered in wood. Deep, dark, cherry wood to match the furniture in the lobby. I guess anyone watching me can see by my face I have never seen anything so magnificent.

We get on the elevator to go up to the eighth floor. This is such an amazing invention. Raffaele tells me we are on that floor because that's where the honeymoon suite is. The porter opens the door to our suite.

"Oh my God," I whisper to Raffaele. I thought the lobby was out of this world. Our suite is more elaborate than I ever could have imagined. It was like walking into a castle. The entire main room's wall is of glass. You can overlook the entire city of Philadelphia. From the drapes and furniture to the wood floors, it's extravagant!

The porter puts our luggage in the bedroom. Raffaele puts a large silver coin in the man's hand and says, "Good night and thank you."

We both walk over to the large window and you can see all the tall buildings around City Hall with the statute of William Penn. There is a full moon plus the gas streetlights are on. I feel almost like I am in a fantasy, and when I open my eyes, this all will be gone. We both gaze out the window and all of a sudden Raffaele embraces me. He kisses me passionately and tells me how beautiful I looked today. He gently holds my face in his hands and again kisses me, but tenderly this time.

He walks over to the coffee table and picks up the bottle of wine, he pours us each a glass of red wine and makes a toast to me: "I will love and cherish you forever."

I am so in love, and I can't wait to really be one with Raffaele. He quickly helps me with the buttons on the back of my dress. I turn and become face to chest with Raffaele, my hands have a mind of their own and slowly reach up to the buttons on his shirt, I begin undoing them. Before I realize it, we are on the bed in a wild embrace. Raffaele tells me to relax because he will be gentle with me. Before I even realized it was happening, my virginity was gone forever. And now I truly am Mrs. Raffaele Pasquariello. I can't wait to see Sofia. She will be very proud of me. I wasn't really nervous about making love with Raffaele. That could also be because I was a little drunk from drinking a couple of glasses of wine.

We are going to have a good time here for the next two days, doing whatever we want to do. Learning more about each other's bodies, getting out of bed late and doing a lot of sightseeing in this city with all of its history. This is a great time for us to be alone and to get to know each other intimately.

Raffaele takes me to see the Pennsylvania Museum and School of Industrial Art. It is a beautiful building that has been expanded many times since opening in 1876. It has things I've never dreamed of. There is a room with oriental pottery and carpets with so much detail. Other rooms displayed handmade lace, and embroidery; European porcelain; arms and armor; furniture and woodwork; goldsmith work, jewelry, sculpture, marbles, and even musical instruments. There is so much to see that we stay for hours, and before I know it, we re starving!

We leave in search of something to eat. We walk a couple of blocks and come to a cart selling food. Raffaele smiles at me and says, "Have you ever eaten German food?"

Before I can answer, he pulls me over to the gentleman standing by a cart, Raffaele orders food for us, and he looks excited to show me something else I've never experienced. When the food is prepared, he hands us what was ordered wrapped in brown paper. We find a stone bench to sit and eat. Raffaele opens the paper; there are two small, fat sausages, but they don't smell of Italian herbs. On top of the sausage is stringy cabbage that is white and tastes sour. My favorite thing is a different kind of bread that is twisted and sprinkled with salt crystals. It is soft inside but only slightly harder on the outside. Raffaele gets up and asks the man who owns the cart something. I can see the man hand Raffaele a dollop of something on paper. When he comes over, he shows it to me; it's dark yellow on the paper, wet, and well, it doesn't look pretty, but I dip the soft bread in it, and it's delicious. It's tart and a little bit spicy. I even dip the sausage with cabbage in it. It's a little messy to eat, and I notice Raffaele watching me intently when I lick the juices off my fingers. His look makes me blush, and he must notice because he leans down and kisses the top of my head. The food is so good that Raffaele purchases two more of the breads—pretzels, they are called—so we can eat them when we got back to the hotel.

We take a horse and carriage back to the hotel. I can't wait to take my shoes off; all of the walking is exhausting. Raffaele orders dinner to be sent up to us while I soak in the tub. Someone is actually going to make our dinner and bring it to the room; I've never heard of such a thing. While I soak in the tub, Raffaele sits on the side of the tub telling me stories of when he was younger. He speaks of his father, and I can tell he misses him. I miss my family as well, and I feel we are becoming closer because we are both missing people in our lives. He helps me wash my hair. It's romantic to me.

There is a knock on the door, and Raffaele goes to answer. It's our dinner. A gentleman comes in with a cart and serves us steak, potatoes, and green beans. We eat dinner by the large window and laugh about some of the things we saw today. As I am telling Raffaele about my favorite part of the day (the pretzels), he gets up and lights a couple candles by the bed. He comes over to me and pours wine for both of us. He gives me the glass of wine and acts as though he is going to kiss me. But right before his lips touch mine, he pulls out a pretzel and bites one end, allowing me to bite the other. We both laugh! This man is becoming my friend as well as my husband. I not only love him, but I like him, which sounds silly, but I guess it's because I feel really comfortable with him. I feel connected to him.

Our honeymoon goes quickly, and soon we are back to our everyday living. I will never forget my special time with Raffaele. I believe my love for him will grow each and every day. I can't wait to start our family and have our first child from our love for one another. *"Per Cent Anni!"* For a hundred years.

CHAPTER 21

It's January 2, 1901.

"Raffaele! Come downstairs and eat your breakfast before it gets cold!" Raffaele walks into the kitchen, looking as handsome as ever. "Sit down Raffaele. I will pour you a cup of coffee."

He stops and hugs me and tells me, "You look beautiful."

His words just melt me every time. I am so in love with my husband. From the first time I saw him over one year ago, I thought he was so handsome. He grows on me more every day with his tenderness.

I giggle at his silliness and motion for him to eat. He will have a big day at the tavern again. I asked, "How was yesterday? Did you have many brawls?"

He rolls his eyes and says, "With the drinking Irish and all the others who wanted free whiskey, I can say I am happy to be in one piece. You can only give out so many free drinks before the patrons get angry at you."

I pour the coffee and ask, "Why would anyone be angry over free whiskey?"

Taking a sip of the hot coffee, his expression is one of bliss as he swallows the dark liquid.

"Ahhh, Carmela, drunk men act similar to children when you take something sweet away from them. Unfortunately, men are much stronger, and their temper tantrums can get someone killed!"

I smile.

"So when you take their whiskey away, they get very angry."

He shook his head.

"Angry is putting it nicely. When you say, 'You've had enough whiskey,' because they want free drinks all day, some become quarrelsome, so we throw them outside and tell them to come back on another day because we have had enough."

As he begins eating his breakfast he continues, "There was one guy who we never saw before. He was out of control and grabbed Peter, one of my co-worker's head and smashed it on top of the bar. Peter went down to the floor. I immediately helped him up. Two longshoremen customers standing at the bar lifted this guy up and threw him out into the street, I never saw him again. He may still be lying in the street."

I ask, "How is Peter?"

Raffaele continues, "When I picked him up, he had blood rushing from his nose. He laughed and told me he hasn't been hit like that since he started working at the bar. He cleaned himself up and went back to servicing the bar and worked till the end of his shift. Don't know what he feels like this morning, but I soon will see." Tilting his head and smiling, Raffaele asks, "Carmela, did you enjoy the parade yesterday? Did you find it entertaining?"

Excited to tell him what I heard, I say, "Yes, having so many people marching down the street. It was freakish, bizarre, odd, but magnificent. Their imaginations were whimsical, but what to me that was astonishing was a group of men standing behind me yesterday. Talking about how they don't accept any Italian men in the parade. This group of men were Italians. Raffaele, do you know what that is about for us Italians here in South Philly? Are there any Italians in the Mummer's Parade?"

Raffaele gives me a dead stare and his eyes are piercing. He lifts his cup to his lips and takes a huge gulp of coffee. Both hands are holding the cup, but they are quivering. I gently touch his hands. I ask, "Did I say something wrong?"

He puts the cup down on the saucer. He smiles and says, "No, Carmela. You can ask me anything. I will honestly tell you what I understand. Don't ever stop questioning me and my knowledge." Raffaele says, "Since the Italians started coming to America, we are considered the lowest breed of people. The men in the parade are Swedish, Finnish, Irish, English, German, and of African heritage. They don't want us in their parade."

I express my disbelief that Italians aren't permitted to be part of the city of Philadelphia.

"Why would they feel like we aren't equal to them? I don't understand that mentality. We are hard-working people. We don't ask anyone for anything. We stay with our own people. We contribute to society. Raffaele, you tell me to stay within our neighborhood, but now I will start to venture outside of here. They come into our living areas. Why are we forbidden into theirs? Why are we different? You can only be different if you allow them to treat you so."

"Oh no. you won't Carmela! I don't want you to get hurt. They feel that we are lowest of lows. That we are dirty, that we came here with no material things. No money! I could go on and on, but I choose not to allow this to make me feel lesser than I am. Because we Italians are good people. Look at the beauty of our church we built. No one has hands to build like us. No one can or will keep us down. They can say and feel any way about us. That's their prerogative. We will raise our family not to have their prejudice affect us. We will keep our heads held high at all cost. Maybe in the future, they will open the door for us to join the parade. But until then, we will carry on. The doors to America opened to us. I will not let anyone close it in my face or yours. This I say for all Italians!

"America is the land of opportunity, and we as a group of people are here to swim in the waters of freedom." As I sit and listen to Raffaele, I watch his facial expressions going from stern when speaking of how we Italians are treated unfairly to loving when he says we are all equal human beings. He has a twinkle in his eyes when expressing his happiness at being of Italian descent.

He suddenly pushes his chair back and stands up straight and tall. Looking at me with such fire in his eyes, he continues to say not once, but twice, "We are Southern Italians. We Italians are a romance ethnic group. Most Italians share a common culture, history, ancestry, and language. Furthermore, Italian people are hard workers, and don't expect anyone to give them anything. What we are in need of, we will work for."

I smile at him and tell him to sit down and relax. He gives me his hands across the table. As we touch, I feel his emotions going through my body. I know he is correct in his way of thinking. I express my love for him in a way that I hope he will never forget how I feel. I say to him, "I married an intelligent man. I will always stand by your side; there is nothing I wouldn't do for you."

As I sit and watch my husband, I am thinking he should be a politician because he cares about people. Not just Italians, but everyone. Raffaele ends his conversation with me as he is walking out of the kitchen with these sincere words:

"As Abraham Lincoln once said, those who deny freedom to others, deserve it not for themselves."

CHAPTER 22

Time has moved quickly from when I first started my journey from Italia. I married Raffaele, and now we are expecting our first child; all of this in 17 months. I am due the first week of February 1901. I will have my baby at home in my bed. Rosa will be there along with a midwife to help with the delivery. Luca delivers all the Italian babies in our neighborhood. So, I am confident that everything will be fine.

I have morning sickness every day. Food isn't as appetizing because I feel like throwing up just looking at the plate of food. The smell of chicken is so nauseating. The ladies in the neighborhood tell me my baby is going to be a *femmina* (girl) because I have gained a lot of weight and also that I am large all over. It's an old wives' tale for us Italians; if the mother looks bad during her pregnancy, she must be carrying a girl because the girl steals the mother's beauty, which happens to be true for me, though Raffaele tells me I am more beautiful than ever. I think he tells me that because he feels guilty watching me get sick constantly. The only thing that settles my stomach is a small glass of Brioschi, and then off I go to bed. It works every night for me.

I feel just like a cow. The shopkeepers on 9th Street are making a wager on whether my baby is a boy or a girl. When I am in their shops, they all try to feed me. Most of them tell me it's a girl. They all love to see me fat and pregnant. When they see me, they all smile and say congratulations. But all I feel is tired, and I have one more month to go. I hope I don't gain any more weight because I don't think my skin can stretch any more without tearing open!

If the baby is a boy, we will name him Michael, the American way of saying Michele, after Raffaele's father. Or if it's a girl, we will name her Rose after Raffaele's mother. This is an Italian tradition. After we have our first boy and first girl, then our next boy and girl will be named after my parents. Rosa can't believe she is going to be a nonna for the first time. Rosa told me that when the baby is born, that's when she will stop wearing her black dresses. Rosa said, "Because we will have a new love in our home, and our house will be filled with joy and happiness. The sounds of a baby crying will be music to our ears." She knows that Raffaele's father would want us to celebrate and enjoy our new happiness.

Her enjoyment of life is coming back to her since the death of her husband. It's almost one year ago that she and the family lost him. He was such a kind, loving man to everyone. There wasn't anything he wouldn't do for you. If we have a boy, I would be honored to have my son carry his name. I would pray that my son would be a good man, just like his nonno.

Everyone in the house is anticipating the arrival of the baby. Raffaele and I couldn't be happier with the way everything is moving along. Giovanni and Orazio have been helping Raffaele build a crib. Rosa bought some beautiful sheets, blankets, and white baby sleeping gowns. I can't stop looking at these tiny clothes. Part of me wonders how a baby can be so small, but another part of me wonders how something so big can be inside me!

On Tuesday, February 12, 1901, our beautiful baby girl, "Rose," is born. What a little dark hair beauty she is, with lots of hair on her tiny head! Rosa and I both are crying. Luca places Rose on my chest. I am so excited to wrap my arms around her tiny waist, but I am afraid I will squeeze her in half. So I put Rose into Rosa's waiting arms. Rosa gently takes her from me. The expression on her face is one of sheer joy!

Luca is rubbing my stomach to get the placenta out of me. She's telling me she can't believe how fast I was with the delivery of my first child.

"I've been here for about four hours, and you are finished. You know, Carmela, with the way you just gave birth to your daughter, you could easily have many babies. The first time a mother gives birth could take hours, and sometimes days." I hear what Luca is saying to me, but my only interest right now is my sweet baby Rose. Rosa gives her back to me because the baby is crying. So, I put her to my breast, and she starts to suckle. She is so small and sweet. I couldn't want more pleasure in my life. I have everything I could possibly ask the Blessed Mother for. I am silently saying a prayer to the Blessed Mother, thanking her for all of her help for making all of this so easy and quick... "But Blessed Mother, please don't have me get pregnant for a couple of years. I sure could use the rest and sleep."

The next day, friends and neighbors are leaving food and gifts at the front door. Family members are stopping in to hold and see Rose. I can't stop smiling when I look at her. I am filled with love for my baby.

Father Angelo Caruso is here because he wants to baptize Rose soon. He wants to know who the godparents will be. Raffaele tells Father that Giovanni and Sofia are going to be Rose's godparents. On Sunday, April 21, 1901, we baptize Rose. She wears a beautiful white satin dress we had made for her. Her godparents have her hat and blanket in white made for her by the same seamstress. Rose looks like a baby saint when Father Caruso baptizes her. When he pours the Holy Water on her head, she doesn't cry. She just lays in Sofia's arms and is staring at Father as he is saying the prayer: "We Baptize you in the name of the Father, Son and Holy Ghost."

Rose smiles at him and falls asleep.

When Raffaele comes home from work in the evening, the first thing he does is pick Rose up and kiss her forehead. He holds her till she cries out and then he places her in his mother's loving arms. Rosa gives her to me, and off I go to my bedroom to breast feed her. She has a good appetite and is gaining weight rapidly.

It's seven months since I gave birth to Rose, and I am pregnant again. I am due in April of 1902. We again are all preparing for a new baby in our house. Raffaele would like this baby to be a boy, but for me, as long as the baby is healthy, I won't complain. Many babies are stillborn or have physical deficiencies. So I try to take good care of myself and have a healthy balance of nutrition. This pregnancy I have heartburn, but not as bad as with Rose. Though I can't eat fried meats; if I do, it will cause heartburn that will last all night. So I believe this is a boy because I feel entirely different carrying this baby.

Rosa tells me she has acid indigestion since I became pregnant. She laughs and says she feels pregnant also. I inform her that she can give birth for me because that would make me happy. That's when she says, "No, not me. I never did well with birthing my three sons. All three of my boys were long and hard labor. Nothing like your delivery. God blessed you with a good birth canal."

While holding Rose in her lap, Rosa asks Raffaele to take her for a moment. Before letting her go, Rosa bends down and kisses her on the forehead and puts her cheek gently on the baby's cheek in a delicate hug. Rosa hands Raffaele the baby and starts to walk in the kitchen and suddenly crumples to the floor. My world suddenly begins spinning out of control. Raffaele quickly hands me the baby and is yelling at Giovanni to get a doctor. I can feel myself shaking uncontrollably, and the ringing in my ears is so loud, I felt like I was in a nightmare.

Orazio's small sobs next to me begin to penetrate my brain, and I tug on him while asking him to help me put the baby to bed. I want to remove him from the situation for a moment; I'm not sure if it is for his benefit or mine, but it just feels right. Once we lay the baby down, we hear a loud noise. Raffaele is letting people into the house, doctors I believe. I look at Orazio and tell him we need to be strong.

We stand at the steps while they carry Rosa out to an ambulance. Raffaele and Giovanni jump in a horse and buggy. I yell at both of them to stop, so Orazio can go with them. I will stay here with the baby. I know in my heart that Orazio will be devasted if something happens, and he isn't there.

On Monday, February 17, 1902, Rosa had a heart attack and died at home. She had already passed away before leaving the house, I didn't know until Raffaele came home. The heartburn she had was her heart beginning to fail her. She won't get to see her next grandchild being born. I already miss her love and devotion towards me. I love Rosa with my entire being. What a wonderful and loving person, just as her husband. We buried her with Mr. Pasquariello. Her coffin was placed on top of his coffin. That way, he can hold her forever in his arms. The two of them were inseparable in life, and I am sure that's how they will be in the afterlife. Together forever!

CHAPTER 23

Although we are very excited about my pregnancy, there is an emptiness in our home without Michele and Rosa. Every time Rose does something new, I want to run and tell Rosa, and then I remember she is not here. I miss her so much! Raffaele and his brothers are wearing the black bands on their arms again. When Raffaele holds Rose, she will often pull on the band to play with it. In my heart, I feel like this is Rosa's way of telling us that she is right here with us, watching over us.

I feel completely different with my second pregnancy. I haven't gained much weight, and I have a lot of energy. The shopkeepers on 9th Street all want to feed me when I visit their shops. They tell me I need to fatten up like I did when I was pregnant with Rose. I think they worry because they know how much I miss Rosa. But I am able to eat better with this pregnancy, and I am happy that I look better.

On Friday, April 18, 1902, I give birth to a boy. Of course, we name him Michael after Raffaele's father. He also has a head full of dark, curly hair. This delivery with Luca by my bedside is even faster than my first, which makes me happy. Luca tells me she knows she will be back before baby Michael turns two. I can't stop laughing at her words to me; that's after I say a few good curse words at her. Even Luca is laughing at what I said, but she is correct.

In August 1902, Giovanni marries Rose, one of the girls from the neighborhood. He moves into her family's house around the corner. We all miss him, but it's nice to have more room in the house for our family to grow. Orazio tells me he isn't leaving home; well, not just yet any way. We laugh together all the time. If and when he marries and leaves, I will be heartbroken. He is such a kind soul and is always willing to lend a helping hand to me. You should see him with Rose. She already has him in the palm of her hands.

I quickly became pregnant a couple of months after giving birth to Michael. I am seven months and not feeling well. I no longer feel the baby move or kick inside of me. I feel myself begin to panic and ask Raffaele to get a message to Luca. I know my condition is serious because I am bleeding profusely, and she will know what to do.

It's been an hour since we sent word to Luca, and I am feeling desperate. Suddenly, I hear the door slam shut downstairs, and footsteps are running up the stairs. Luca comes into my bedroom, and the look on her face is of panic. Her fear is causing me to react with overwhelming feelings of anxiety. I just want to run and run as fast as I can...

Raffaele takes both of my hands and tells me to calm down; Luca is here, and she will do whatever she has to. We must have faith in God and pray for His help.

Luca is pushing on my stomach and asking me questions, but for some reason I just lay there and stare at Luca's hands pushing. She's trying to get my baby to kick or move. But there is no movement from my baby. Just my sobs and my praying to the Blessed Mother. I am thankful that I have my Catholic upbringing, for my faith has helped me with many trying moments in my life. But this is truly way beyond my understanding. I pray that my baby can wait to be born for a few more weeks. Because I don't feel this baby is fully developed enough to come into the world; not yet anyway!

Luca stays with me for hours. I must have fallen asleep because I am physically and emotionally exhausted. When I awaken, I know my baby is not going to make it; my baby is going to be stillborn. Luca is sitting in a chair next to my bed. She, too, had fallen asleep, probably from being here for hours tending to me. I called out to her, "Luca...Luca!" but my voice is very weak.

Suddenly, she jumps up startled! I tell her to get prepared because I feel sharp pains in my womb. My baby is getting ready to be born. Raffaele is standing next to me. He is holding my left hand tightly. I can't stop shivering out of fear for my baby; I can't believe this is happening! I hear Luca telling me to push harder because the baby's head is coming out. I am bearing down as hard as I can. I feel the baby's body touching my inner thighs as the baby comes out of me.

Quickly, I look down at my baby in Luca's hands. There's not a sound. I never heard such silence before in my life. I sit up and reach down for the baby. I want to hold my baby. Raffaele is telling me to lean back, and Luca will give me the baby in my arms. I see Luca wrapping the baby in a blanket, but I don't hear the baby crying.

I ask Luca, "Did I have a boy or girl?" I can't help but cry out in agony because I know my baby is dead. I feel Raffaele holding me in his arms. I can feel his body shaking with quiet sobs, but he is trying to console me. Luca quietly says, "It's a baby boy," and puts him in my waiting arms.

I am rocking him back and forth; I can't control my sorrow. I keep repeating, "I am so sorry...I am so sorry." I kiss his face and give him to Raffaele. He takes the baby from my arms and walks away with him. I tell Luca I will name him Domenic after my father. I ask Raffaele how he feels about the name. He turns to look at me with a tearful expression. He tries to smile at me and says, "Domenic is a beautiful name, and he should be named after your father."

He puts baby Domenic back into my waiting arms. I look at every inch of his face, and I unwrap his blanket. I lay him on my lap and see his entire body. He is slightly blue in color, and his body is totally formed. He has 10 toes and 10 fingers. Such little tiny fingers. I find myself kissing his face, arms, and hands. I can't let him go, but Luca tells me I must. She will have the ambulance come and take baby Domenic to the city morgue. Before I allow anyone to take my son, I tell Raffaele to send Orazio to the rectory to get Father; our baby needs to be blessed first.

Luca takes our baby and again wraps him in the baby blanket. She tells me she will take care of everything and that I should rest. She takes baby Domenic over to Raffaele, and he kisses Domenic's forehead. I reach out to hold my baby one more time before I never get to see him again. I kiss his cheek and tell Domenic he will always be in my heart.

"May the angels take you with them. Goodbye, my baby Domenic."

When Father walks into my bedroom and he sees Domenic, he immediately walks over to us, I am holding Domenic in my arms. Father says the prayer, and we are all softly praying with him. Father has Holy Water, and he blesses baby Domenic.

Luca has him in her arms and gives me one more look of sadness. She turns and walks out of the room with Raffaele and Father. I listen to every footstep they are making while carrying my baby downstairs. I sit in my bed in stillness, waiting to hear the front door close. As it does, Raffaele walks into the bedroom and gets into bed with me. I put my head on his shoulders, and he wraps me in his loving arms. We both cry and express our sadness to each other. We make a promise that no matter what happens to us, we will always love and protect our family. And that God took our baby for whatever reason and though we don't understand and probably never will, at least he will have his grandparents there to watch over him. We will have each other and Rose and Michael; for that, we must be thankful for our blessings.

Raffaele stays in bed with me as we share our grief. I don't sleep at all that night because I can't stop my brain from racing. The next day, I am out of bed by late afternoon because I have two children who need me. I have to push myself to get up and move around. Life must go on no matter how hard life gets. Baby Domenic will have a special place in my heart forever. I know the Blessed Mother will watch over my baby.

We bury our son Domenic in our family plot at the Holy Cross

Cemetery. Domenic is in the same coffin with his cousin Antonio, who passed away five days before my son Domenic. Antonio was also stillborn. The two babies will be together through eternity, holding each other just as they were placed inside the coffin.

CHAPTER 24

Every time I turn around, I'm pregnant. It's nine years since we married. We already have six children, one boy and five girls! Rose is in third grade, Michael is in second grade, and the four youngest are home with me all day. My days consist of cooking, cleaning, and doing laundry. There is so much laundry every day, the diapers alone are a full-time job! Every morning, after breakfast, I put the large pot on the coal stove to get the water hot. Next, I begin to handwash the dirty clothes on a wash board made out of wood and zinc. I add bleach in the pot, so all the whites will come out looking and smelling clean. Then I hang them on the clothesline outside in the yard. This happens to be the chore I hate most, but my time spent with the kids is wonderful. They are so full of energy and curious about everything.

Now that Orazio is married to Mary, he is busy with his own family, and we don't get to see him as often as we like. I do miss his laughter, sense of humor, and all the help he used to give me with the children.

To break our days up, I bring the kids down the street to the park unless one of them is sick. I love to hear their laughter as they run in the sunshine. When it rains in the summer, I let them jump in all the puddles outside; it cools them off and tires them out! I am kept busy, but there is much love in my home. I couldn't ask the Blessed Mother for any more happiness. I feel complete being with Raffaele and our children as a family.

Raffaele got promoted to full-time bartender and assistant manager. He will be a bartender at the bar on Dock Street in South

Philly on the waterfront. This is a new profession for him, being a manager, and he is looking forward to serving more than alcohol to the customers. He thinks he will do well at this job because he is talkative and friendly. I am not thrilled about this because I am leery that he may start to drink every day. I did express my concerns, but Raffaele says that I have nothing to worry about.

"It's my job, and I am there to work. Don't worry, I won't drink when I am working." He says, "Besides, we have many babies now. I need to bring home more money. What I make out on the street will never be enough to feed all of us."

I am learning English from the kids when they come home with homework. They are teaching me the English language. They tell me all the time when we sit to do their homework that I should go to school with them, and the nuns could teach me English. I do prefer to speak Italian in the house, but when the kids come home from school, they speak English among themselves and with Raffaele.

Last month, I had a miscarriage. I was only a month or two pregnant and felt sick all the time. After the miscarriage, I felt good again. Luca told me not to worry; that miscarriages just happen and usually early in the pregnancy. I was telling her that I had a sore on my vagina at the entrance, but after a few weeks it went away. Then I noticed I had a rash on the soles of my feet, and lately I have been feeling feverish, and I didn't have much of an appetite. Luca's face got very serious, she held my hand and said, "Carmela, you must let me take you to the hospital to see the doctor. We should go as soon as possible." When I started to shake my head, she continued, "On Raffaele's next day off, I will come and get you, we will go together to the Pennsylvania Hospital at 8th and Spruce Streets.

When I told Raffaele what we were going to do, he became visibly upset. I thought he was very worried about me, but then he told me not to see the doctor. I asked him, "What seems to be the reason you are upset? I am not feeling well; seeing the doctor is a good idea, and it is helpful that Luca will go with me and talk to the doctor, her English is so much better than mine."

He again insisted I not go but gave no reason. I did listen to him until I started to lose hair. I had three good size bald spots on the top of my head. That's when I knew I needed to see a doctor. So, Luca came and picked me up and off we went with the kids to the hospital without informing Raffaele.

I went into the exam room by myself because Luca stayed with the children in the waiting room. Luca did fill out the paper questionnaire for me. The doctor did speak to me, but we really couldn't understand one another. He looked me over, checked my eyes, ears, and throat. I showed him the bottom of my feet with the rash. He excused himself and went out to get Luca. She came in and informed me that he wanted to get some blood for a test, which he did in front of Luca. He told Luca to come back in two weeks for the results.

Ateleta, Italia, circa 1881, Geltrude's birthplace

Geltrude's Birth Announcement, Ateleta, Italia. June 27th, 1881

SS Tatar Prince - built 1895 - January

Geltrude's Manifest, Line #14, 1899

Statue of Liberty, circa 1899

*Our Lady of Good Counsel Church, 816 Christian Street,
Phildelphia, PA*

Registrum Matrimoniorum in Ecclesia *Beatae Mariae a*

Consilio Diœcesis *Philadelfhiensis*

Nomen Familiæ.	L.D. /900 Die Mensis.	REGISTRUM MATRIMONIORUM.	Dispensationes.
Japone	Maj 12	Ego infrascriptus *prae* missis *tribus* denuntiationibus et mutuo contrahentium consensu habito, per verba de præsenti matrimonio conjunxi *Vincentium Japone* ex loco *Montella* Filium *Johannis* et *Rosam Trotti* ex loco *Montella* Filiam *Salvatoris* Præsentibus testibus *Rocco Adessi Anna Spaventa* *r. Augustinus pogliani O.S.A.*	123668
1900 *Pasquariello*	Maj 14 Monday	Ego infrascriptus *prae* missis *tribus* denuntiationibus et mutuo contrahentium consensu habito, per verba de præsenti matrimonio conjunxi *Raphaelem Pasquariello* ex loco *Morra* Filium *Michaelis* *Raffaele* et *Carmelam Gelsudenisi Lullo* ex loco *Atelela* Filiam *Antonii* Præsentibus testibus *Rocco Calamanni* *Angela Marinelli* *r. Augustinus Pogliani O.S.A.*	123022 *my grandfather* *my grandmother* *priest*
Bunn	Maj 20	Ego infrascriptus missis *tribus* denuntiationibus et mutuo contrahentium consensu habito, per verba de præsenti matrimonio conjunxi *Georgium B. Bunn* ex loco *Philadelphia Pa* Filium et *Margheritam J. McfJuly* ex loco *Philadelphia* Filiam Præsentibus testibus *Augustino Gatti Maria Gatti* *r. G. Coleman O.S.A. Sup*	124373
	Maj 21	Ego infrascriptus *praemissis tribus* denuntiationibus et mutuo contrahentium consensu habito, per verba de præsenti matrimonio conjunxi *Jacobum Decaro* ex loco *Messina* Filium *Francisci*	124013

Our Lady of Good Counsel Church Registration Matrimoniouim Raffaele amd Geltrude Pasquariello. Monday, May 14th, 1900

Hotel Lorraine, 1899. Philadelphia, PA - Honeymoon

United States Census, June 2, 1900.
Pasquariello Family Philadelphia, Pennsylvania.
837 League Street, South Philadelphia

Philadelphia Mummers Parade - 1901
"Here we stand before your door
As we stood the year before;
Give us whiskey, give us gin,
Open the door and let us in."

Anti-Italian Cartoon of the 1880's, New Orleans magazine,
"The Mascot" in 1888

Dock street, Philadelphia, circa 1880s

Typical Dock Workers Bar, circa 1900

Michael Pasquariello's Baptismal Certificarte
Born April 18th, 1902 - Baptized August 3rd, 1902

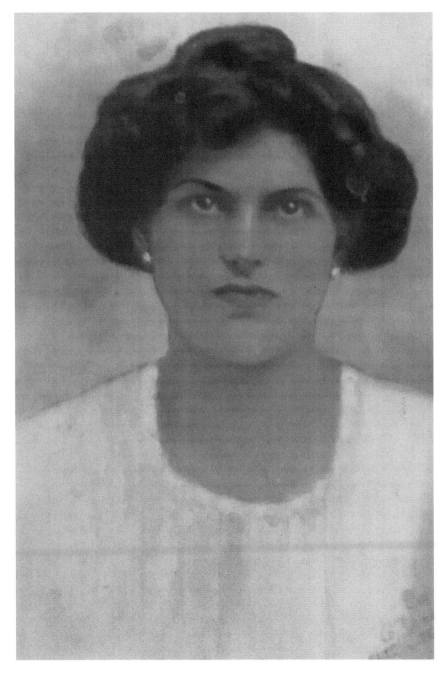

Geltrude Carmelo DiLullo Pasquariello, 28 years old, circa 1910

Raffaele Pasquariello, 32 years old, circa 1910

A Paison, Michael and Raffaele at Coney Island, circa 1910

The Family in Turmoil: Look at my Aunt Anna - standing next to grandmother on the right. That is not her face. She cut that picture of the face out of a magazine because she liked how the face looked. Also, note the strap that is on my Grandmother's lap goes to Aunt Millie's hand. Aunt Millie always had to be connected to her mother.

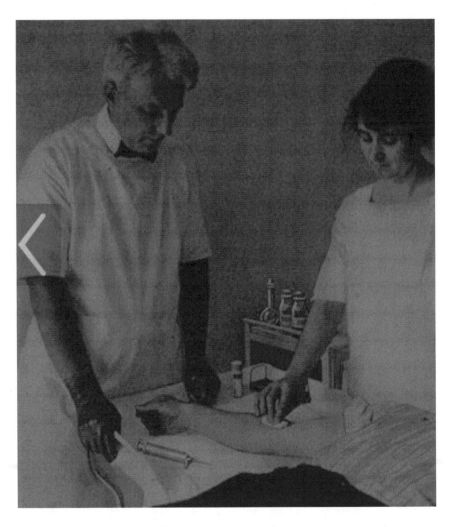

The treatment of syphilis mercury injections, circa 1912

Michael Pasquariello, 13 years old, circa 1915
Look how beautiful he looks in his wool coat and his hat.

An anti-spitting sign on top of the Fourth Liberty Loan sign; City Hall is in the background. Temple Urban Archives

Spanish influenza, 1918: Our family lost one member at the age of ten-years-old.

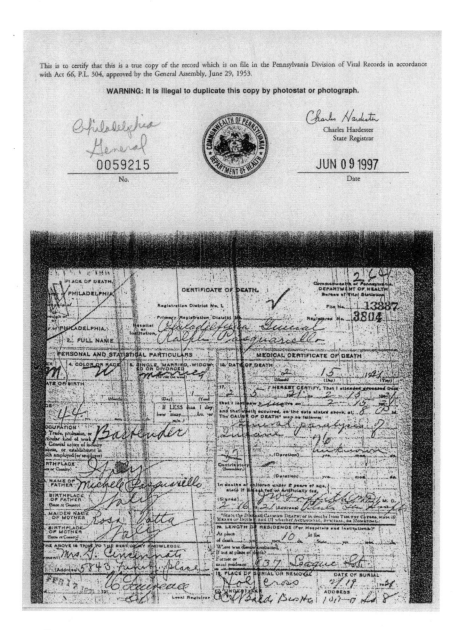

Raffaele Pasquariello death certificate, February 15, 1921.
44 years old!

Philadelphia Italian market, 9th Street, circa 1920

Family working on a New Jersey Farm, circa 1922

Geltrude's death certificate, February 23rd, 1925, 43 years old

Washing the sheets in South Philadelphia, 1927
The immigrants like to keep their steps and streets clean.

Beginning the next generation. Rose Pasquarello (oldest child)
wedding, circa 1928

Michael Pasquarello marries Romania Pescatori Pasquarello on Monday, November 7th, 1932 at City Hall of Philadelphia

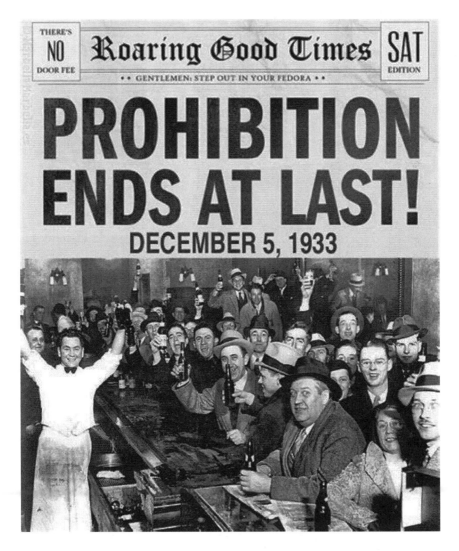

Prohibition ends at last.

Michael working his wooden cart on 9th Street, circa 1933

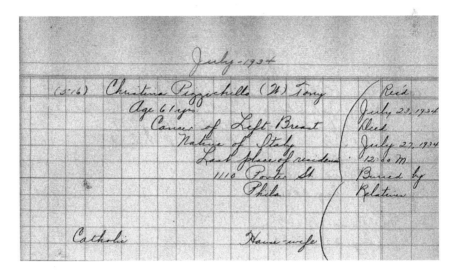

Christina DiLullo Pizzichillo, July 27th, 1934 –
died Home of the Incurables, Philadelphia

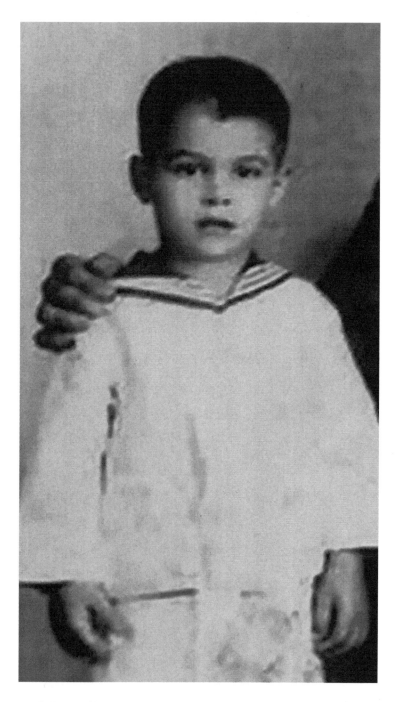

Ralph "Raffaele" Pasquarello
First child of Michael, circa 1936

Michael's brother Domenic with Ralph at his Confirmation at
Saint Nicholas, Philadelphia Church, circa 1942

Michael (left) with his brothers-in-law, circa 1950

Michael Pasquarello - 50th Memorial 2005 with some of his children

CHAPTER 25

On the day that Luca comes to the house with the results, I still haven't told Raffaele that I went to see the doctor with her for some tests. I will never forget this day for as long as I live. My entire world shatters right in front of my eyes. It is just a year after I gave birth to Antonetta. It is a windy, cold day in March. All the windowpanes in the house were vibrating from the cold air pounding against them.

I put some more wood in the stove to keep the downstairs warm. The kids are running around the house, playing nicely with each other. They are up for the rest of the day because they just got up from their afternoon naps. I still have them take a morning and afternoon nap, so I can get more accomplished around the house.

I hear someone knocking on the front door. When I answer the knock, it is Luca standing there with much sadness in her eyes. I open the door wide and tell her to come inside. She walks past me and goes straight into the kitchen. She doesn't even kiss me hello or say anything to the children, even when they are all saying hello to her.

I tell the children to be quiet and to play in the living room. As I walk into the kitchen, Luca is standing at the stove with her back towards me. I tap her shoulder and ask if she is ill. She doesn't turn to look at me and replies, "I am not ill. Carmela, we must talk now. I have news from the doctor about the bloodwork and your results are not good."

She turns and looks me straight in the eyes for a split second, turns away, and says something indistinctly, making it difficult for me to hear.

I hear myself saying to her, "Just tell me what it is. I need to know."

Luca puts her arms around me tightly, then she hands me a piece of paper from the hospital. As I take the paper, I quickly give it back to her.

"You know, Luca, I can't read the results from my test. Could you tell me what it says?"

She tells me we should sit at the table, and she will read me the results. As she unfolds the paper, she won't take her eyes off me. I sit and watch her nervousness, and it makes me feel uneasy.

She tells me that the test is accurate and that it came back positive that I have bad blood disease, known as Sifilide. She reaches for my hand and says, "This disease is untreatable; there is no cure, and the outcome is fatal."

Her eyes fill up with tears and the look of sympathy on her face makes me angry for some reason.

"Are you telling me I have a sexual disease? Is that what you want me to believe?" I can feel myself becoming more annoyed at Luce and her words. I instantly jump to my feet, standing there staring at Luca.

She too stands up and walks over to me. She is saying something to me, but I can't hear her. I only hear my children laughing in the other room. Luca takes my hand and leads me back to my chair.

"Please, Carmela, sit down and collect your thoughts. We need to talk and figure out what procedure we should follow. The doctor would like for you and Raffaele to come back and see him at the hospital. That should be done as soon as possible. He also needs Raffaele to take a blood test for syphilis."

I look at Luca as I quietly weep, so the children don't hear me. I don't need for them to get upset because of me.

I tell Luca, "When Raffaele comes home, I will kill him. First, because he has infected me with this disease, then secondly because he is, or has cheated on me with a puttana."

CHAPTER 26

"I want to thank you, Luca, for all of your time and help getting me to see the doctor, but I think you should leave before Raffaele comes home for supper. This conversation has to be just between Raffaele and I. He has a lot of explaining to do, and I want to hear how I became infected with this disease other than having sex with my husband. For now, I must save all of my thoughts and words for him."

Luca walks over to me as I stand looking out the kitchen window staring at space. My thoughts racing through my head are moving swiftly. But I see and feel nothing. I think I am frozen in time. Numb to all emotions except the rage racing through me.

Luca embraces me, her voice is soft and gentle as she says, "Carmela, if you need me to stay with you for any reason, I will. Maybe I could help with the children while you and Raffaele have a much-needed conversation tonight."

As Luca is holding me closely in her arms, it's a moment of great relief. I need someone to tell me that I will be fine. I take one step back and look at Luca's beautiful green eyes. She is such a beautiful Italian lady; not many Italians are red haired and green-eyed beauties. This is the first time I see all of her beauty and tenderness. She is a very good friend, not only to me, but to my family. She's such a caring, good-hearted person.

As I try my best not to break down, I take Luca's arm and walk her to the front door. I thank her for her friendship, and we say our goodbyes for now. As I am turning the doorknob, the door pushes open, and it's Rose, Michael, and Mary coming home from school. Seeing their beautiful faces and hearing their laughter for a brief moment makes everything feel fine. But I don't truly feel that I will ever have happiness as I had before today. Luca and I kiss each other without saying another word as I close the door behind her. I walk into the kitchen with all six of my children in tow.

I pretend that this is a normal day in our home, I prepare supper and get the children to do their homework. My head is a thousand miles away, but I know I have to pull myself back to reality when Raffaele walks through that front door. He will walk into the loving arms of our six children, and into the hands of someone who is hostile. I don't know in my heart what is going to happen. On one hand, I can't wait for Raffaele to come home, so he can help me understand to a degree what is happening to our lives. And on the other hand, I just want to put him out from our home forever. But what I want may not be what is best for my family and home. I can only pray for guidance and leave this into God's hands for the sake of my family.

I hear the front door open, and as usual, I hear Raffaele call out to the children that he is home. This is his greeting to the children whenever he comes home. All of them go running into the living room and whoever gets to him first, he picks them up off their feet and spins them around a few times. There is so much laughter and yelling because they all want him to pick them up and spin them around in his arms. The children's laughter makes me even angrier. How selfish can one person be? He not only cheated on me, but on his children as well. This disease will take us from them eventually, and what will become of them at that time! Will I ever get to hold my grandchildren? I just want to hurt him! I can feel myself starting to shake with rage.

I take a couple deep breaths; I can't let my rage go in front of my children. So I don't walk out there to greet him because I still don't know how to handle this situation. I must keep my composure, but I need to blow up in his face for me to feel better. I need to explode. Raffaele walks into the kitchen and grabs me from behind. He asks me, "How's my beautiful wife?"

I turn to look him in the eyes, but before I can say anything, he asks if I am upset about something. I know I can't hide my feelings because of my facial expression. My face has always been an open book, and I feel as stiff as a board. I hear the children run up to their rooms to get ready for supper, and before I knew what was happening, I hear myself yelling at the top of my lungs, "**What have you done?**"

Raffaele looks at me in amazement. He hasn't a clue what's going on until I scream at him.

"Luca took me to the doctor two weeks ago. The doctor did some blood work and ran a *sifilide* test on me. It came back positive! How did I get syphilis?" Raffaele stands there staring at me without saying one word. I am still screaming at him; I can't seem to control myself. "Do you know there is no cure for this disease? That we are going to die from this, and it will be a horrible death?"

I don't need Raffaele to respond to me. At this time, I feel anything coming out of his mouth will only be lies. I realize the man I married was untrue to me and unfaithful to our marriage. I am crying and yelling at him, "Raffaele, can you be honest with me? You're not a trustworthy man. I can't believe this is happening to me—to our family. Do you understand what your actions have done to us and our children? I just want to choke out the last breath you have in you, just as this has done to me. You're a no-good bastard. Leave our home. I can't look at your face. And whatever you say to me now is only going to be lies. Get out of this house. Take some clothes or all of them, and get out."

Raffaele tells me he will tell me the truth from the beginning if I can calm down. I sit down on a chair because I don't have the strength to stand. I feel so empty inside and weak. I look at him across the room. I ask that he stand there because I don't want him to sit across the table from me. I can't look at his lying eyes. They make me want to throw punches at him. I am telling him that he has broken my heart and my soul and that I can never forgive him. He looks at me and again says he will tell me the truth.

"I know I have only been the manager at the bar for a few short months. I really like my job, and my boss tells me I am doing a great job. Because he told me that since I have become the manager, the bar is making good money, and everyone likes me. On Saturday nights, the ladies' entrance is busy with the prostitutes coming in and out looking for customers because the dock workers get paid on Saturday. There is this one girl who recently moved up from Virginia, and we became friends."

I interrupt verbally to his blabbering with, "What's her name, and how old is she?"

He looks at me and says, "This has nothing to do with her. Her name and age are irrelevant to our problem. "

I scream, "Yes, it does. I want answers to everything I will ask. So, I repeat to you: her name and age. NOW!"

"Her name is Mae, and she is 22 years old. There is nothing special about her. As a matter of fact, she isn't allowed in the bar any longer because she and another woman were fighting over a customer in the bar. So, I won't ever see her again; she hasn't been around for a couple of months."

I glare at him, "Is this supposed to make me feel better? She had to leave, so you won't have sex with her any longer?" I want to throw something at his head but hold on tightly to my chair instead and continue, "If she was here, would you still be sleeping with her? She has already infected us, the damage is done, right?"

"No, Carmela, no! I was full of regret after it happened, you should believe me. I love you more than words!" He has tears in his eyes, but I have no sympathy for him.

"How did you and she begin having sex? Which I don't understand because we have sex every week. If I am tired or sick, we have sex. Why did you need sex with her? A stranger."

"I was really stupid. I was only thinking of myself and not my family and most especially you, Carmela. Carmela, I do realize what I did was a huge mistake. I shouldn't have had sex with her or anyone other than you. But I did have sex with her, and she was infected with syphilis, which I did not know. Now we both are infected. My selfish actions have ruined our and our children's future. God help us!"

"When were you going to tell me, Raffaele, that I was infected?" I am still shaking with rage.

Raffaele says, "I was hoping that I would not pass this scourge onto you."

I can't stand the sound of his voice any longer, so I stand up, slam my hands on the table and say to him, "I need to take care of the children. Give them supper and put them to bed. I would like for you to not sleep in our bed or come into our bedroom. So, please sleep with Michael till I know what I am going to do with this. I can't talk with you about this anymore. The feeling I have is that there is nothing further to be said. Your actions have spoken for you, and now I will no longer be your wife, and I no longer respect you! I will do what I do best and that is to take care of the children. Because their well-being means everything to me! It seems to me that you were only thinking about you and not about us."

As I walk round the table to leave the kitchen, Raffaele reaches for me. I pull my arm away with such force, he almost falls out of the chair...

I should have pulled harder!

CHAPTER 27

After I put all the children to bed, Raffaele asks if he can come into our bedroom and talk. He will tell me when he went to the doctor and answer all of my questions. I look across the room at him standing in the doorway; he looks pathetic, as if I should feel sorry for him. I look him up and down, shake my head in disgust, and look the other way. I want him to know that I have no pity for him!

I sigh and tell him to sit on the chair. I sit on the edge of the bed across from him and say, "I have many questions and expect them to be answered honestly." He nods his head and looks directly in my eyes. I hold my chin up and look right back at him and begin my questioning, "First, when did you see a doctor for this problem?"

He nervously says, "I went about eight weeks ago to see the doctor. I knew something was wrong because I had a sore on my *pene* (penis), but after several weeks, it was gone. About the same time, I had a large area of sores under my left arm; they were painless and went away on their own. I really didn't think anything about those sores because it's been so hot; I thought they were caused from sweating so much. But there were sores on the bottom of my feet that became painful and made it hard to work on my feet all day."

Raffaele starts to look away from me in shame, but he takes a deep breath, looks back into my eyes, and continues, "When the doctor examined me and I told him all of my symptoms, he took blood from my arm. I went back three weeks later, and he informed me that the test came back positive for syphilis, also known as bad blood disease." He rubbed his face with his hands as if to wash a bad dream away. When he looked back at me, I could see he was fighting back tears. "My Carmela, I love you with all my heart and didn't know how to tell you. How could I tell you about my having sex with a prostitute? It was my mistake for being a complete fool. I was only making myself feel better for a few minutes. There is nothing more to it than that."

He gets up and moves his chair closer to me. He reaches for my hands, but I pull away. He continues with his hands, still reaching out to me.

"I beg you to forgive me. I don't know how I could have done this to the loving wife you have been to me for the last 10 years. I don't want to live without you and the children here with me." He puts his hands down, stands up, and begins walking back and forth, but before he can speak, I jump in.

"Raffaele, why?" He stops and looks at me; my voice is almost pleading. "Why another woman, Raffaele? Was I not enough for you? Did I not make you happy?"

All of the air seems to drain from his body, his eyes became red again, his voice cracked when he replied, "Why I had anything to do with this girl? Maybe because I wanted some excitement in my life. I am always working at the bar, and you are here with the children, and you are tired when I come home from work. You haven't had much time for me."

"Excitement! You needed excitement?" A sound comes out of me that starts as a laugh and quickly turns to tears. I shake my head and take a deep breath. Raffaele takes a breath to say something, but I put my hand up to stop him from talking. "No, it doesn't matter; there would be no correct answer to that question. Let me continue: Raffaele, why didn't you tell me about this disease we both have? Did I not mean anything to you? It seems to me, the last person in this family who you showed love and affection is you! Tell me how I can ever trust you again after you didn't take our well-being to heart?"

"Carmela, I didn't know how to tell you that I cheated on you. Or, how was I going to tell you I had given you such a horrible disease?" He walks over to the window and looks out for a moment; he is trying to compose himself. He turns back around and says, "I know you and I wanted more babies. That may never happen now. I have ruined everything for our future. The future you and I talked and dreamt about for our family. I didn't tell you about this because I was afraid you would leave me. If I have to drop to my knees, Carmela, and beg for your forgiveness, I will. Tell me how do we go from here? I made so many promises to you, and now I have failed you miserably."

I feel a rush of emotions going through my body as I watch Raffaele. Through my tears, he looks as if he is defeated, but I can't forgive him. I tell him that I am tired and need to get some sleep, and we will talk tomorrow.

"Please, Raffaele, you will sleep with Michael. I can't have you sleep here with me." I turned to walk him to the doorway, and he says his goodnight. He leans in to kiss me, but I turn away from him. I tell him to leave me alone with my pain.

As I lay in bed, I am thinking this is my first night in 10 years that I haven't slept with Raffaele. He always held me in his arms till I fell asleep. But not tonight. I am in bed by myself. How can I ever get over this betrayal by the one person who I thought would always protect me? Now I have to deal with the possibility of being alone. Also, the social stigma of our having syphilis. How will our family, friends, and the world look at us? The disapproval from the church will be the hardest because I believe in my faith. The church will never grant me a divorce because they don't believe Catholics should ever divorce, no matter what the reason could be. Because of this, I could never ask the church for a divorce. Will we now be outcast in our own neighborhood with our own people?

Oh, this is too much to think of. I will go and see Sofia because she will understand my feelings. She will tell me how she feels.

Because at times, she is brutally honest. I need that now from a dear friend. She will only express her real feelings on all of what has and is happening in my life. Maybe this is the end of my life as I have known it.

CHAPTER 28

I get the children up and send the three oldest off to school. Raffaele is in the kitchen reading the *Inquirer* and drinking coffee. We haven't spoken since last night. I am waiting for him to go to work. Then I will take the youngest three over to Sofia's house. I wish he would just leave, so I can talk with Sofia. I need her now more than ever. She always makes me feel her love and compassion for me. Only Sofia will understand my hurt and rage towards Raffaele.

I hear him calling out to me from the parlor, saying, "Carmela, I am leaving for work. I will be home at the regular time." The front door closes, and I rush to get the kitchen cleaned up from breakfast. Off we go to Sofia's. I need to talk and to hear her say that everything will be okay.

As I am pushing all the babies in the baby carriage down Washington Avenue, I think I know exactly what I will do, and I'm sure Sofia will think my idea is great. When I reach her house, I knock on her front door and quickly she opens the door and her warm smile melts my heart. She comes down the three steps and grabs me tightly and says to me, "What a wonderful surprise to see you and the babies. Here, I will take the back of the carriage and you, Carmela, take the front. We will carry this up the steps and into the foyer."

I do just as she says, and once in the foyer, I feel myself shaking and crying.

Sofia looks at me and says, "Carmela, what's wrong?"

We both take the babies out of the carriage and off they go running. I look at her and say, "I need desperately to talk with you. Raffaele has done something that will change our lives forever."

She stares at me for a second and says, "What are you talking about? What did Raffaele do that makes you so desperate? Come, Carmela, let's sit at the table. I will put a pot of coffee on the burner. Sit down, and get your composure and thoughts together. Start from the beginning of your story."

I can't stop my voice from shaking and the occasional sobs that come out, but I rush on to tell her, "I noticed sores on my body, and I haven't felt well for some time. When I told Luca about a sore that was on my private parts, Luca said we needed to go to the hospital and see the doctor. I had been feeling tired and weak, but I have all these children. I kept on pushing through each day, feeling exhausted. Luca took me to see the doctor because my English is poor. The doctor told Luca that I was to give him some blood to run a test. So I did." The sobs start again, and I have to calm myself to continue. "The results were not good, and I am embarrassed to say what I have. What Raffaele has given to me." My tears are running down my cheeks like a stream of water. I am sobbing so hard, I don't recognize my own sounds because I don't think I have ever expressed such sorrow before now.

Sofia looks at me and says, "Carmela, no matter what this is you shouldn't be ashamed to tell me anything." Sofia slides her chair next to me. She puts her arm around my neck and pulls me close to her. "I don't care what he gave you. You are my sister for life, and that means that no matter what happens, I am and will always be here for you and your loving family. We are and always will be sisters. No person or thing can take that from us. What is this all about?"

I whisper so low that I couldn't hear my own words.

Sofia says, "What are you trying to say? I can't hear you."

I stand up and slam my fist down on the tabletop and shout out loud, "Raffaele and I have syphilis." I feel the need to vomit, but I don't have anything in my stomach since yesterday morning. I feel Sofia take me gently and sit me back down in the chair. I tell Sofia,

"I need some bread to eat because I am starving and a cup of coffee. Maybe I will feel a little stronger if I eat something."

She puts a plate of food in front of me and pours a large cup of black coffee, tells me to eat and then asks me, "What do you want to do?"

I tell her, "Well, this is incurable, and we both will die a terrible death."

She looks at me and says, "I know exactly how people with *sifilide* die. I witnessed my grandfather back in Italia die from *sifilide*. So, I understand how frightened both of you must feel.". She goes on to say, "but you could have many good years together before this deadly disease takes your lives. What have you and Raffaele decided to do knowing this?" Sofia stops for a second and angrily says, "Carmela, who was she?" She could see I was confused by the question and continued on, "I know it wasn't you; you were a virgin when you got here and would never cheat on your husband, so it had to be him."

I nod and say, "Raffaele cheated on me with a prostitute from the bar. You know those girls are in and out of the bar all day, looking for the long shoremen when the ships pull in at the docks. They know the men have money. I can't waste my time thinking about him and her. I have a deadly disease running through my blood. Sofia, you know what I would like to do? I want to go back to Italia with my six children. Never see Raffaele or America again. I came here to have a good life, and look at me. I will go home, and my family will be deeply upset about how my life has turned out. My coming here has not resulted in the dream my parents had for me. This did not make my life better."

Sofia says, "Let's think this out for a while. Don't rush into any decisions for a few days." Sofia looks at me with a smile and says, "Carmela, how about I write to your sister? Maybe she can come to America now to help you with this and the children? You both miss each other."

I grab Sofia's arm.

"Oh, what a great idea. I would like for you, Sofia, to write to Christina. Maybe she can come here. I need her courage because right now I feel lost. The person who I thought was by my side has failed me. If Christina was here, I would be happy. We should write to her now so she can get her arrangements started!" I stop for a minute and sigh. "I am only fooling myself, Sofia. Christina won't leave my parents. She takes care of both of them. My father wouldn't allow her to come here for me, but I must still try to get her here."

As Sofia is writing the letter, I ask her to tell Christina not to tell my parents about my disease. I don't want them to worry about me. They are old now. I want them to have as much peace as they can. I tell Sofia to ask Christina to get back to us as quickly as she can. Please Sofia, tell her I miss and love her dearly. Let me sign my name on this letter." Sofia hands me the letter. "I will stop at the post office and mail it to Italia today."

She hands me the envelope and says to me, "Carmela, promise me you won't do anything irrational because I am worried about you."

I smile at her and say, "I couldn't do anything that would hurt my children. Besides, Sofia, I know there isn't anything you wouldn't do to help me. And for that reason only and my children's safety, I won't be stupid."

She expresses her love for me and kisses me goodbye. I smile at her as we are carrying the baby carriage down the front steps. She laughs and says to me, "That's my sister, the one who always has a big smile no matter how hard life is to her. That's you, Carmela. You are incredibly strong, and you will make the best out of this." She kisses me goodbye and for a brief period of time, I feel clean. Not dirty from this disease. Sofia doesn't make me feel contagious.

CHAPTER 29

As I walk home from Sofia's house, I feel empty and sad. I find myself walking up the steps to the rectory to ask if I could talk with Father Foglia. When the housekeeper opens the door, I feel a rush of anxiety going through my body. I ask her if Father Foglia is in, but then I hear Father calling out, "Who is at the door?" Before I could say my name, he is standing there. "Oh, Mrs. Pasquariello, come inside, and bring the girls with you." So we all took one baby each into his office. Father Foglia looked at me and pulled a chair out for me to sit in. "Well, Carmela, what is on your mind today?" I can't tell him what I feel because he will think I am not a good Catholic. I sit straight up in my chair. I cross my arms tightly across my chest. Father smiles at me and says, "Go on Carmela, tell me why you came here today."

"Well, Father Foglia, Raffaele and I need to talk with you. We have an enormous problem in our lives. If we could get Raffaele to come and talk with you, maybe you could help us. I don't know where to go and how to get help with this problem."

Father Foglia stands up, walks around his desk, and leans against it. He is a few inches from me, and I feel as if he is overpowering me with his physical stature. He is such a tall man and broad. Yet, he is gentle and understanding. He has helped me many times since I have arrived from Italia.

I look at him, and I start to tell him my story.

"Father Foglia, we have a disease called syphilis. Raffaele got it, and naturally, I became infected. I would like to leave him and take the children back to Italia. But I don't think that Raffaele will allow me. We have the money, but I don't control the account at the bank.

Only Raffaele does. If you could talk to him, you might be able to convince him to let me and the six children go. We could leave as soon as he could buy the tickets, one way of course."

Father Foglia tells me that it would not be fair for the children not to have their father. And for Raffaele not to have his children here in America. "But I will tell you what I will have you and Raffaele do, and that is to come see me. We will talk this out, and go from there. I will stop at the bar today and talk with Raffaele, and you both will come see me in the morning after the 6:00 AM Mass. Meet me here in the rectory. Stop worrying, and let's put all of this to rest. You and Raffaele should be together as a family for your children. In the eyes of the church, you can't get a divorce."

I put the girls in the carriage and off I walk home. I am not happy with what Father Foglia wants me to do. I will go tomorrow with Raffaele. I am not happy at all about how Father thinks we should stay together.

The next morning, we get to the rectory before the 6:00 AM Mass is over. I am sitting nervously, waiting for Father Foglia. This morning could turn out to be a disaster for me. I am willing to try anything for my children. Not the same for Raffaele! Father walks into his office and sits at his desk. He clears his throat and says, "Are the two of you talking to each other?"

My response is sharp and clear, "No."

Raffaele looks across to me and says, "Carmela told me she has nothing to say to me. So, no, we aren't talking to each other."

Father says to me, "Carmela, do you love your husband?" I don't reply. Then he says, "Do you want to live your life without him by your side, and what about the children?" Still I don't reply. I feel as if my lips are sealed when it comes to Raffaele. Then he asks Raffaele, "How would you feel if Carmela and the children went over to Italia, just for a visit? They could all return in one year. And the two of you could start all over again. Some time away could be good for the entire family."

Raffaele reaches for my hand, but I pull it away. I won't even look at him. Father Foglia tells me, "Carmela, you have to learn how to forgive. We all make mistakes, no matter who we are and no matter how good we think we are. If God can forgive us our sins, then Carmela, you can forgive your husband for his poor judgment."

Raffaele and I lock eyes. I can see the tears running down his face.

"Carmela, don't take my family to Ateleta. I am afraid I will never see any of you again. And what good will that do for our love for each other? What about the children? I couldn't bear to wake up every day and not hear the children playing in our home. You and the children are the joy of my life. How lonely I would be without each and every one of you."

I look across the room at Father Foglia.

"Well," Father says as he is walking to me. "Tell me how you feel to hear Raffaele express his love for you and the children?"

Raffaele stands, walks over to me and gets down on his knees. He puts his head in my lap. I can feel his heart against my legs. It's beating so fast. He lifts his head and looks me in my eyes.

"I beg your forgiveness for my selfish act and not thinking of you. Now we both are sick. But the doctor said we should have many good years to live. Why can't we share those years as a family? I will do anything you ask, just don't take my family and your love away from me."

I look at Father Foglia, then I look Raffaele in the eyes.

"Raffaele, I love you more than I could ever express in words. I have never known such happiness as I have with you. But for now, I can't forgive or forget. So, if you truly love me, then you must sleep in Michael's room. Because you and I will no longer sleep together. Let time pass, and maybe someday I will see things differently. Just not now! I will continue to pray to God for his guidance."

Father Foglia expresses his happiness with us staying together. He tells Raffaele and I that whenever we need to talk, not to hesitate.

He is always here for us. Before we leave, Father asks us to say the "Our Father" prayer. As we are praying, we are at the end of the prayer, and all I hear is, "And lead us not into temptation but deliver us from evil. Amen."

I guess it is going to take time for me to heal.

CHAPTER 30

We go on living our lives as we had before. Except for one thing, probably one of the most important aspects of our marriage: We no longer have sex. It is strange enough to get on with our lives as if there was no betrayal; I just can't bring myself to accept him back in my bed. Many times, he will say, "I would like to sleep in our bed."

But the answer to that is always no.

This morning I wake up and find an envelope on my pillow addressed to "Carmela, My Love." I open the envelope, and it reads:

> *Monday, November 7, 1910*
> *Please, darling, don't leave me.*
>
> *My Dearest Carmela,*
>
> *When I first saw you 10 years ago, I watched as you stepped off the train. I immediately fell in love with you. You were my beautiful angel, and I had to have you in my life forever.*
>
> *I am writing this letter to you to ask for your forgiveness. I have no excuse for why I had no self-control. I acted as a stupid man. Can you ever forgive a fool like me? I can't express how much my deceit has damaged our marriage.*
>
> *Please, I don't want to lose the love of my life, the mother of our children. You are the only woman I will ever want or love.*
>
> *When I think of you, I feel a soft breeze come across my body. I sleep with thoughts and many images of you.*

I see your beautiful face, and I can smell the sweet fragrance of your hair. I cannot live without your tenderness, to wake up in the morning and not have you close to me and feel every beat of your heart has been torture, but to know it is permanent is unbearable.

Together we can get through this storm in our marriage. I will put trust back into our marriage. I have love and the ability to do so. If you would allow me the honor of doing this for us, I want to take all the suffering away from you. I only want to hold you in my arms again. Hopefully someday you may feel the same towards me.

Faithfully Yours,

Raffaele

My love for Raffaele was always in my heart. He had to break down my hate for him to receive my love again. This letter had done just that. Tonight, Raffaele will be invited back into our bed.

I started to feel sick in the morning. I realized I was pregnant. I had sex with Raffaele the first time in a few years, and now I am pregnant. Raffaele and I went over to Pennsylvania Hospital to see the doctor. We were hoping there was a cure for this dreadful disease. Dr. Willow talked with us on how they had a few treatments, but he wasn't sure they would help or cure us.

They have a treatment where the patient is put in a hot, stuffy room, and rubbed vigorously with a mercury ointment several times a day. The process goes on for a week to a month or more. Another toxic substance was arsenic. Both have terrible side effects, such as kidney failure, loss of teeth, mouth ulcers, and many die of mercurial poisoning rather than from the disease itself. Treatment goes on for years and has given rise to the saying, "A night with Venus, and a lifetime with Mercury."

The doctor looks at Raffaele and says to him, "Syphilis is a dreaded disease for many reasons, and it often mimics many medical disorders. When you both came to see me, I wasn't sure what your sores on your bodies were. The blood sample I took from the both of you told me it was syphilis. Now, if I were you, I wouldn't take any of the treatments because the side effects could be worse than the disease. You both are clear of sores, and you have no physical effects and it may lay dormant in your bodies for some time. Come back to see me whenever you need to see or talk with me. And Raffaele, please no more interaction with anyone other than Carmela." Raffaele shakes his hand and thanks him for taking the time with us to educate us on our disease. "And believe me, Doctor, I will only be with my darling wife."

I walk over to Dr. Willow and tell him that I may be pregnant.

"Are there any problems with giving birth to a baby?"

Dr. Willow looks at me and says, "If I were you, I would try my best to not get pregnant. You have many children to take care of now."

I nod my head and continue, "But Dr. Willow if I am pregnant, could there be problems with the baby?"

He tilts his head sideways as if to study me for a second.

"Well, Carmela there are effects on the baby. A pregnant mother who has syphilis can spread the disease through the placenta to the unborn infant. The infant while in the womb could be infected and die shortly before or after birth. Some defects like blindness, deafness, and deformed bones could affect the baby. Also, there are some babies that aren't affected at all."

This news is not what I was hoping to hear, but there is nothing to be done about it now.

"Well, Doctor Willow, I am in fact pregnant."

Doctor Willow says, "I suspected that was the case. Let's hope for the best."

We both are so happy with the prospect of having another baby in the house, so we decide to think positive, since there is nothing we can do but wait. It takes some time for our lives to feel normal, but we both are pleased that I and the children never went back to Italia.

I receive a letter from my sister Christina a couple months after writing to her. She says our mother isn't well and that our father is quite old now. So she can't leave until our parents are gone. But when that happens, she will be on the next ship to America. She will be thrilled to meet Raffaele and all our children. She isn't happy with him for what he has done to me. But she will love him because she knows I do.

It's August 1914 and extremely hot in our house. Raffaele came home this evening with a big German Shepherd dog named Charlie. The dog belonged to the owner of the bar. He asked Raffaele to take "very good care" of his dog while he is on vacation in Atlantic City because his children love their dog. I am not thrilled to have this animal in my house with all the kids. I am afraid the dog might get too excited around all the children.

After being at our home for two days, the dog stops eating. I am upset because I don't want anything to happen to the dog. I feed him his dog food in the morning, and as Charlie is chewing his food, he begins to choke. I put my hand into his mouth to get the food out of his throat. Charlie bites extremely hard on my hand and bites one finger almost off. I am bleeding profusely. The dog is agitated and foaming from his mouth. I put him in the backyard, so I can get to the hospital. I wrapped a towel around my bleeding hand.

My next-door neighbor is home, and she comes and stays with the children. I go by trolley into town. When the doctor sees me, he tells me I am lucky to still have my finger connected to my hand. Raffaele comes to the hospital soon after one of our neighbors sent their son over to the bar to tell Raffaele about the dog biting me.

The dog catcher picks up the dog and finds that he was infected with rabies. To prevent illness and even death, I now have to come to the hospital to get many shots. The doctor calls it "rabies vaccine." They give me an injection, which is followed with 12 additional doses administered over the following 10 days. The only thought that I had is, *What is going on with my baby?* The doctor told me that it would not affect my pregnancy at all. The baby will be born normal as long as I continue with all the doses, and I do exactly what the doctor tells me to do. Now, I not only have to worry about syphilis but also rabies and its effects on my baby.

In November, I give birth to a boy. We name him Ralph after Raffaele. As usual, Luca delivered him. I can always count on her to be by my side when I give birth. But Ralph is under four pounds and has a tiny body. He is the smallest of my babies. As time goes on, his growth is not like his brother or sisters. He is smaller than them. His mind is good; it's his body that is not developing as fast as the other children. Raffaele and I would tell each other "Little Ralph" is going to be small. We thought this was all due to the dog bite. The doctors said they weren't sure if it was or wasn't because the vaccine was fairly new, and they didn't have much research on it.

Raffaele is doing great at work! He surprises me with a deed to a large piece of ground in Willow Grove, Pennsylvania. He says one day that's where he is taking us. He will build us a large home, and it will have many bathrooms with toilets in every one of them. We are all happy to hear we wouldn't have to stand in line to use the bathroom. My thoughts are happy ones, but I will miss South Philadelphia and all of my neighbors. For that matter, I will really miss Sofia. Who could I talk with especially in time of need?

My sister Christina just arrived from Italia. Both my parents died within six months of each other. It's 1916, and she is living with us. I just gave birth to my son George. And 15 months later, I gave birth to a son Domenic. We now have nine children. Christina is a big help with the children. She never married in Italia, and after my parents died, she came over to America, just like she said she would. Oh, how I love her. All the children love her, and she loves them dearly. She is stern with them but really loving to them.

I couldn't be happier. Little did I know our happiness wasn't going to last.

Raffaele is showing signs of late-stage syphilis. He doesn't see as good as he used to. He is only working part time due to his weakness. The entire neighborhood knows he is sick with syphilis. I am no longer ashamed of our illness.

CHAPTER 31

I have asked myself many times, what, if anything, do I care about what others think of me?

This question runs through my head often. But I do care about my children, and I do not want them to be made to feel ashamed about being Italian. So, I question why other Americans look at Italians differently. Is my skin color too dark? Am I too poor because I was raised on a small farm? I can only speak Italian, not the language spoken here in America. I try to be strong, but often I just feel inadequate about people, places, and my life.

At times when I am not in the Italian section of South Philly, people stare at me and often call me names, like Dago and Wop. Sometimes they tell me to go back to Italia where I belong. The funny thing about what they say to me is they themselves also are immigrants from other countries. But yet I don't say those things to them. What right do I have to talk to anyone like that?

It's not been easy adjusting to the American way of life. I did what I had to do for myself and family, always wanting to become American. There are so many terrible stories about the treatment of the Italian people when they came to America. How unfairly we were treated. Like in 1891, they lynched 11 Italians in New Orleans. All of those men didn't do anything wrong. They broke no law. It was all due to the anti-Italian sentiment felt by the other nationalities. This also led to calls for more restrictions on immigration. The Italians felt frightened and were in fear of their lives. Americans don't understand us. We don't give up. The Italians just push through, and we hold our heads high like no other nationality. We are fierce in our pursuit of living a good clean life.

We all came across to give the next generation what we didn't have. We want our children to read and write, to get an education; always to be proud of oneself and work hard, no matter if it's in the dirt as a farmer, or in books as a teacher. We are no better or worse than any others. So, we will stay in our Italian communities and thrive. We will make our lives improve with time and with the expansion of our families. We Italians don't have to prove anything to anyone but ourselves.

We keep within our own community. Our children go to schools and churches that we built for them. The teachers and nuns speak Italian and English to our children. As a group, we stay in the same neighborhoods in large cities because we have a better chance to find a job. Even though we have been treated unfairly, we still survive. There isn't one Italian parent in South Philadelphia who doesn't want the same thing for their children, and that is for them to become better than we are. We want to look at them with pride in our hearts. We came with nothing, and we made do with what we had and became Americans. That's what we Italians worked towards, and we are accomplishing our dreams here in America because we are now Italian Americans. I want my children and their children to know and understand the hardships we endured at the turn of the twentieth century. Our persistence made us stand out to the rest of America.

What the people here in America don't realize is that we Italians come from a country with a long and rich history. That each and every one of us is willing to fight to keep our place here. We aren't going to run away from anyone for any reason. We ruled the world for over 500 years, and we learned a valuable lesson from our ancestors. Work and work hard every day to make something of your life. We, as a group, aren't going to give up. I am so proud of Raffaele, myself, and our children. This is the one lesson I can give to my family, and they to theirs.

My family in Ateleta were industrious and fond of work, loved the fields, the flock, the family. Abbruzzese women are the rulers of the home; they are excellent housekeepers, take care of the children, and their parents. They make all the clothes for the family and prepare all the food. Abbruzzese men work in the dirt and tend to the flock. They are hard workers. Up early and go to sleep many hours later.

The people from Abruzzo are known for their strength and kindness.

CHAPTER 32

My girls and I are in the backyard cleaning up the garden. It's the end of the growing season, and our tomato plants have produced bright red and pulpy tomatoes this year. It's the best it's been in 10 years. Rosie and Mary made enough sauce to carry us through till spring. Annie and Millie are gathering the remaining squash from the sprawling vines. This year, we didn't have any of our squash get fungi or bacteria. Taking care of the fruit and vegetable garden is a huge job for the girls! They plant, grow, and harvest everything out here, just like Christina and I did as young girls in Italia. We also have 15 chickens in the chicken coop, but cleaning out the coop is Michael's chore. He doesn't seem to dislike that dirty job. Michael talks to the chickens and chases them around the yard. I believe he takes joy from having to take care of the chickens. He will also choose one for dinner. He breaks their necks using the kitchen cabinet drawer, he puts the chicken's head inside the drawer and slams the drawer hard. The girls scream, "That's the end of that chicken!"

The girls like to watch Michael when he is killing the chicken. They think their big brother is funny. We all enjoy eating chicken, especially seasoned with rosemary seeds. I will put potatoes and carrots around the chicken. Pour olive oil on top of the bird and put the pan in the oven. The house will have a good aroma for when Raffaele comes home for supper after a long day at the tavern handling the troublemakers coming in and getting into brawls. He tells me that's what happens when you drink too much whiskey. You feel as though you can take on the place and everyone in it. Raffaele has a list of troublemakers who no longer are allowed inside the tavern.

I hear Michael in the basement shoveling the ashes. It's time to clean down there and get more coal for the hand-fired coal furnace. He fills the metal bucket with the ashes and puts it outside on the curb. It's really heavy for him to carry up the steps and through the house. He works so hard to prove to his father that he is a good kid. When he is finished, he will be covered in soot from head to toe. He never complains about any of his chores. Just like his sisters, they all work hard to help keep the house running properly.

I hear a ruckus going on out front in the street. I can hear people singing, "I love Sweet Rosie O'Grady, and Rosie O'Grady loves me." An Irish song. We all rush through the house to get to the front window to see who is out there. I see three men standing in the street in front of my house. One big man is yelling out loud, "Carmela Pasquariello, come outside. My name is Timothy Calhoun." I am thinking I don't know this person or his friends. What does he want from me?

The front door flies open, and thank God it's Michael on the other side. He is standing on the front stoop and extends his hand towards me.

"Come outside, Mom, and meet Timothy Calhoun. He is a friend of Dad's from the tavern." I step outside, and Timothy extends his hand towards me. I shake his extra-large hand. He is enormous in stature. I would think he's over 6 feet tall. His weight must be close to 250 pounds. He's a giant.

I smile at him, and I tell him what a pleasure it is to meet one of my husband's acquaintances from his job. Timothy smiles a warm, friendly smile. He tells me that he and his two cousins are stevedores on the waterfront, that's how he came to know Raffaele. He goes on to tell me that Raffaele has been serving them alcohol for over 10 years.

I look at Timothy and his two cousins; they are having such a hard time standing up. They are drunk and extremely loud. They start singing again, "I love Sweet Rosie O'Grady, and Rosie O'Grady loves me."

I tell Timothy, "If the policemen come down the street, all three of you will get thrown in jail. Could you be quiet? That way you won't have a problem. Besides, don't all three of you want to go home and be with your families today?"

They all seem to ignore my question though their voices did quiet down a bit. So, I question him on what he does on the waterfront because I don't know exactly what stevedores are. He turns his back towards me and on his waist, he has a large metal hook. He tells me, "This is the hand tool of my trade. I use this hook for the loading and unloading of the vessels. It's used for the ship's cargo."

He then yells to his cousins, "Boys, turn around and show Carmela your hooks."

The hooks are frightening! They have a long metal hook, and you hold it with your right hand. At the top of the hook is a six-inch piece of wood that you use as the handle. As the hook comes down, the metal gets thinner and thinner. Timothy is trying his best to be jovial because he can see how upset I am. I don't want my children around this. I ask Michael to bring all the children inside the house. I tell Michael I will join them shortly. After Michael says goodbye to Timothy, he gathers the girls and brings them in the house out of harms' way.

Before I can say anything, Timothy walks over to me and expresses how he didn't mean to show disrespect towards the family. He and his cousins have been working for two straight days. So, when they got off the dock yesterday, they went to drink, and that's where they came from about two hours ago.

"To be honest with you," he says in a quiet voice with a twinkle in his eye. "I am afraid to go home to see my wife. She will probably have a cast iron pan waiting for me. This isn't the first time I have done this." He smiles a gentle smile and in a much louder voice he continues, "Well, Carmela, it was nice to see you and the children. I hope we can be friends and that you're not upset with me. I would hate to lose my friendship with Raffaele."

I give Timothy a kiss on his cheek and tell him in Italian, "*Sei mio amico per sempre.*"

He laughs and tells me, "I don't speak Italian. What did you say?"

I laugh back and tell him I don't speak Irish, but I translate my words for him, "You are my friend forever."

He gives me a sincere smile, bows slightly, and we both laugh as he turns to walk away. I go in the house, and all the children are waiting for me. Rosie is the first to ask what they were doing singing in the middle of the street. Then all the kids are jumping up and down and laughing, "Mommy, why were they singing about Rosie O'Grady?"

I can't stop laughing myself. I tell them that they, all three of them, just got out of the insane asylum.

Michael asked, "Mom, are they crazy or just drunk?"

"Oh, please, all of you, leave me alone, and allow me a really good laugh at just what happened. Besides, I just got myself a new friend. The Irish Giant."

CHAPTER 33

"Rose hurry! You have to go to Esposito's Butcher Shop on 9th Street! Mr. Esposito will have five pounds of veal, beef, and pork wrapped waiting for you, along with a package of fatback. Get moving because your father's brothers and their families are coming for Sunday supper."

Rose, while allowing me to dress her like a ragdoll, asks, "Mom, how many of us will there be for supper?"

As I am pulling the dress over Rose's head, we both begin to laugh because I forgot to unfasten the top button, and her head can't get through the small opening. Quickly, I unfasten the button while Rose puts her shoes on.

I hand her the money and tell her to come straight home from the store. I begin scooting her out of her bedroom while I tell her, "We have to put the pot of gravy and meatballs on as soon as we can."

As Rose is going down the stairs and walks to the front door, she turns and again asks, "How many of us today?"

I smile at her beautiful face and reply, "There will be 18 of us for supper. Hurry now, get moving." My voice is getting louder as she turns to open the door, "When you return, I will have breakfast for you and your siblings." I continue to watch Rose as she opens the door because Rose has a habit of slamming it so hard that the front window rattles. Just before she closes the door I yell, "Don't slam the door, or the window is going to fall out of its frame."

She didn't fail at showing me her strength. I hear the familiar sound of the window shaking. I sigh and shake my head. In a blink of an eye, Rose is gone.

I turn around and quickly go back up the stairs to awaken everyone. I tell them, "Dress and come downstairs as soon as possible because today is family day with your uncles, aunts, and cousins. We have a lot of work to do after you get home from Mass."

All five girls are helping me in the kitchen. Michael is helping his father in the yard. They bring in basil, parsley, garlic, and endive with a few tomatoes for a salad from our garden. I will use the garlic and parsley in the meatballs. The aroma in my kitchen is like a typical Italian home. These are smells I am very accustomed to having in my kitchen, but my husband and children never get used to it; they all agree that Sunday supper is their favorite meal.

On a day like this, I feel so much love for my family. This feeling of complete happiness I always have when we all are working together. Everyone takes a part in preparing this meal; this is how we show love for each other.

The girls are giggling as they roll the meatballs in their hands. I am frying the fatback in the cast iron skillet. Each girl has a particular job at the table to do and they take it seriously, they don't want to let anyone down. Mary is cutting the garlic, Annie is washing and pulling the parsley apart, Millie is rolling the meatballs along with Nettie. As always, Rose is the director; she is in charge of everything my girls do. I can always depend on her to make sure everything is getting done to my standards.

She is my little "foot soldier." Rose comes up from the basement with the spaghetti maker in her arms. She's yelling at Michael that when we are done making spaghetti, he's carrying it down to the basement because it's too heavy for her. Michael rushes over to her and takes it out of her arms and puts it on my small wooden table. This is the same table on which Raffaele's mother made her spaghetti on every Sunday. I smile at the memory.

Rose gets me all the ingredients I need to make my spaghetti. Flour, salt, and eggs. The girls always help with this because it is fun making the mound of flour with a well in the center. Mary and

Annie are doing a great job bringing all the mixture together. Rose steps in to knead the dough with help from Millie and Nettie. They make more of a mess, but it's how we all learned to cook. It's rewarding to me as a mother to see my girls all learning to cook, especially as an Italian mother, because family and food are heartwarming in any Italian home.

As the girls clean the kitchen, Rose and I work the spaghetti machine and hang the spaghetti on two wooden rods, so they do not stick together.

On Sundays, our family supper is at 3:00 PM. We do this because that gives us plenty of time to socialize, and also the men have to get up at 5:00 AM the next day for work. So early is always better for the entire family.

When Giovanni and Orazio bring their families over, we will all be excited to see each other. We all will kiss and hug like we haven't seen each other in months. We Italians are very affectionate. We are always kissing and hugging; that's part of our makeup. If someone in the family doesn't kiss and hug you, you know they are mad at you for something you said or did. And what this is, you may never know.

The house smells of basil, garlic, tomatoes, and meat cooking. The kids are all dipping a piece of Italian bread in the gravy pot. I act stern and tell them all to get out of my kitchen and to wait to eat until everyone gets here, but secretly, I am smiling.

The girls are now setting the table while Raffaele and Michael are bringing up extra chairs from the basement.

Today, we will use my fine china; it has apple blossoms on it. This china makes me smile because it reminds me of the day Raffaele came home and told me he got the set from one of the guys off the ship that day. It took two of them to carry the boxes home with Raffaele. There are a couple hundred pieces to this set. It is extremely beautiful! The dishes also have to be carried up from the basement. It is fun setting everything up, but not so much fun carrying all the china and chairs back to the basement.

Someone is knocking on the door, so it's time to be happy and enjoy each other. And that's exactly what we do! Everyone is happy with the food. No one needs to tell you the food is good; you know it is when everyone asks for more. Giovanni and Orazio both brought their homemade wine, and they did a stop at Termini's Bakery for dessert with coffee. Even the kids drink black coffee with their cannoli. Needless to say, while the adults are relaxing after a big meal and having adult conversation, the kids are running all over the house, and there is so much laughter that the house is full of love.

This is what life is all about for us Italians. Good health, laughing, and eating! What else could we want in this life? This is what I call happiness!

CHAPTER 34

It's 1916. Our son Michael has to help our family survive because Raffaele can no longer do it. Raffaele has Michael selling produce on 9th Street. We no longer have Raffaele coming home with his full salary. So, Michael has to work and work long hours out there on the streets of South Philadelphia. Raffaele, at this time, is still working, but not as many hours.

We have to take Michael out of school when he finished eighth grade. At 14 years old, my son has to become a man. We are in need of money; there are a lot of mouths to feed here. Raffaele explains to Michael exactly how to get the guys on the docks to give him the produce for the day to sell. All the dock workers know Raffaele from going into the bar, so they are all helpful with Michael because they know about Raffaele having syphilis. Raffaele has already explained to the dock workers about his illness and how Michael has to be the one coming home with money. They have all come to his aid because most of them know or have someone in their family with the same illness. Raffaele believes he should prepare Michael for when he and his sisters are the ones paying the bills.

There is also a side business that Raffaele is teaching Michael: Raffaele gives loans to people and makes a profit from the loans. We do not loan money at an extremely high rate, so we are not loan sharks. We loan the money at a fair rate, so we can also make some money. We don't swindle or gouge anyone. He explains to Michael, "When my family came to America back in 1888, we also had to work hard. When my two brothers and I turned 14 years old, we were able to quit school and work. We all were laborers, along with my father. My father also gave loans to the other workers. Within 10 years, we could buy our house on League Street with cash. My father provided a good life for our family."

Raffaele gets up slowly and pours two small glasses of wine; he hands one to Michael and sits across from him. He continues, "In 1910, I worked a short amount of time as a grocer on 9th Street. But I didn't like doing that kind of work, so I went back to bartending and became a manager. Whatever job I was working, I always continued to make money on the side with the loans."

I watch Michael looking up at Raffaele, and my heart breaks; my little boy has to become a man whether he is ready or not. Michael looks both afraid and excited. I know he is excited to prove himself to us but nervous he might fail. Raffaele must recognize that look because he reaches over and puts his hand on top of Michael's hand.

"Now I will teach you as my father taught me. First and foremost, always treat everyone with respect, and never overcharge for any reason. You will always be looked upon as a man with honor. As men, honor is all we have; don't ever lose it. Your grandfather and I had the rare opportunity to be regarded as good men. I hope you do the same for yourself and continue to carry our family name with respect for the next generation."

Raffaele takes a drink of his wine, and Michael does the same.

"Michael, I would like to give you my father's ring. He gave it to me, and I would like you to give it to your first-born son." The ring is a gold band with a ruby in the center and diamonds on both sides. Michael is speechless and just stares at the ring. "By the time you give this family heirloom to your first-born son, you will have already taught him to respect everyone until proven that he shouldn't. As long as I am mentally able to help you, I will."

Michael takes his new responsibilities very seriously. He goes out seven days a week to work. He doesn't believe there is a day of rest for him, but I force him to attend Mass on Sunday, I get all the children to an early Mass, and Raffaele comes if he is able. Then Michael runs off to work for the rest of the day. But as a Catholic, I believe Sunday is a day of rest and worship. But not for Michael! Michael wants to prove himself to his father.

Raffaele is becoming quite sick. The doctor tells me that Raffaele is in the latent period of syphilis. At this time, I have no signs of the disease. But it still may affect my heart, brain, nerves and other parts of my body. The doctor tells me this could go on for years since I'm still in the dormant stage or the hidden stage. I have no visible signs. Raffaele appears to be well but isn't. I believe I am ignoring all the mental effects of this disease.

Looking out the back window, I see my sister Christina telling the kids a story in the backyard. I smile and look up to heaven, "Thank you, Blessed Mother, for sending me my sister Christina; I don't know what I would do without her, she is a great help with the children. They listen more to her than me!"

I laugh at how she tells them what to do, and they all march as if they were in the army! She does this with love, and they do love her back. I always thought I was hard on them, but watching Christina, she has me beat by a long shot. Life is much easier now that she is here in my home, always walking the children to school and walking them back at the end of the day. There is nothing that could break our bond, but now Christina will leave us for a new life.

Amid the chaos in my home, my sister Christina has found love with one of the men from our church. His name is Antonio Pizzichilli, born in Italia. He is a widower with three small daughters. His wife died a few months ago. Their relationship happened quickly. Someone in church introduced Antonio to Christina, and one month later they married in 1918. Christina is now a married woman and the mother of his three daughters, who happen to all be beautiful and sweet girls. I couldn't be happier for my sister and her new family. But, secretly, I miss her and all of her help. She did need a husband and children in her life. Christina looks so happy and content. Again, there she goes taking care of everyone else but herself. She has such a kind heart. In addition to Christina's marriage, we are in the midst of the war in Europe.

Raffaele is becoming worse each clay. I have to battle his pride just to take care of him. He is a proud man ,and I see it killing him that he has to depend on me to feed him, wash him, and even change his diaper. When I bathe him in the bathtub, I pour Epsom salt to reduce the inflammation of the sores on the back of his arms. He can no longer walk, so he lives in his bed. Thank God for the children. They help me a lot.

Every day brings a new challenge. Raffaele is beginning to lose his mind. Some days are good, but other days, he doesn't recognize me or the children. I, at times, go into the bathroom and just sit on the floor and cry. Watching my husband become crippled is too much for me to handle. In front of the children, I put on a good front. I know this situation is bad, but the only thing I feel is helplessness. As I watch what Raffaele is going through, I know I also will walk the same path. For some reason, I am stronger than him. He is quickly losing his bodily functions. The doctors believe I will outlive him for several years. That's how advanced his illness has grown. He becomes weaker every day, and I become anxious, not knowing where the future of my family lies. Somehow, by whatever means possible, I will keep my family together. Always in time of need, I find myself praying to the Blessed Mother. She is who I lean on. I can't go to Christina now. She has her own family to take care of. I will get through this as I have gotten through everything else.

I took my scapular off of me and put it around Raffaele's neck. This scapular has been with me since I was 10 years old. I feel such an important part of me is gone. But Raffaele needs to be protected with the help of the Blessed Mother.

CHAPTER 35

I haven't been feeling well. My daughters, especially Rose, have been helping me with their father. I suspect that I may be pregnant. I am 38 years old, and Raffaele and I are not prepared to be parents again. He, with his condition, and me, taking care of him, I won't have much time in my day to take care of a baby. My three youngest boys now are five, three, and two years old. How will I ever take care of a baby, along with everything else I have to do every day for Raffaele?

On a beautiful day in October 1919, I gave birth to a boy. We named him Rocco after Saint Rocco, the patron saint of those with contagious diseases. Luca was here to help me give birth to him. But I felt there was something wrong. She took him immediately away and wrapped him entirely in a blanket. I couldn't see any of him. I knew in my heart there was a big problem. I was so emotional. I kept my eyes on her the entire time, until she looked at me and smiled. She brought him up to me and said, "He is a little small and deformed and has a rash on his body under his arms, back and stomach. He is small, and there is something wrong with his legs. We need to take him to the hospital as soon as you are able."

I started to cry and said, "Please, give me Rocco. I want to see him and hold him."

Luca places Rocco in my arms, and I can feel that he is underweight. As I unwrap the blanket from his body, I can see the rash on him. Oh, he is so fragile. I feel completely sad. I see his legs are deformed from the knees down. They are bent and thin. His entire body is small. He cries a small whimper at first, but now, he is still and quiet. He looks lifeless to me, but I can see his chest going up and down from his heart beating slowly. I immediately put him to my breast and put him on my nipple, and he starts to suckle as all of my babies did.

Luca asks if she can come back tomorrow to see Rocco and maybe when I feel strong enough, we will bring him to the hospital because the doctor needs to see him. I tell Luca I would be happy for her to get us to see the doctor because I know Luca knows that Rocco is born with syphilis. But what is strange to me is that the three boys born before him were healthy. Except for Ralph because I got bit by the rabid dog, and I had rabies and all those shots.

I am so shocked to see Rocco ill with this terrible disease. Only I, his mother, can see his beauty. He has chancre or ulcer sores on his body. His nose is running, and the doctor called his nose "saddle nose." That's when the nose is flat to the face.

We are at the hospital with Rocco, and the doctor's expression is very serious. Luca and I are here to talk with the doctor. Maybe there is something we can do for Rocco. I want the doctor to look at Rocco and help me to take care of him and to make him feel more comfortable. His little body goes into seizures, and he becomes stiff as a board. I can't get his body to relax. The doctor gives Rocco a thorough exam, and he answers all of Luca and my questions. He tells me that the outcome was going to be grim. That there isn't much they can do for Rocco. The doctor didn't believe he would live past one month old.

The doctor asks if Raffaele and I are going to continue to have sex. He says he hopes that we don't, so I won't become pregnant again. I told him I would make sure that we don't. That getting pregnant with Rocco was something that just happened, but I won't let this happen again.

"Well, Carmela take your baby home, and make him as comfortable as you can. Take good care of him as you are tending to Raffaele. When Rocco becomes too sick for you, we will take him here at the hospital, or we could wait for when he passes away. And you can sign the paper for us to take his body for research here."

Oh, how I wish Raffaele could be here with me; I feel so alone and guilty. What have we done to this innocent little baby? The doctor sees my sadness and continues, "This research could help other families in this situation. Perhaps we can find a cure or at least a remedy to help with pain."

I look up at the doctor, but his face is a blur behind all my tears, I nod and say, "Before I leave the hospital today, I will sign the paper that when Rocco passes, the hospital will take care of him with a burial. Raffaele won't understand because most of the time he isn't coherent about what's going on around him, but if he was, I know he would agree."

I am shaken to my core about my son, but there isn't anything I can do. I love Rocco and will cherish every minute I have with him. I wish sometimes that I were young and living in Italia with my family; life was so much easier. I have visions of little Rocco playing on the beautiful hills of Ateleta with my parents. They would have loved to be grandparents. I hold on to this dream as long as I can because reality is so hard.

Rocco lived for three months and died in his sleep. Rose went over to the hospital and informed them about Rocco. They came and took his body, and we never saw him again. I pray every day for his soul. When I go to sleep at night, I talk to him. I tell my son that I soon will be with him. That I will carry him in my arms when I get to see him again in heaven. I tell him how much I love him, as I love all of my children, the ones here on Earth and my other children in heaven. I end my prayer with, "Please, Blessed Mother, take care of all 12 of them. Keep them protected."

CHAPTER 36

America was in the waning months of World War I, and there was enormous pressure to sell war bonds. A big parade was staged here in Philadelphia to rally the public behind the war bond effort. They had it on Saturday, September 28, 1918. The Health Commissioner, despite warnings about a new influenza virus, went ahead with the parade. He refused to cancel, believing it was fine and no one would get sick. The Spanish Flu pandemic had a devastating health consequence here. Over 200,000 people attended the parade. Within a week, 45,000 people were infected, and the entire city had shut down. Within six months, 16,000 people were dead.

Giovanni's son was 10 years old and died about a month after the parade. We buried little Giovanni in the family plot in Holy Cross Cemetery. His father took his death extremely hard. They were at the parade on that Saturday, and within one month, his son was gone. We all were saddened by his death. We are doing our best not to get infected. But when you see and hear so much about death, you believe it's close to you, and you start thinking you have the Spanish Flu. We were lucky that we lost only neighbors and friends, but no one else in our immediate family became ill or died.

First, we made it through World War I, then the Spanish Flu pandemic. Now, side-by-side comes the Roaring Twenties and Prohibition and the 19th Amendment. We females finally have the right to vote. It is ratified on August 18, 1920.

There is so much happening at this time. The Roaring Twenties and Prohibition, I feel, go hand-in-hand, people wanting to drink and dance and enjoy life. We have been through so much hardship lately that drinking and dancing for a lot of people is their way of trying to stop worrying about their troubles. Friday, January 16, 1920, every tavern, bar, and saloon in America has to close its doors and no longer can sell liquor. Michael, to make more money, is now selling liquor to the speakeasies. That's where people get to dance and drink, but they are illegal. If you get caught, the police will arrest you, and you will have to pay a large fine. But that doesn't stop most people from having fun. The liquor trade is now underground.

Some of the liquor being sold is bad. It could cause brain damage, so, you have to be careful what you are drinking. However, that didn't stop people from drinking. If they could find liquor, then they would drink it. Michael tells me stories about the speakeasies and how he makes his deliveries to them. Most of them have peepholes on the front door of the illegal establishment. They look out to see if it's the cops. If it is, they run out the back door. One guy jumped out the third-floor window, so he wouldn't get caught, but he crushed his head when he landed on the cement slab below and died there.

Michael believes this law is because the middle class, white Americans want to assert some control over the unruly immigrant masses who crowd the native cities. I don't know whether Michael is right, but he sure does make a lot of money selling liquor. I don't know what I would do without his money.

Michael tells me his schedule for the day. He wakes up early, and down to the docks he goes to get his fresh produce for the day. He then goes back to South Philly on 9th Street and fills his wooden cart with his fruits and vegetables. His cart has three levels, and the top two are his produce and the bottom one is for his liquor. He gets his bottles of illegal liquor on the wharf every day. He has become a great businessman, and the older guys down there help him with his supplies. Since prohibition, his sales have quadrupled because of liquor. His produce sales have also taken off. Michael's cart has become a one stop shop for his customers.

Last night, Michael came home at 1:00 AM from a card game. He set this up at a store front on 7th Street in a second-floor apartment. He pays the landlord a fee and then charges the guys three times that amount. He sells liquor to the guys and gets food for them while they play cards. Michael makes money off of everything while the card game is going on. It's all becoming extremely lucrative for him. Since all the guys on the docks know Michael, he can get as much liquor as he can sell for his illegal business.

He makes enough money to pay all the bills and even has some to save. He wants to get into the real estate business, buying property to rent out for his card games. He thinks he can make himself a rich man.

CHAPTER 37

The new year 1920 and a new decade has come. We haven't had a good start with the new year because of Rocco dying. But Rose and Mary are working in the garment industry here in South Philly. They are vest makers and help with bringing home their paycheck.

Michael still is selling produce on the street and continues to work seven days a week. The younger girls all help me with Raffaele. He has become unbearable at times. He yells at us, but we know he doesn't mean to be harsh. The girls' expression is of hurt because they love him all through this.

While I am cooking for the family, they take over the care of him. He can't get out of bed because he has paralysis, he has bladder incontinence, so I feel we are always changing him, trying our best to keep him dry and clean. Every day, he gets worse; he also has organ damage, and his brain and spinal cord have been affected. He no longer speaks and can't see. What a way to die! I am watching him wither to nothing. The only thing left for him is to deteriorate until he takes his last breath. This seems so unfair for such a proud man to die this way! Michael says to me, "Mom, we need to send Dad to the hospital."

MICHAEL'S POV

We sent my father to the Philadelphia General Hospital because we no longer could give him the proper care he was in need of. Dad had become utterly helpless. We took him to the hospital in an ambulance, and Mom went with him. He was put in the psych ward because he was not coherent and at times would be violent.

I will never forget the moment Mom knew that my Father had died in his sleep.

As we were all preparing to go to work, the house was quite busy as normal. With three girls in the kitchen trying to have a cup of coffee before they are off to the garment factory and my two brothers sitting at the kitchen table trying to get their homework complete from the night before, everything seemed like a typical day to all, except my mother. She seemed to be very quiet today; she was just staring out the window. Since Ralph and George never liked to do their homework, I decided to step in and leave my mother to her thoughts. I told the boys, "If you don't get good grades on your report cards, the two of you will grow up to be stupid." Which, in this day and age doesn't mean a thing to them. Not yet anyway.

Even though there was a lot going on in the kitchen, I could hear Aunt Christina bursting through the back door into the kitchen. As soon as she saw my mother, she put her arms around her. My mother's body became stiff as a board. She looked at Aunt Christina straight in the eyes. They were speaking without words. You could see Mother slipping out of Aunt Christina's arms and falling on the cold linoleum floor.

She fainted! Aunt Christina, Rose, and I were helping my mother off the floor. We put her in her chair, and she moaned; it is a sound I know I will never forget. There was so much pain in this sound. She opened her eyes, and now her tears are streaming down her face. Rose and I looked at each other; we had no idea what was going on, until my Mother spoke:

"Did my Raffaele die?" Even before Aunt Christina can answer, Mother looks at me and says, "Michael, I knew your father was gone. I woke up in the middle of the night, I thought I heard foot-steps coming up the stairs. When I opened my eyes, he was standing in the hall at the doorway watching me and extending both of his arms out to me. I couldn't reach his arms, and before I knew it, he was gone!" She was speaking between sobs, her small body was shaking, and she looked so helpless; I don't know what to say. She continued, "What will happen to my heart? Does it die with him? Will I become a widow and die with a broken heart?"

She blessed herself with the sign of the cross and said, "Dear Blessed Mother, thank you for taking Raffaele out of his misery. Now at last, may he rest in peace. Please, keep him in your arms till I am with my True Love again."

CARMELA'S POV

He lived for two weeks. The nurse from his ward told me he went to sleep and never woke up. He died on Tuesday, February 15, 1921. On his death certificate, they have the cause as "general paralysis" of the insane in late-stage syphilis. I feel both sadness and relief. Sad because the love of my life has passed. And relief because he is finally out of his misery. In addition, I am afraid for the future because I know I will go through the same final years myself.

Today is Raffaele's funeral, and I feel completely numb of all emotion right now. I hear someone coming down the living room stairs. I can hear the sounds of agony coming from my son Michael. As he walks into the kitchen, I walk over to him and put my arms around his shoulders. His strong body feels so weak and hollow today. His beautiful, dark brown eyes are half shut from crying; they are swollen and bloodshot. This is the first time since he was a baby that Michael is just my son. I feel so lost with that thought. I hear myself saying to him, "Today we are going to bury your father. We all have to say our goodbyes to him and pray for his soul so that he rests in peace through eternity. Michael, it's only a few days since your father died. We will all miss him dearly." I held his face in my two hands and said, "Michael, I need you to be strong now. You must carry on with taking care of this family as you have been doing for the last couple of years. Your family needs you now more than ever!"

I take his hand and walk him over to the table so we can sit. I move a curl off of his forehead and wipe a tear from his cheek, his resemblance to his father gives me a slight chill. I look in his eyes and continue, "I know we put all the responsibilities on your shoulders. When your father became too ill to work, he needed you to go out and work the streets of South Philly and bring home money. Michael, you amazed us with how hard you worked and how smart you handled the family business."

Before I can continue, Michael reaches for my arm and speaks in a quiet voice, "Mother, I worry that I won't be able to keep doing all of this on my own. I know I have been working seven days a week since I turned 14, but I am already tired and weary of life. Now that my father isn't here, I feel lost. I can't believe he is gone from me forever, never to see his face or hear his laughter again." Michael sits back in his chair, looking older than his years, and the smallest of smiles touches his face. "Remember how he liked to play funny tricks on me, so I would laugh at him? That's what made me go out there and make money for our family. My father's love for me."

"Oh Michael, look at the smile you have when you speak of your father. Remember his kindness and his strength. I hope you will be a good man as your father was. I am very proud of you now. You were your father's first son. In the Italian tradition, the first son will be a good son. You, Michael, are all that your father prayed for as a son. He loved you dearly. You always gave him the love and respect a father should receive from his son. What more could an Italian father expect from his son? Your father was extremely happy at the love you expressed to him every day. To see you both every day interact always put joy in my heart.

"Michael, please eat something. Here's a cup of coffee and some toast that should help settle your thoughts down. Today will be a very long and emotional day. We will move slowly, so we don't wear ourselves out too quickly. You must help me with your eight siblings.

You know the girls will be hysterical. I will need your help with calming them down and trying to keep things moving along.

"Hurry Michael. The funeral hearse from Baldi's Funeral Home will be here shortly to take us first to Our Lady of Good Counsel Church for your father's Mass and then they will take us to Holy Cross Cemetery for his burial. We won't get back home till dusk."

I shoo him from the table to get him moving. I know he will become less emotional when he is busy with his siblings.

"Go upstairs and make sure everyone is washed and dressed, then send them down to me. They should all eat a little something, so they won't get sick to their stomachs today. This is going to be a very sad day for all of us. We will come together and make it to the other side of today." Michael stops and looks back for a moment as if he wanted to say something, but I stopped him. "Michael, please go, and do as I have asked of you. Please, be gentle with them. They also are shattered, just as you and I."

Michael walks over to me, puts his arms around me tightly and squeezes me so softly. He whispers in my ear, "Mother, please don't worry about anything. I am here to take care of you and my brothers and sisters until each and every one of you no longer need me."

I pull away from him. I do not want him to carry the whole weight of our family on his shoulders. How unfair life can be to us. But it is life, and we have to accept our fate. As quickly as he said those words of comfort to me, he was out of the kitchen and up the stairs to gather the children for breakfast.

CHAPTER 38

At this moment, I know our lives are going to change drastically. But I can't think of tomorrow. I must make it through today.

Rose walks into the kitchen like a mother duck with her ducklings behind her. All of my girls are showing sorrow. They are all crying. We all knew Raffaele was going to die soon, but we still are in shock when it happened. Annie says, "We can't believe he is gone from us forever."

I hear Michael and the boys jumping down the stairs to go outside. The door slams with great force. Michael and the boys are out there with the driver. He is telling Michael we all can fit into the vehicle, but it will be a tight squeeze.

Today is the worst day of my life; there is no getting around it. I will be totally lost without Raffaele. I know he hasn't been able to do much of anything in the past few years, and I know how much it bothered him that he was not able to work and not contribute much financially.

Thankfully, Raffaele was able to give Michael the knowledge of who on the street and on the dock to deal with. If he wasn't able to teach Michael, I don't know how we would have made our bills. Michael is a fast learner and was eager to help his family and to prove himself to his father. I know it gave Raffaele peace knowing he was leaving us in good hands. Yet, it is still devasting to me and the family that Raffaele will not be with us here in this house.

All our children looked up to him and respected him, especially Michael. In all of this, Michael has never said one bad word about his father. Michael has always done whatever Raffaele or I have asked of him, even though what he did outside of the house was not always legal. But when your nationality is looked down upon and you are not able to make a fair living as others do, then you find other ways; we Italians are survivors.

If it came down to starving or feeding the family, we were going to eat! Raffaele always warned Michael about staying away from the "Blackhand," a society engaged in criminal activities. They were always known for taking young Italian boys away from their family and turning them into lawless criminals who were taught to be savagely brutal to get what they wanted. Now I have four sons who I must look after because I don't want anyone of my boys hurt or killed. With Raffaele here, my boys were left alone, but now, I am afraid they will try and lure my sons away.

We all stayed at the cemetery till everyone left. There were so many people there. Raffaele had many good friends. They will all deeply miss him and his ability to make everyone feel welcome and loved. That's what was so special about my husband: he was a kind soul who never spoke badly about people. If he felt you were not a good person, he would tell you and leave it at that. He didn't really argue with anyone and always saw the good in people. But don't mistake his good nature, if you proved him wrong about you, he was finished with you forever. This is an Italian trait that many, if not all Italians, are born with. We don't forgive or forget.

When we leave the cemetery and arrive home, the house is full of people. So many of them are family, business associates, and friends. This makes my heart secretly cry with happiness for Raffaele. There is so much love everyone was showing him. When I walked in, everyone stands up, and it becomes an overwhelming feeling to me because all of these people are showing how much of a good man my husband was to them. Even when he was ill and he was showing mental disorder, he still would try to help in his small way.

Everyone came to express their sorrow for me and my family for losing Raffaele. Kissing, hugging, and many tears are shed on me that were not mine. I wear those tears as a soldier wears his armor. They make me realize even more how Raffaele was looked upon as a good person. Someone would and could count on him in times of need. Men were putting cash in my hands. The ladies all made food. Pans, pots, and plates full of meats, macaroni, and vegetables. Some of the ladies also put cash in my hands. One neighbor told me she took her husband's cash from the top of his nightstand. When he asked where his money was, she told him that he donated it to Raffaele Pasquariello's family. He said he was happy to give his money to us for all that Raffaele did for him when he first came to America, and he will never forget his kindness. I feel that everyone in my home at that time was my family because I felt so much love and respect from everyone. We are the romantic people of the world. Our hearts are full of so much love that we have to offer it to others. We are givers, not takers; this is the Italian nationality. We always want to help someone in need. We are offering our love to everyone. We Italians stick together because no other nationality can or will understand ours. Each and every one of us accepts each other. As Michael has expressed to me on many occasions, "Mom, I have your back always." We love to love.

People are saying goodbye to the family. Everywhere you look, you can see people kissing and hugging. Michael and I are standing at the vestibule door to express our thankfulness to each person as they leave. I stand there until Sofia and Matteo, the last guests, leave. Christina walks over to me and says as she is carrying a kitchen chair, "Sit down and don't say a word. I will make you a cup of coffee. Just relax now. It's only your family here. I will spend the night with you and stay for the day. You need to rest and slow yourself down. Carmela, I love you."

Before I can respond to her, off she goes to get the coffee. All the children are cleaning up the mess. The girls, as usual, are all talking at the same time. Their chatter at times is loud, and I can't understand a word of it. I am sitting watching them and their every move, thanking God for all of them! The boys are putting the furniture back in place in the living room and dining room. Last night, I had the boys bring Raffaele's bed back upstairs. I didn't want to see it down here any longer. It was here for two years, and it was full of bad memories. So, it's best that it's back upstairs in the boys' room. With all the ugly memories when he became so ill, he couldn't walk up and down the stairs, so he had to use the bucket when he needed to empty himself. He laid in bed and did nothing all day. I don't want to think of those things. Now I must move forward and get my family in a good place. Tomorrow, Christina and I will talk about this and what my plans are to keep our family together. Christina is smart and tells me she has a few ideas to help me and my family.

Christina brews me a cup of coffee. After I drink my coffee, I will go to bed, though I probably won't be able to sleep, but at least I can rest my body. We sit together, and for the first time in our lives, we don't say one word, but our souls are one. I sit there staring into space with my thoughts of hopelessness and sorrow. But come tomorrow, I will get my plans together with the help of my sister. I know in my heart that I also will die this horrible death. But I also know that when I do die, I again will be with the love of my life. Until then, I will take care of my children, and I will work hard to keep the memory of Raffaele in my children's hearts.

CHAPTER 39

How would I feel if Raffaele was still alive? I have this thought inside my head for the last few days. Today is Monday, June 27, 1921. It's a fantastic day to celebrate my birthday. It's sunny and warm. I am 40 years old today and feeling lonely. I no longer have Raffaele by my side to make me feel special on my day, but today, I will see my life as I have had more happier days than not, with much joy and laughter.

Raffaele and I worked hard, but we loved even harder. I couldn't have asked God for a better husband. I know deep down inside, there are people like my sister Christina who would disagree with me. She feels he only thought of his needs. No one knew Raffaele the way I did. I knew his strengths, and I knew his weaknesses like no other.

Sure, at first, I was angry at him for his cheating and then giving me syphilis. In the beginning, I was on the verge of leaving him for good. It took me a long time to forgive him. And also to forgive myself. I had so much anger inside of me. This was not the person I wanted to be. If it wasn't for my Catholic faith, I don't know how I would have forgiven him or survived without him in my life and the children's lives. It wasn't just about me. I had to mature and look at the total effect on my family. Do I think I did mature during that time in our lives? Immensely! I did become a complete person, a better and more understanding person. I am happy I had all those wonderful 21 years with Raffaele, even if some were the worse in my life. I became more loving towards him. Life was just not about me or Raffaele. It now was about our six children. Who knew, we would love again and would go on to have more babies?

I am stronger now. I am not a naïve, young girl as I was when I stepped off that boat years ago. I am stronger now with much experience and wisdom from living life. I will proceed with my children to have a good, happy life. I am able to take care of them and my house. The older children will work and bring home their salaries. As for the last three boys, they are in school and will continue with their education. Raffaele would be happy with how I moved on with life. He always said to me, when he became bedridden, that life is for the living.

"And, Carmela, when I die, let me go, and you go on living with our children."

Mr. John Reed came to the house about a year after Raffaele passed away. He is Raffaele's realtor who sold him some ground in Willow Grove. Raffaele's dream was to move us out of the city and into an open space with a country setting. And why not Willow Grove? It's open with a lot of fresh air and looks a lot like Italia with all the trees and grass. It's an area with many farms. You can see cows, horses, and it smells of a farm. When I went with Raffaele to see the parcel, it had belonged to the Moore family. They were selling the 200 acres left to them by their grandfather in two-acre parcels. As soon as I saw the beauty and smelled the familiar odors, it was amazing and friendly to me. I smiled at Raffaele and said, "Oh, I would like to live out here. To feel and smell the dirt again; I couldn't be happier! You could see for a very long distance into the corn fields. This place feels like home." Raffaele purchased a two-acre parcel of ground that day. He paid the realtor in cash, and it now belonged to us

Since we married, we have done well. We own our home on League Street, purchased from his two brothers in 1908; we purchased the property in Willow Grove; had all of these babies and put them in Catholic school. We all dressed nicely, always had plenty of food, and never did the family go hungry. We helped family and friends when they were in need. God blessed our family with much and that's what I most remember when I feel lost and I am missing Raffaele. I will wear black for the next two years in mourning because that is what an Italian widow does to show her love and respect for her departed husband. I think of myself as the "*La Vedova,*" the Widow.

I hear someone knocking on the front door. When I open the door, I am shocked to see Mr. Reed standing there. He hands me a box from the bakery and steps into the foyer even though I haven't invited him inside my house. I stretch my arms out to reach both sides of the archway to quickly block him from entering the parlor.

I ask him, "Why are you here at my house?"

He quietly says to me that he knows Raffaele has passed, and he wants to talk to me about the property in Willow Grove.

I ask him, "What about the property? We paid for it, and now it belongs to me and all the children. I have to go and get the deed changed, but I have been busy with everything since losing my husband. I will get to it soon enough."

Mr. Reed asks if we can go inside and sit down and talk just for a few minutes. He wants to tell me about how the property had gone down in value. The sympathy on his face doesn't look sincere, but he quietly continues, "Now is the time to sell it and not lose a lot of money. Every day you hold the deed, you are losing money. You need all the money you can get to help with the raising of the children on your own."

I invite him to sit at the dining room table. Rose puts on a pot of coffee. The kids all sit around the table to hear what Mr. Reed has to say. They can't wait to open the bakery box and eat the French pastries, which look delicious. As the kids are enjoying themselves, I ask Mr. Reed to tell me what is happening in Willow Grove with our land and ask how I could help him.

He says, "The parcels are selling at a much cheaper price now. It is best to sell the land as soon as possible, especially since you are in need of money. I know you and the older children have been working hard to keep your house in South Philly and what you have in Willow Grove. But you still have to pay taxes. Are the older children still working?"

I reply, "Yes. We could use some money to pay for Raffaele's funeral. I still haven't paid it all off to the funeral home."

I ask the older three children what they thought about selling the property. They all look at me and say, "Ask Michael what he thinks."

But before I allow Michael to voice his thoughts, I say to Mr. Reed, "I would like to sell the property because there is a larger house on 10th Street that I want. It belongs to a friend of Michael's, and they are moving back to Italia. This may be the right time to move out of this house. I have too many memories that aren't happy ones. And we could use a bigger house for the girls. They are all getting to be young women. They need to have privacy. More room for the five of them would be helpful."

Mr. Reed tells me he will go ahead and promptly get the property up for sale. He comes back in two days and tells me he sold the property, but for a lot less than what we paid for it. He needs me to sign the papers. At first when he tells me I lost a lot of money on this deal, I think something doesn't seem right. But he seems concerned that the offer will drop in price if I wait any longer. He pleads with me to act quickly because every day I wait, I lose more money.

Well, hearing that I am losing money makes me cringe inside. So, I act in haste and surely move too fast and sell Mr. Reed the property.

But I soon realize Mr. Reed is indeed no friend to me or my family! I learn he sold it for much more. So I go to see him at his office in Willow Grove. I take Michael with me. Or, I should say, Michael was not going to allow me to travel to see Mr. Reed without him! I have Michael promise me that whatever the outcome of our visit, Michael will behave in a manner suitable for a young man. A man with the last name of Pasquariello!

When we walk into Mr. Reed's office unannounced, he is shocked to see us there standing in front of him. Mr. Reed says to me, "What a nice surprise it is to see you, Mrs. Pasquariello. Please have a seat and you, Michael, please sit down. I will be right with the both of you."

As we are waiting, I can see Michael is getting uneasy sitting in his chair. I grab the leg that can't stop moving and in a stern manner say, "Please Michael, no commotion here today. Mr. Reed will call the police on us. I just have one thing I must get off my chest to a scoundrel like him."

When Mr. Reed comes over to his desk, he stands there and says to us, "What is it that I can help you with today? Are you looking to buy more property here in Willow Grove?" He is thinking we are still ignorant to his actions. He continues, "I do have a nice piece of land to sell."

Before I can say one word, Michael jumps up, and Mr. Reed runs into the office next to his and locks the door. Michael is banging on the door, and he is yelling at Mr. Reed, "Come out like a man and hear what my mother wants to tell you. You're a coward, Mr. Reed. You stole my mother's land for hardly any money, and you said it was for a client. You lied because it was for you, and you sold it for more than twice what you paid my mother. Come out and face my mother and explain yourself to her. I would like to hear why you did to her what you did."

From behind the locked door, in a shaky voice, Mr. Reed says, "If you don't leave, my co-worker will call the police. Get out of here now and don't ever come back."

I walk over to Michael and whisper, "Let's go home, he already did what he did to us." As I turn to the locked door, I knock on it and yell as loud as I could because I have to let the anger out of me. "I hope, Mr. Reed, you rot in hell with all the other devils!"

I am shaking because I am so mad at Mr. Reed. I would like to have hit him hard in his mouth for all the lies he said to us. I reach for Michael's hand and press hard. He looks at me as I am crying. I tell Michael, "It's fine now. I said what I came to say. Now, we will go home and forget about this. We cannot change what he did, but you and I know if your father was alive, Mr. Reed would have never gotten away with this. He is a coward! He never would have done this to your father in fear of what your father would have done to him. We will let this go for good. Let us let your father rest in peace."

A few months pass, and I hear that Mr. Reed got into a fight in a bar and that two men beat him so badly, he was never able to return to work because his left leg was broken in so many places. He couldn't walk on it. Do I feel bad for him? Absolutely not! On this Earth, you will get what is coming to you, good or bad. God will see to it!

CHAPTER 40

The only one still at home with me is Dominic. All the other young children are in school and my three oldest girls work in the garment industry. Michael is selling produce; they all tell me how much they like to work and make money. They all bring home their paychecks to me. I don't know how I could take care of this house and the family without their help and love.

Christina stops over to visit with me and to say she has a great idea of how I can survive. She told me there is a farm in Sicklerville, New Jersey, which would take me and the kids for the season to work on the farm. Without hesitation, I agreed that we would go, and the four oldest would work in the factories and stay here in Philly. They could take care of the house and themselves until we returned in October.

We leave in April to go to New Jersey. They have a cabin for us to live in for the months we work on the farm. Mr. Sickler tells me he can't pay us much, but we can stay in the cabin and work the farm Monday through Saturday. Sunday would be our day of rest.

It is a large farm and has quite a few families working on it. We all work extremely hard. I have forgotten how hard it is to work on a farm. It's an endless job that you work all day from early morning to dusk. They have a large barrel of water that sits out all day directly in the sun for when you are in need of a drink, though the water is hot and disgusting. But, if you are thirsty enough, you will drink the water. It is so hot you could make a cup of tea out of it. That's what all of the workers complain about and then laugh at themselves.

At the end of the day, all of us are exhausted and hot, go to our cabin, have dinner, then go to bed, only for morning to quickly come to us. The sun comes into our cabin through the windowpane and wakes us up. It is our alarm clock!

Today, it's a rainy day, but we still will pick the peaches off the trees. No matter what the weather, there is always work to get done. It makes me proud of my family that we can and will work in any element. We all are hard workers, even my three young boys.

On Sunday, our day of rest, I get the children up for an early 7:00 service. We are Catholic, but there is only a Baptist church down the road that we can walk to. I feel God understands why we aren't at a Catholic church. I taught my children that every time they thank God for what He has given us, that God will be pleased with their love for Him.

Life is hard on them, but they don't seem to mind. They smile often. No matter how hard it is on the farm, they never complain. Unlike me; I complain to myself all the time. There is a blind horse named Smokey the boys play with on the farm. Smokey carries the food baskets, and when the baskets are full, the boys take the reins, face the horse in the right direction to go to the barn, and off the horse goes. Since the horse is blind, the boys watch to see if he will walk into the trees. Smokey knows how to get back to the barn every time. All the children love Smokey, but he must be 25 years old and moves so slow.

It's starting to get a chill in the air in the evening, which is good because that means the first frost is coming, and we will all get to go home. The children will go back to school, and I can go back to my house in the city. I miss my bed, but in a way, the farm is good; at least the children get to experience life on a farm.

We now have been working the farm for three years. When we get home this year on October 8, 1923, we are moving into a new house we just purchased at 2308 South 10th Street. It's larger than the house on League Street. We have three bedrooms, one bathroom, and a kitchen with a small backyard. But it's still bigger with more room for us.

My family couldn't be happier. Rose, Mary, and I, before we moved in, went to the house and poured salt at the front door. Then swept it all out onto the street to get rid of any evil in the house. Father Foglio met us there, and he blessed the house with Holy Water.

I am feeling weak and tired, and it's harder keeping up with my daily chores. I see myself going down quickly with my disease. Michael brings my bed downstairs because I am too fatigued to climb the steps to my bedroom. So I stay downstairs except for Saturdays when Rose and Mary bring me up to bathe me. I really enjoy my bath.

The girls cook all the meals, clean the house, and do the laundry. In my head, I want desperately to help but physically I don't have the strength.

At times, I don't remember where I am. It's getting frightening to me not to understand my surroundings. I try really hard to remember, but my mind goes blank on me. I remember Raffaele losing his mind. It was horrible watching him go through that, and now, this is what is happening to me—the exact same thing.

Christina comes over to the house every morning to check up on me. She washes me every day. Brushes my hair just as she did when we were little. I remember more about when I was younger than I remember about what is going on now. I thank God all the time for all the love my family has for me.

Christina and I talk more openly now than ever before. We don't get upset at each other if one of us says something the other doesn't like or want to hear. For me, I have to say what I feel because I am afraid if I don't now, I won't have another chance.

We laugh a lot as we did when we were kids, talk about how life didn't turn out the way we dreamed about. I can see in her eyes the sadness that she never was fulfilled with having her own children.

She once told me that life had been unfair to her while it had given me so many babies. When she said that to me, we both broke down and cried for the love she never felt and the loss she had in her heart.

I told Christina that when she dies, if she wants, she can be buried with the Pasquariellos. Because her husband, Antonio, is going to be buried with his first wife and his daughter, Domenica, who died this year at the age of 17. She had TB (Tuberculosis). Antonio wants to save a space in case one of his other daughters doesn't marry. I am not happy about that; after all, Christina has been with him now for six years, helping him with his three daughters. But Christina's not complaining about Antonio, so I will keep my mouth closed for her sake. When I ask her, she tells me, she will think about what she should do but, this is not the time to worry about her.

But how can I not worry? I want Christina to be taken care of after I am gone. She has no one but me for family. I know my Michael will look after her. I will tell him to treat his Aunt Christina like she is his mother. What a good young man my Michael turned out to be. To know that whatever I request, he will take care of it.

CHAPTER 41

MICHAEL'S POV

Millie and Nettie are in my room, yelling as loud as they can to wake me up. I am still drunk from last night. I am 21 years old and like to drink and have a girl every now and then. Probably more now. I find myself laughing because I had so much fun last night. Drinking, gambling, and females. What young guy doesn't want a life like this!

I tell my sisters I am getting up and getting ready for work. Millie tells me it's going to be sunny and warm for late October. It's Saturday, and that's usually a busy day in the Italian Market on 9th Street down here in south Philly. The housewives are all in need of fresh vegetables for their Sunday Supper. I will have to make sure my produce cart is full to the top, all three layers. Before I go anywhere, I need a large cup of black coffee; I ask the girls to please get me a cup and then I am off to work for the day. It will be dark by the time I get home tonight.

It's real busy with the customers this morning. Everyone is out shopping today. I am having a really great day with sales and making a lot of money! Two older ladies approach me and tell me that there is a ruckus going on down the block on 9th Street near my house. Before I can question the ladies, I see and hear my brother George yelling, "Michael, I need your help! It's Mom, she has gone crazy on the street." The ladies tell me to go with George, and they will stay with the pushcart till I return.

I grab George's arm and off we run, down 9th Street. George is explaining that he woke up to our mother throwing dishes in the kitchen against the wall.

"Every time, she threw a dish against the wall she would yell, 'The devil is not dead!' She did this till almost all of the dishes and cups were gone. Our sisters were crying and trying to hide the dishware from Mom and trying to get her to stop. But Mom wouldn't listen to any of us! Then after 10 minutes of her throwing dishes, she sat down and drank a cup of coffee, not saying a word. She just sat and drank coffee; she looked like a zombie to me, just a blank stare. The girls all tried to get her to say something, but she refused to talk. The next thing I know, Rose and Millie were trying to block Mom from the front door. When I came out to the vestibule, there was Mom, pushing her mattress out through the front door, onto the steps, and out into the street with the girls behind her trying to stop her. Mother kept pushing them away, I couldn't believe her strength! She pulled that mattress down the street until she got to the Italian Market. There were so many people shopping on the street. Everyone was looking at her. She was pushing through the crowd like she was the only one on the sidewalk."

We are both running out of breath and stop and put our hands on our knees to catch our breath, then quickly start running again. George continues, "I caught up to Mom and tried to talk with her. But Michael, she wasn't there mentally. Her eyes were big, dark, and cold looking. Our mother's face was twisted in some strange way.

"We were trying to get the mattress from her. She was so strong. We didn't want to get her any more upset than she was. We just didn't know how to handle this situation. Then with the broom she found on the sidewalk from the hardware store, she started to beat the mattress, screaming the entire time, asking the Blessed Mother to take the evil out of the mattress, so she wouldn't get syphilis. Now the entire neighborhood knows she has syphilis. So, I ran to get help from you. Hopefully she will listen to you and calm down."

As we run down the street, you can hear and see a large crowd of people in a circle. Inside the circle is my mom with the mattress and my sisters are standing there with a look of fear on their faces.

Every time she gives the mattress a good hit with the broom, she yells, "KILL THE DEVIL...KILL THE DEVIL!" The mattress is laying on the sidewalk next to her.

I come into the circle and stand behind her, telling George and Rosie to both grab the broom from her. Then I will take her from behind and keep her arms down at her sides. Both of them for a split second look at me with such a frightened look; they are worried that we may hurt our mother. I tell them, "On the count of three, we all go at her at once. One...

"Two...

"Three!"

We have her physically under control, but she is screaming and trying to bang the back of her head into the front of my head. I feel tears streaming down my face. This is happening to my loving and caring mother in the street.

I carry her home in my arms, holding onto her for dear life, I don't want to lose her. My heart can't take another loss. I am sobbing the entire way home, thinking to myself, if Father would have known that his actions would have caused such destruction to our family, would he have done what he did not only to himself and our Mother, but to us nine kids they had together, made from their love?

We know she is losing her sanity, and she won't live much longer, because that's how it was with our father. My mom is on a road to no return called insanity!

CHAPTER 42

CARMELA'S POV

As I lay in my bed unable to move my limbs, my dear sister Christina is here to help take care of me. With her bowl of warm, soapy water and wash cloth in hand, I watch as Christina walks across the room towards me. I can see the worry in her face, but she will put on a brave front for me and my children, always carrying herself as a strong, fearless woman; most would miss what I can see, fear! Oh, how I adore my sister. She never walked away from me in time of need. Even when she had much turmoil going on in her life, she was always taking care of me, helping me as if I matter more to her than her own well-being. With such love and admiration, how could I not love her above anyone else on this Earth for all the love she has given me?

She walks over to me and kisses my forehead, looks me in the eyes and smiles her warm smile at me.

"Geltrude, how are you this morning?" Laughingly Christina says, "Oh look what I just did? I washed your dirty face first instead of brushing your teeth." Then she steps back and says, "I realize I called you your birth name and not by your middle name, but sometimes it just slips out of my mouth. So, excuse me for calling you by the wrong name, Carmela." Then she comes in for a kiss, and I close my eyes. Oh, how I wish I could turn my head, but now I am becoming paralyzed from my disease. So, I am at the mercy of anyone taking care of me. When I open my eyes, Christina is laughing at me saying, "You think, Carmela, because you close your eyes that I won't kiss you." Now Christina is kissing me all over my face saying to me in between kisses, "So, Carmela, what are you going to do to me?" She lifts me up by my shoulders and says, "I will always kiss and hug you forever. As long as we are together, that's all I need." She is hugging me like this will be our last hug.

I can only concentrate and say a few words because my mind is becoming stale. It's unable to function as it once did. I know all of my symptoms because of Raffaele going through this four years before me. I, too, am becoming an almost totally disabled invalid. Knowing my death is soon to follow and there is no medical help that could work for me. There is no cure for syphilis, just medical procedures they do or give you, but nothing truly helps, but I still have not given up hope. I will never give up hope as long as my mind tells me to fight this battle. I will!

"What's on your mind this morning, Carmela? I can feel the tightness in your body. What is bothering you today?" As Christina is washing my arms and back, I am starting to relax, and I am preparing myself for a much-needed heart-to-heart talk with Christina. Although I can hardly speak, there is something I must say to my sister, yet I am still fearful of what she may say. I tell Christina to please prop me up against the pillows, so I can sit and look straight into her eyes. Once our faces are at each other's level, I tell Christina I am ready to tell her about my love and life with Raffaele:

"I had a wonderful life from the moment I was born, having a good family as a child. We didn't have money, but we were raised with love, and we were protected against the evil in the world by our parents.

"When I came to America and married Raffaele, I couldn't have asked the Blessed Mother for a man better than him. We had many babies all made from our love for each other. Yes, he did give me syphilis. That means he cheated on me. He was dishonest in our marriage. But I overcame the horror of his cheating and making us both sick. We have had our battles in life because that's what life is at times, a war. Do I wish we never were sick from this deadly disease? Yes! It's the way God has mapped out our lives on this Earth. We did continue to live and enjoy our lives with our family.

"I know, Christina, if it was up to you, you would have preferred I left him and gone back to Italia, but that's not what I wanted. In my soul, I had the most beautiful life, and I am extremely happy that God has blessed me with so much happiness. That's what I want to take with me to my grave.

"My love and happiness! I will leave everything else behind me."

I take a couple small breaths and concentrate to make sure my words come out correctly, "Not only the love I have for Raffaele and my children, but the love I have for our family and the abundance of love I have for you. If I leave this way, I will rest in peace with much happiness in my soul."

Christina is crying uncontrollably. She is wiping her tears with the sleeve of her blouse. In between her sobbing, she expresses to me how sorry she is, that she didn't have the right to judge Raffaele. Her words are broken between her sobs, I take another breath and say, "Our lives and how we lived them were of our own doing."

Finally, I get Christina to maybe be forgiving towards Raffaele and his improper behavior.

Christina looks at me and is finally smiling a very gentle smile. She says, "Carmela, your eyes look like stars. They have such a bright sparkle to them; I can tell you are so happy and in love with Raffaele still to this day. For that, I am happy that you found happiness with Raffaele. Please forgive me from the bottom of my heart. If you are happy, then I am happy for you."

Christina gets into bed with me and holds me until I am falling asleep, I feel secure in my sisters loving arms. Before sleep consumes me, I whisper to her, "Now that's what Italian sisters are all about."

CHAPTER 43

CHRISTINA'S POV

Geltrude is slipping away slowly, and there is nothing I can do about it. I am her older sister, and never dreamed I would have to bury her someday. I fall asleep each night, thinking about holding her in my arms as she falls asleep, feeling selfish because I beg God to let her wake the next morning, even though I know she is suffering. I love her children as my own and can't stand to see them suffer as they watch her slip closer to death, yet we can't seem to let her go. I often wonder if the strong, innocent people are sentenced to a slow death because those around them are weak and cannot handle life without them. I feel my dear sister is in hell right now suffering because I am not strong enough to say goodbye.

I hear banging on my front door, and this interrupts my thoughts. It sounds like they are breaking into my house. My heart is jumping inside my chest. What do I do? I am home all alone; everyone has gone to work. I know I can go out the back window and jump the two stories down to the dirt. Hopefully, the dirt will be soft enough to break my fall, so I won't break my legs. As I lift my left leg through the window, I see my skin. In a panic, I forgot: I don't have my dress on, only my undergarments. I drop my leg and run to my bedroom and grab my dress off the bed. Oh God, please get them to stop. If they continue to keep banging, the hinges on the door will loosen, and that wooden door will come crashing down to the floor.

I am running down the hallway to the back window and putting my dress over my head. Sliding my arms through the sleeves of the dress, hoping I don't bang my head into the wall. I can hardly breathe. I am sweating so bad. I get to the window, and I see my nephew, Michael, standing in the backyard. He is looking up at me and yelling, "What is taking you so long to open the front door? Come on, Aunt Christina, let me in, my mother needs you now. She can't move her legs since last night. She won't go to the hospital, and we need your help. She will only listen to you. My sister, Rosie is home with her, and we need for you to help us. Please, open the front door, and let me in to talk with you."

I turn and run down the flight of stairs to the front door. I open the front door and in rushes Michael. This poor kid, he has so much to deal with for a young man. But he now is the man of the house with my sister, his mother, and his eight siblings all home. He watches over them like a hawk because if anything happens to any of them, he wouldn't think of himself as a man. His father passed away, and all the responsibilities are now on him. Michael is only 23 years old, and my heart breaks for him.

We are standing in the living room, and you can see in Michael's eyes the panic. I put my arms around his shoulders, and I kiss his right cheek then his left cheek. I tell him how much I love him. I can feel how tense his body is, but he will never say that he is frightened. He moves away from me and looks down at the floor. He whispers, "Aunt Christina, my mother can't move her legs. She is getting the same symptoms as my father. First his legs, and then quickly everything else will begin to shut down. We know each and every symptom. I don't know if I can now watch my beloved mother die a slow, painful death. Can you come home with me and talk to her about going to the hospital? My sisters have taken good care of her through the night, but she is delirious, thinking she is back home in Italia with her parents. My mother keeps calling out for her father, telling him she is sorry. Sorry for what? What did she do back in Italia, Aunt Christina?"

I tell Michael, "Let me grab my shawl, and out we will go to see your mother."

As we hurry down Washington Avenue, I put my hand into Michael's hand. He looks at me with his big, brown, warm eyes and you can see both old and new tears in them. I tell him for now, "Your mother did nothing wrong, but one day I will tell you the complete honest story about your mother and grandfather Di Lullo. I will tell you your mother was his pride and joy. She was his angel on this Earth. So, put your mind at ease Michael, you have enough to worry about. Let's take care of your mother."

When we reach my sister's house, I take a deep breath of air. *For God's sake, what will we all do now?* I am thinking. *Are we going to go through this with my sister, just like with her husband, Raffaele?* I don't know how we will all stand up to her illness and death. Every day is a day closer to her dying, and we all recognize this. Raffaele was 43 years old when he died. He left his wife and his nine children—Rosie, Michael, Mary, Anna, Millie, Nettie, Ralph, George, and Dominick. The oldest, Rosie, was 19 years old, and the youngest, Dominick, was three years old. In an Italian household, the oldest male becomes the head of the family. That is what Michael inherited when his father died. Michael was to keep the family safe. To protect his sisters from being taken advantage of by men and to teach them to keep a house filled with love and food. He had to teach everyone how to work hard and make money to support the family. But Michael still has some years for his brothers to get old enough to help him with money. So, for now, the financial end is entirely on Michael's shoulders. I say the rosary every day for my sister's family and extra prayers for Michael because he needs all the help he can get.

In the streets of South Philly, it is not easy, and my nephew can get lost out there. Some men are like vultures, looking for their prey. And Michael at this time is an easy mark and a catch for these sorts of men. As long as Michael is working hard and he is tired, I know he will not get into trouble. I thank God for my sister raising her children to be hard working, respectful and respected children who go to church. Please God watch over them!

I hear my sister, Geltrude, yelling, but I can't understand what she is saying. Now Michael opens the door to the living room. There is my sister in bed, and my oldest niece is washing her mother's face with Ivory soap and water. They have a bed in the living room for my sister since she became sick. I walk over to my sister and say softly in her ear, "Calm down, baby sister. I am here now to help you." I say this just like when we were kids, and it still does calm her down. She relaxes her body and puts her head on her pillow. Geltrude has always been full of fire. But now it's her illness that controls all of her outbursts. She has syphilis and has lost all physical and mental control. There isn't anything the doctor can do to cure her because there is no cure for this dreadful disease. Her husband died from this disease because he enjoyed the company of a whore. At first, my sister would get a little discharge that wouldn't last long and always believed it was just normal for a female to have something going on in her female organs. Well, at least that's what Raffaele would tell her.

"Besides," he would tell her, "how many females do you know who have been pregnant 12 times? So, your body is responding to everything you did to it." But he never told her how her body would respond to what he was doing with his body. But enough about him. I have a bigger problem here with my darling sister.

I tell Michael and Rosie to get her clean underwear and a night-gown. We will wash her body and hair today. Oh, what beautiful hair Geltrude has. Not one gray hair! It's still chestnut brown with red running through, and it is so long, hanging down to her mid-back with beautiful waves. She has hair just like our mother did. I really could use the insight of my wise mother right now. But she died several years ago in Italia, and one year later, my father died. Now it's only me and Geltrude.

Rosie tells me she's going upstairs to get clean items for her mother. And Michael goes into the kitchen to get a large bowl to fill it with hot water. I call upstairs to Rosie to get a new bar of Ivory soap. We will clean her up and put clean clothes on her, so she will feel better.

As Rosie is walking down the stairs with her arms full, she says to me, "Aunt Christina, I also have a clean set of sheets because my mother soiled the sheets, but it didn't go through the mattress because Michael lines the top of the mattress with rubber. So, we should change everything for my mother, and maybe Aunt Christina, you could get her to eat something? My mother hasn't eaten anything in two days or drank any water either."

As Rosie comes over to me, I can see she is overwhelmed with taking care of her mother now. It wasn't long ago that she helped take care of her father. I feel so bad for my sister's family, but this is what God put in front of us to do.

"So be it!"

CHAPTER 44

MICHAEL'S POV

As I am walking down 9th Street pushing my produce cart, I am thinking about what I would like to say to my Aunt Christina. How do I tell her my thoughts about being the oldest son in the family? That if I could get on a ship and sail across the ocean, I would. If I could run, I would. I can't tell Aunt Christina how I feel about the weight put on me since my father became ill and not able to work and care for the family. Most of the everyday pressures and demands of the family are on me.

When my father first became ill, I was only 12 years old. Within two years, I was out on the streets doing whatever I could to make money. By the time I was 16, my father was unable to work; he could only lay in bed. This disease he had took him over with a slow, painful death.

When I get to Aunt Christina's house, I'll take a deep breath to keep calm; I don't want her to see me upset, I don't want her to think I can't handle this. I just need someone else who is strong and can help me be strong for by brothers and sisters. I hope she can help me with preparing for my mother's death. Only she can understand the agony I'm in. I stop the cart, look up at her window, take a deep breath, and walk up her steps.

CHRISTINA'S POV

Someone is knocking at my front door, and within seconds, I hear, "Aunt Christina, open the door for me. It's your nephew, Michael. I need to talk with you."

I turn the knob quickly, and there stands Michael, looking much older than 23 years. I can see he has tears in his eyes, and he is extremely upset. I know he has been going through a lot with the loss of his father four years ago and now his mother having to go in Philadelphia General Hospital, the same place his father died due to his disease. This will be Geltrude's last stop before she dies from the same disease. It's hard on the children to witness such a horrible death for their parents, yet there isn't anything the doctors can do. The doctors could give them mercury to help with this disease. But the truth is, you probably would die from mercury poisoning. They haven't found anything that can save their sanity or their lives. This disease has been killing people for years.

I ask Michael to follow me into the kitchen, so we can sit and have a cup of coffee. Even before we reach the table, he is crying uncontrollably. I put my arms around him and tell him to sit, and we will talk. I don't know how long before my tears start to run down my cheeks because this poor kid has been carrying the brunt of his father's sins. Michael is paying the price for his father being unfaithful to his mother. His father getting infected and passing it onto Michael's mother. My sister!

I see Michael taking deep breaths trying to control himself. With one more deep breath, he says, "Well, Aunt Christina, we had the ambulance come get my mother this morning. They took her over to Philadelphia General Hospital. My sister, Rosie went with her to fill out all the paperwork. We will never have her home with us again. She will die in there, like my father did. This is how and where their lives have ended, in sheer misery. My father died in so much pain, and this will happen to my mother."

I see Michael look up to the ceiling, and the pain on his face is unbearable to see. I move closer and put my hand on the side of his face, so he will look at me. It is hard for me not to burst out in tears, but I feel like he needs my strength, and I owe him that much. He seems to relax slightly as he looked into my eyes and continues,

"Since now I am the man of my family, I feel helpless. I can't protect my mother from this disease."

I try to tell him that I was proud of the way he is handling this, but before I can talk, he reaches up and holds my hand, moves it to his heart, and says, "I would prefer that it would be me dying in that bed. I should feel the agony, not my mother who I love and worship. She is an incredible person and a loving mother. Not only to me, but to all of my siblings. There will be a hole in my heart forever. Not one of us will ever forget her and her tender ways to us."

I have to walk away from Michael because I can feel a storm brewing inside of me. My anger and disgust towards his father are like a volcano ready to erupt. Look at what he has done to his wife and children. When he died, Domenic (the youngest) was only three years old and Rosie (the oldest) was 19 years old. Where does this family go from here? My heart aches for each and every one of them, as it does for Geltrude, my beloved sister.

I pour Michael a cup of strong, black coffee. He looks up at me and smiles that warm smile he has for me. He says, "You know, Aunt Christina, my mother always spoke of you to us with an enormous amount of love. You are and have always been her idol."

We both are laughing at her foolishness.

"Her gentle, naïve soul is what I will miss most about your mother," I say. "I don't know how I will carry on knowing she is not here with me. Even when I was in Italia and she was here in America, I spoke to her every day in my thoughts. I will miss her smile and her warm, gentle touches." Thinking of her calms my anger, and I sip my coffee and continue, "She never realized what she meant to me. I am fortunate and grateful that God gave her to me as a sister. However, we must carry on, Michael; not for ourselves, but for the love we both have for your mother. We will never forget what she gave us. Her loyalty and love. What else could we have wanted from her?"

Michael smiles and says, "Aunt Christina, you forgot one more thing we could have wanted: for her to be here just a little longer in our lives."

"Michael, you are right, if she had just a little more time on this Earth."

We both are just sitting here at the table not moving, just staring at each other, knowing we will never feel love like the love we have for her and she for us. Finally, after a long, silent moment, we come back from our intimate thoughts of Geltrude.

I get up from my chair and walk over to Michael, put my arms around him and squeeze tightly on his shoulders. I kiss his cheek and whisper in his ear and say, "Michael, go to work and keep your mind occupied on your customers. Talk and laugh with them today. Because when you walk back in your house tonight, it will all come boiling up inside of you that your mother isn't there. She mentally hasn't been here for quite some time. Now go to work!

"As for me, Michael, I will at times break down and cry for the loss of my sister. I will cook and do my house chores. Carry on with life every day. But I will never forget her, and neither will you. For whatever reason, if you need me, I am here for you. So, tomorrow, we will go to the hospital and visit with your mother. She won't even know we are there, but you and I will still go and talk to her as if she can understand us. We will do this for her till the end. Now, leave me here with my own feelings and thoughts."

Michael smiles very sympathetically to me; he understands that I am trying to be strong for him so he can be strong for his brothers and sisters. We hug and kiss each other goodbye. I walk Michael to the front door. He opens the door, walks down one step, turns to me, wanting to say something, but changes his mind. He shakes his head, and down the steps he goes walking towards Snyder Avenue. I watch as he is pushing his produce cart to sell his vegetables like he does every day.

I close the door behind him and fall to the vestibule floor. I can finally allow myself to feel the emptiness in my soul. I can only break down like this when I am by myself and not in front of anyone. I must stay strong for Geltrude's children. Now they will be without a father and mother. I have no children of my own and have always felt that they were the closest thing to my children, sharing them with my sister. I will stand in her shoes and protect them, just as Geltrude would have me do.

CHAPTER 45

MICHAEL'S POV

Today is Monday, February 23, 1925. My dear mother passed away today at the age of 43 years. No matter what age she would have been, I would say that she was too young to die. The doctor confirmed through a blood test that she died from "general paralysis" due to the disease syphilis.

She lived in the hospital since Friday, October 31, 1924, till today. She no longer knew who she was. Her mind was gone. Physically, she was incapable of walking. Her muscles could no longer function. She was no longer the mother I knew. Watching my mother become insane was heartbreaking for all the family. She died in the psych ward. I, at times, still get angry at my father for infecting my mother, though I am sure, I am not the only one; however, not one of us will speak badly of my father. We still honor and respect him because our mother would never have allowed us to speak of him disrespectfully. She never once accused him of cheating or giving her syphilis. Therefore, neither did any of us, except among ourselves.

Now, on the other hand, my Aunt Christina openly talked with my mother about my father cheating and giving her that deadly disease. Not once, but on many occasions, whether my father was there or not, Aunt Christina always let her feelings be known to him. This would always upset my mother because she loved him dearly. When my father walked into a room, my mother lit up like a light bulb, and all her worries disappeared in that instant. Nothing could affect her love for him. He was her everything. Even with all of their children, he was the world to her.

We will bury her with my father, her casket will be on top of his, so he can hold her up for eternity. This is what she told me when my father passed away: "Michael, make sure when I die, that you put my heavy casket on top of your father's, that way he can feel the weight of our lives forever." She would always wink and then laugh, but we would never say this in front of anyone else, not even her sister, Christina! I think she felt Aunt Christina would have joined in with much happiness at the thought of my father holding up her casket above his for infinity. My mother would never have given that joy to her sister. Why? I don't know. It could have been sisterly rivalry. Aunt Christina believes she had control over my mother, which happened to be true 99 percent of the time. But when it came to the love she had for my father, my mother would never allow anyone, even Aunt Christina, to get in between them. My father was the one person my mother wanted all to herself.

We held my mother's viewing at Baldi's Funeral Home on 8th Street. This is same funeral home we used for my father and his parents. She, too, will be buried at Holy Cross Cemetery in the Pasquariello burial plot. There are nine of my family members buried there. Aunt Christina asked me if the 10th place could be for her, so she could be buried with my mother, her sister. I told her we would not bury her anywhere but next to her sister. That way they could lay next to each other throughout eternity. She told me how happy she was for me allowing her to lie next to her sister for all eternity. Her eyes filled with tears, and she stuttered while speaking. Finally, her words came out clearly.

"Michael, you are like a son to me. I know I didn't give birth to you, but you have always treated me with high regard. I am and always will admire your tender and loving heart towards me. I love you!" She kisses my forehead and walks away. Even at one of the darkest times in my life, she still has a tendency to make me chuckle at her seriousness. My chuckle is inward, so I don't embarrass her or hurt her feelings. Aunt Christina has such odd ways of behaving. Just like now, at a tender moment, she is gone in a flash. But I understand her more than she knows. If she would have stayed holding onto me, she was going to break down.

Oh, no, not Aunt Christina; she won't allow herself to break down in front of anyone. She portrays herself as a tough woman. God forbid anyone find out she is as soft as anyone could be! My aunt, the marshmallow. She has the softest and kindest heart. just like my mother.

Everyone is walking into Our Lady of Good Counsel Church and taking their seats. My sisters and brothers along with Aunt Christina are sitting in the first two pews from the altar. Here come all of my uncles, aunts, and cousins taking seats behind my siblings. I, on the other hand, am welcoming everyone. Shaking hands, kissing cheeks, and expressing my gratitude for their attending my mother's funeral mass. They are offering many prayers to God and the Blessed Mother to protect her soul and for her to rest in peace. That's what we Italian Catholics do at funerals.

Now, the friends and neighbors, along with my father's business associates, are filling the pews. The Church is almost at its full capacity. I hear Father Foglia say, "Would everyone please stand." I go up front to join my family in a moment of silence.

Father is expressing the love my mother had for God and the church, but I find myself daydreaming about her true love, the Blessed Mother. Then I hear the church bell tolling, and the Mass is over. I have never felt such emptiness before now, not even when my father passed away. Maybe because now I no longer have either one of my parents here. I can hear the brass band outside the church playing the death march, as the pallbearers, including Timothy Calhoun, carry her casket to the waiting hearse. It's a beautiful white hearse to carry her to Holy Cross Cemetery from South Philly to Yeadon, Pennsylvania. This will take the rest of the day to get there and back. I hear my sisters all crying and whispering to one another. They all want to get in the hearse with my mother, but we all get into a second car.

When we reach the cemetery and turn to go to the family plot, I then realize that I haven't been back here since we buried my father four years ago. I am flooded with emotions all at once. I start to shake and think that I haven't paid my father or grandparents the respect they deserve from me. I know my siblings go to visit with them and bring flowers. They even bring their lunch. They make a day of it. I, on the other hand, don't go with them. I am always so busy with trying to make enough money. There are nine of us, my three younger brothers are only 11, nine, and seven years old. I am always worried that I will fail them. I won't tell anyone of my fears. Never! There are things that I know I should do. Like be here when my family comes to the grave, but I can't do it all, so some things get pushed aside. I know my parents who watch over us understand the toll all of this has taken on me. I don't feel sorry for myself in any way. Since I am the oldest male in my family, I do have a responsibility that comes along with being from an Italian family. The males always take great pride in taking care of the females in the family.

Everyone is gathered around the open grave where her casket will sit on top of my father's casket. I look down through the opening, and I can see his casket with a silver cross on the top. My mother chose my father's casket, cross, and his suit. She took charge of it all. One of her friends sang at his viewing. She sang about five prayer songs for him. Her voice was magical, and listening to her sing put me at ease. But she died recently, so we couldn't have her here for my mother's funeral. I will take care of my family. My siblings will always look to me and respect me as the head of the family.

Father Foglia is asking us to say our goodbyes and to always keep Geltrude in our prayers. Sofia, my mother's oldest and best friend, drops to her knees and says, "Carmela, my sister, I will miss you forever."

Then Aunt Christina walks over with my sisters to place flowers on the casket. They are all crying and showing their grief. Father Foglia walks over to me and asks me to get them to move along.

"We must get back to the city. There will be many people at your house, waiting for you to return."

Aunt Christina, the family, and I all say our last prayer to the Blessed Mother. My stomach is turning as I watch my siblings all kiss her casket. My mother told the girls a few years ago to put her in a cherry wood casket with a gold cross on the top where her head would be. My sisters went to Baldi's Funeral home and dressed her in her favorite olive-green dress. The dress was the fashion of the day. My mother had a natural talent for fashion inside of her, and she always looked beautiful. I will miss her and her creativity.

Now we must watch as the grave diggers put her casket in the ground and put dirt on top of it. I am pacing back and forth because now is the time I must say my goodbye. Uncle Giovanni and Uncle Orazio walk over to me. One stands on the left and the other on the right side of me. I feel myself become too weak to stand on my own. They both are holding me up by my arms. I regain my composure and thank them for standing by me. Both of my father's brothers are good, decent men. My mother had a closeness with Uncle Orazio. She always felt that he was her younger brother, someone who she had to take care of and watch over since he was so young when he lost his parents.

We all get back into the car, and my sister Rosie is telling us how proud our mother would be at such a heartfelt day in her honor. Mary is laughing and asking if any of us saw Mr. Vito peeing behind one of the large trees. We all laugh because Mr. Vito is drunk all the time. Mary is telling us that he is always wetting his pants. So, now is he going behind a tree to pee?

Annie chimes in on our conversation but is laughing so hard her words can't come out of her mouth. When you have all five of my sisters together, you have to watch because anything can and will happen with them. They get such amusement out of life and the people who they surround themselves with. When we are all home together, even we four brothers find ourselves laughing at something silly they are doing or saying. But being around our sisters, it's catchy that when one starts to laugh, all nine of us are laughing. To me, that's one of the finest things that could happen in a large family. Someone is always entertaining someone else. It feels good to laugh with them now; I feel a heavy veil lift from my shoulders at the sight of everyone's smile. Perhaps our mother is sitting next to us laughing as well.

We finally reach our house. When we walk inside, there are people everywhere. There is food all over the kitchen and on the dining room table. Enough homemade food to feed everyone in the neighborhood. All the family and neighbors have brought food to my house to show love and respect for my mother. Bottles of home-made wine and grappa are on display. All of this delicious food and drink is to show us "the family," how they feel about my family, but especially my parents.

I hear my sisters laughing and carrying on because Mrs. Nina Lombardi, is here. She's a neighbor from League Street, and she and my mother were close friends. She is always yelling at the girls not to show any part of their legs. Their skirts and dresses should be down to their ankles. They should always cross their legs, so no man can see up their skirt. We all think she is a little crazy. She is never without her pocketbook; it hangs off her arm, and she never puts it down. That pocketbook is part of her arm. My sisters are trying to get her to open it to see what she has inside. It's small with black beads and a linen handle. Mrs. Lombardi is telling my sisters that it's none of their business what is inside her bag. She tells them to shut their mouths and walks away to sit down next to Aunt Christina. Aunt Christina puts her arms around Mrs. Lombardi and settles her down. If we didn't have some kind of drama like this going on now, I would totally feel out of place.

I feel like someone else is inside of my body, hearing and watching everyone. But I am still mentally back at the cemetery, watching my mother's casket get lowered into the ground. I will never forget seeing them lower her casket. The sorrow I feel, knowing I will never see my mother's beautiful face again, is almost unbearable. I have to put my emotions aside for now and get through this day. My mother would have been astonished at how many people showed their respect towards her because my mother was shy and humble. She always went to everyone's funeral in our neighborhood and always made a large plate of food for their family. She was always there to help anyone in need. Seeing all of this kindness returned to her makes me proud to be her son.

CHAPTER 46

It's 1925 and summertime here in South Philadelphia. I just woke up and got out of bed quickly, so I could wash and dress. I have to get out on the street to sell my produce before it gets too hot to push my cart in the late afternoon sun. I make my way down the stairs and walk into the kitchen. Aunt Christina is there making breakfast for the family. I don't know why she isn't making breakfast for her family. Instead, she's here taking care of me and my eight siblings. She turns to look at me, and the sun is on her face. Her hair is a lot grayer than it used to be, and she has more wrinkles on her face. It's only been four months since we lost my mother. Aunt Christina has gotten quiet, only speaking to me when no one else is around. She, too, has had a hard life raising her stepdaughters. That's why her husband married her shortly after his first wife died. He wanted Aunt Christina to step in and take care of everyone but herself. She takes care of her husband and the girls, and now us as well. She is so kindhearted.

Aunt Christina gestures for me to sit down. She puts a plate of eggs and ham in front of me. My sisters are all yelling their goodbyes into the kitchen as they leave because they start early at the clothing factory. Aunt Christina and I are laughing at them because they are so loud. I do understand, it's five of them, but they each have a big mouth. You can always hear them no matter where they are. I guess that's because they are girls.

The three boys are still in bed and will help me sell produce later in the day. Aunt Christina sits next to me and tells me that my five sisters are having a problem when walking to the trolley car in the morning.

"There is a man in the alley at the end of our block on 10th street. When your sisters walk by the alleyway, he jumps out and opens his coat. He has his pants down to his knees, and they can see his private parts. Then he starts to play with himself in front of them. Your sisters are afraid to tell you because they know about your temper. They fear you will kill this man. I am telling you this because I want you to hurt this man, but not kill him. Hurt him badly, so he doesn't continue to do this to your sisters or something much worse."

I look at Aunt Christina, and she is serious about what I should do. I tell her I will take care of this tomorrow morning, and every morning after until I get this man to stop.

"Don't worry, Aunt Christina. When I get finished with him, he won't want to show himself to anyone."

The next morning, I tell my sisters that I am walking with them to the trolley stop.

"But first, I need you girls to help me get dressed like a woman." They all look at me like I lost my mind, it's the quietest they have ever been. I continue, "Aunt Christina told me about the alley man."

At first, my sisters are hesitant to help me; now Mary and Nettie are complaining that I will hurt this man and then I will end up in prison. I hold my hands up, so they will listen to me.

"Assuming he is right-handed, I am going to break his right arm, so his hand won't be able to reach his penis. That way he can't play with himself any longer in front of anyone." I turned to question Rose because she is the oldest. "Rose how long has this been going on?"

Before she has a chance to respond, Millie jumps up and yells, "Mike, he's been in that alley many times, and he is so disgusting to look at. I could throw up every time he is there."

My sisters are all laughing at his lack of physical characteristics, meaning the size of his penis.

"I don't want to look at that ever again." Annie says, "Mike, beat him up, and I will help you. You know we can take care of this."

Rose hands me a red dress and says, "Put this dress on, but you will have to wear your own shoes, your feet are too big to fit into any of our shoes."

Nettie comes over with red lipstick and puts it on my lips. They wrap my head in a silk scarf to cover my short hair. The girls are laughing and telling me that I am the ugliest girl they have ever seen. I think they are having too much fun at my expense!

Rose says, "Maybe when this man sees you, Mike, he will run away."

The girls are now laughing so hard they have tears in their eyes. I sigh, knowing I will never live this down and say, "Let's go find this guy!"

When we go outside, I tell the girls to surround me and keep me in the middle so I can somehow blend in with them.

"Just carry on as usual and talk loudly so he can hear you coming down the street."

As we are reaching the alley, I can see the man walking out and getting closer to us. I push through the girls, and they are yelling at the top of their lungs, "That's him Mike. That's the man who shows us his penis."

I don't give the guy a chance to open his coat and enjoy himself. I punch him on the side of his head. He goes down with the first blow. The girls are screaming at me to kick him in his head... And they were worried about my temperament!

I think I broke my hand when I punched him in the head. It really hurts, and this guy isn't moving. I hope I didn't kill him by accident. Before I can think of what I should do next, some of the neighbors are coming out. They can hear the commotion outside, and now the police are on their way. When the cops asked my name, I told them my name is Michael Pasquariello. These two cops are laughing at me and asked if my name is Cathy. What are they talking about? And then a cop told me how pretty I looked in red. The dress! I forgot I was wearing a dress!

Before the humiliation kicks in, the cops put handcuffs on me and tell me I am under arrest. My sisters are all talking at once to the cops; I almost feel sorry for the poor cops They can't get a word in because my sisters won't shut up.

The cops call for an ambulance. The guy does wake up, but he is crying that his head couldn't move. So, off to the hospital they take him. The cops release me from the handcuffs after my sisters explain what had been going on in our neighborhood and how I was there to protect them. The cops tell me they know him because he was arrested last month down on Lombard Street for the same thing.

One of the cops said, "The only reason he went to the hospital was most likely to avoid getting locked up for indecent exposure again."

Another cop added, "If he keeps it up, he will end up dead; especially if he runs into someone as crazy as he is."

When I tell Aunt Christina about the incident, she smiles from ear to ear, gives me a tight hug, and tells me she is proud of me for taking care of my family.

"But Mike, how did he go down on the first punch?" Aunt Christina asks.

I laughed and say, "Well, Aunt Christina, I had my brass knuckles on my right hand. And I put them in Millie's pocketbook before the cops got there." Aunt Christina just laughs and gives me a wink.

CHAPTER 47

"That son of a bitch!"

I don't realize I've spoken out loud until I hear one of my sisters ask, "Why is Michael so mad?"

I'm too furious to care though. My mind keeps racing. I can't believe some idiot thinks I am just a kid and that he can push me around, especially now that both my parents are dead. Good luck with that! I've been taking care of my family for years now and won't let anyone disgrace my parents' name. Anyone who knows me, knows I don't allow anyone to walk on me or my family. I know there is always someone who thinks they are wiser, and at times that is true; but not under any circumstances will you get to take advantage of one of my five sisters. That could only happen over my dead body. Treat me and my eight siblings with respect, and I will show you the same respect.

I sit down, sigh, and begin to rub my temples. Trying to handle the love life of one of my sisters is exhausting. I really don't understand the way my sisters think. My youngest sister, Antoinette, who is 15 is involved with one of the neighborhood boys who is only 14. She tells me she is in love with Jim, and she would like to move into his family's home. He lives just a few blocks away on Passyunk Avenue. He comes from a good Italian family. They are hardworking people, and Jim has always been respectful to Nettie and our family. To me, that's the most important factor, how he treats her and does he really care about her. But if she wants to be with him all the time, then he should marry her and treat her as his wife.

When I tell her how I feel, and that matrimony is the only way she will ever live with him, Nettie gets all her four sisters to tell me how unreasonable I am being. They tell me that females can now vote, so therefore females can live with their boyfriend and his family. That the times are changing, and females are now equal to men. My sister Rose tells me that Jim and his father are coming to our house to talk to me. They would like to have a talk about Nettie living with them. When I question Rose about her feelings regarding Nettie not being married and living with Jim's family, she tells me that no matter what we say and do Nettie has told her that she is going to move out and live with Jim and that we can't stop her and him from being together. His parents think it is fine.

Rose looks at me quite seriously and says, "Michael, we can't hold her hostage here with us. She's old enough to do what she wants. If we tell her she can go, then we won't lose her forever. If we tell her there is no way we will allow her to go, I am afraid she will still go and never look back at us. Our mother would never forgive us if she was still alive. Nettie was her baby girl. When our mother died, Nettie was only 14 years old. She is lost without our mother. I think Nettie needs love and found that love with Jim. We should let her go and pray that this all turns out for the best for everyone involved. He is a good kid and works six days a week."

Needless to say, I don't need to have a sit down with Jim's dad. I will do whatever is necessary to change Nettie's mind. Rose asked me to make her a promise because she believes that I am harsh and blunt. She says, "I don't want you to offend them in anyway, Michael. Let's keep everything peaceful, and hopefully, it will be good for all of us."

I say, "I will try my best not to be too honest with my feelings. Don't ask me again to keep my thoughts inside my head. Who allows their kid sister to go live with her boyfriend and his family? After I have a talk with our other sisters, I will follow your suggestion. I am going to tell her she can go, but she can't come back here if it doesn't work out. I will tell her, 'You've made your bed, now lie in it.'"

When I meet with Jim and his dad, it doesn't go well. I don't think I should let her go but I do. I really don't have anything bad to say about Jim or his family, but I am mad. If I had sat and talked with them for a lengthy amount of time, all hell would have broken loose. We three shake hands, and I walk out of the house before I explode.

My kid sister calls to me as I am walking down the street, trying to calm down. She runs outside and hugs me. She is crying. She tells me her crying is out of happiness with my understanding of her situation. Nettie moves out of our family house the next day.

But it isn't to last long. After six months of Nettie living with Jim's family, his dad comes to see me on the street. He came to me on 9th street at my produce cart. When I see him walking down the street, I know that this isn't going to be good. He shakes my hand and says that we need to talk about something important. I ask him," Are we going to do this here, or would you like to meet later away from my business?"

He replies, "Oh this won't take much of your time."

Before I can agree to this meeting, he tells me that his son, Jim, no longer wants my sister, Nettie, to live with them and she needs to move back to her family home. I can't stop laughing at this guy. When I get my composure together—meaning, before I allowed my temper to control me and punch him in his mouth—I think to myself, *I allowed this to happen. I should have said no to her from the very beginning. I should have told Nettie you can't do whatever you two have decided to do. Now, he wants to throw her away after a short period of time.*

I am trying my best not to grab him by the throat and squeeze his neck until his eyes pop out of his head. I repeat to him what he just said to me, "Your son wants to send my little sister back home? What is the reason for Jim wanting to do this?"

He smiles and says, "Well, my son thinks he is too young to settle down. Maybe later when he is older, they will get married but not now. Come on, Mike, they are just kids. They don't know what they really want."

I feel my blood boiling at what he just said to me. Without blinking an eye, I tell him, "You know what? I feel the same as you. They are too young, but you knew that, and so did Jim. You came to my house to convince me that you and your son would take very good care of Nettie. You would treat her like she was your daughter and watch over her and make sure that nothing or no one would harm her. Now, all has changed, but I really do understand what is going on here.

"So, for the safety of my sister I will have her come home. When you send her home, you also will send one of your daughters with her. I really don't care which one of your daughters it is. Just send one!"

He looks at me perplexed.

"Why would I send one of my daughters to you?"

I am now laughing as my eyes are burning holes into his forehead. I can feel my blood rushing to my head. I am telling myself not to jump over my produce cart to choke the last breath out of him. I pull myself together and regain my composure as I walk around the cart to him.

He takes a few steps backward, puts his hands up, and says, "Mike I am not here to fight you. The kids made a mistake."

I interrupted him and told him one more time, "Send one of your daughters to me. I will keep her for six months, and when I am finished, I will get my sister to walk her back home to you. Then, I will feel as if I have evened the score for allowing my sister to be with your son."

Well, Nettie never came back home, and she finally got Jim to marry her. The old man never sent one of his daughters to me. I thank God that he didn't because I really didn't want to have to take care of one them for six months. So, it all ended the way it was supposed to. Without being brutal, I defended the honor of my kid sister.

CHAPTER 48

It's 1927, and I feel as if life has turned against me since both of my parents died. Everything has me feeling as if the weight of my responsibilities is turning me into someone I no longer understand or recognize. The well-being of my eight siblings means everything to me. I feel exhausted every day. There are no longer any physical or mental resources left inside of me. I am overwhelmed with being the man of the family.

Something really trivial happened to me today. It involved my youngest brother, Nick, who is only 10 years old. Nick is a really good kid. He works with me every day after school and all day on Saturday. Every one of us either goes to school or works. The ones that go to school have chores after school. They either meet me on 9th Street, go home and clean the house, or take care of the garden in the backyard. We all are extremely busy with concentrating on our routine tasks. There is always a lot to get finished each and every day before it's time for bed. We all work extremely hard to achieve our goals. I am very proud of my family.

Today, I am a lost soul, feeling as if I have no value or purpose other than worrying about my brothers and sisters. Maybe I should stop drinking every night. I go to the bar on 10th Street every night except Sunday. I don't drink on Sunday at the bar because of the "Blue Laws." These laws are meant to preserve Sunday as the Lord's Day, so the bars are all closed. Though this doesn't stop me from drinking; I just go to one of my friends' house, and we all get drunk there. I like to get drunk because then I forget how I truly feel. How much I blame my siblings for all of this. In reality, I know this is not true; but when I am drunk, it no longer matters to me. That is, until I wake up the next morning and nothing has changed. It just means that I made it through another day, hopefully without exploding on anyone.

Unfortunately, I did explode on my kid brother today. After school, Nick came over to my produce cart and told me to put tomatoes, peppers, eggplants, onions, garlic, and lots of fruit in his wagon. He pulls the wagon down the side streets and sells door to door. As soon as the housewives hear him yelling, "Come get your fresh vegetables and fruits," they all come outside and buy his goods. The ladies all love Nick because he is so gentle to talk with and he is a handsome kid. The ladies all call him "The Good-Looking Boy." Nick enjoys all the attention they give him. When he sells everything in the wagon, he brings the wagon and money back to me.

But this day is different. When he returns, he takes the money from his pockets. As usual, it is all silver coins and pennies that he puts on top of my cart. We never count the goods against the money because I don't feel that I would ever not trust my kid brothers, Nick, George or Ralph. We all work together in my business to help the family. As Nick is putting the coins on my cart, I see a nickel fall onto the pavement. Nick bends down to pick it off the sidewalk and proceeds to put the coin in his pocket. It surprised me that he did that, so I shout at him and tell him in a very stern and loud voice to give me the nickel. Nick pulls the coin from his pocket. He slams the coin on the wooden cart and says to me, "Mike, that is my nickel. I have been saving it for a long time. I did not take it from your money. It's been in my pocket all month. It belongs to me. I found it in the street, and I kept it."

This infuriated me! I have given every last penny to my family, never keeping anything to myself, yet this 10-year-old thinks he has a right to keep it?

I lost control and smacked his face. He fell backwards and let out a loud shriek.

All of a sudden, I hear someone yelling to me, "Michael keep your hands off of Dominic! You can't hit him he is only a kid!" Well, it's Aunt Christina grabbing my arms and screaming at me. "You will never hit Dominic again!"

That was a reality check for me instantly. Here I am on 9th Street with many people walking by or standing at my cart and shopping. Two of the ladies at my cart are cursing at me. One lady tells me that she will hit me in my face, just like I did to Nick. She says that he is just a baby. I think I am most angry at that statement; I never had a chance to be a baby or kid brother.

Aunt Christina tells me to come with her. As we start walking, she puts her arm around my waist. She stops abruptly and stares at me with more anger in her eyes than I have ever seen. Not my loving and caring Aunt Christina! She is now expressing her hostility to me.

"Michael, I know you are doing all that you can. But you can never display such threatening behavior towards anyone in the family like that ever again. Especially to one of your brothers!" She puts her arms around my shoulders and puts her head into my chest. She is standing on her toes and whispers in my ear, "Please Michael, pull yourself together and act as your father would have in this situation. Send Dominic home and talk with him later. I don't even know what this is about, and it doesn't matter. What could a kid have done to deserve your hitting him so hard in his face?"

We walk back to the cart. I grab a paper bag and put all the coins inside the bag. I hand it to Nick and tell him to take it home and to put it in our hiding place. We put the bags of coins in our basement on top of the pipes. If anyone robs the house, hopefully, they won't find the money. As Nick takes the bag from me, I can see the hurt in his eyes when he looks at me, and I never want to see any of my siblings ever again look at me with such fear in their eyes.

When I get home for dinner with the family, Nick sits next to me. He puts the nickel on the table next to my plate. He smiles at me and tells me, "I really don't need the nickel. So just go ahead and keep it."

I pick up the nickel and place it into his hand. I say, "Nick, under no circumstances would I ever believe you stole money from me. I know I can trust you, just as I trust our brothers, Ralph and George. I don't know what happened to me today. I just lost control of myself. If it weren't for Aunt Christina stopping me today, I don't know what my actions would have caused you in bodily harm. As for my actions today, I promise it won't happen again. You are my little brother, and I will always love and watch over you. Please excuse my insulting behavior towards you."

Nick pulls his chair away from the table and stands up and looks around the table at each and every one of us. When he came to me, we locked eyes. His eyes are filled with tears. With a small grin he starts speaking softly, "Michael..." He clears his throat and starts all over again. We still have our eyes staring at each other. "I respect and love you as my father figure. I was only three years old when our father died. I know this has to be much more on you to handle than anyone of us. I am now 10 years old, and I will do whatever you and Rose think I should do to help the family; I don't need or want this nickel. To be honest, Mike it just felt good to have a nickel in my pocket to play with. I want you to add this nickel into the bag from today's sales from my wagon. This will make me feel good, and it could make you feel better about me."

Now, I am up standing next to Nick at the table. Everyone else is sitting and staring at us. No one is saying a word. You could have heard a pin drop. I put my arms around Nick, and I am sobbing silently. I am holding onto him as if he was my child. I feel the fog lifting from my brain for the first time since my father became too ill to work. I drink every night to try and escape my reality, But I finally realize, just as I didn't choose to lose my parents at a young age, my siblings didn't choose it either. We are in this together, and I am lucky to have them, it's far better than being

CHAPTER 49

Aunt Christina stopped to pick up some produce today. She doesn't look healthy. She has lost weight, and her coloring is ash white. Usually her skin is flawless, and her color is medium brown. She is beautiful like my mother. They both had a lot of hair; it was thick enough for two heads, and the color is brown with a shade of red when the sun is shining on it. However, she has lost about half of her hair, and today, Aunt Christina looks haggard and weak.

When I asked if she is sick, she smiles a very gentle smile and says, "No and stop worrying about me."

I put my hand on her shoulder and realize I can feel her bones.

"I would feel terrible if anything was to happen to you."

She pats my cheek and gives me one of her warm smiles. There is a hint of a tear in her eye, but she quickly straightens her shoulders and tells me she needs Nick to carry her bags of food home. I yell over to Nick, "Help Aunt Christina and return back here as soon as you're done."

There is this group of women that come every day on their lunch break to buy vegetables. But in the crowd is one girl who stands in the back of the line. She is beautiful and speaks only in Italian. When she gets to the front of the line, she only wants me to help her. My brother, George, laughs all the time at her. Today, he asks her, "What is your name?"

She stands there for a few seconds, unable to speak. When one of her friends says, "Her name is Romania, and she was born in Roma," I quickly walk over to her and extend my hand; she hesitates to touch me. I tell her, "I won't bite you. I promise." Now, I have her laughing and she shakes my hand. When she puts her hand into mine, I feel a surge of sweet energy like I have never felt before. I've been wanting to talk to her since she's been coming to my cart.

One of her friends tells her, "Romania, we have to get back to work. You know our supervisor will be mad at us if we are late."

I put her peaches in a bag and tell her, "These peaches are on me. Enjoy them, and maybe when you have more time, we can talk."

Before she can respond, one of the girls pushes her and says, "We have to go now!" And off all of them run down 9th Street.

She comes to see me every day for a week. And every day, I give her peaches until she says to me, "My father is tired of peaches, and he wants to know if you have cherries or grapes." That's when I asked her to go to the movies with me. She tells me she will have to ask her father. The next day she comes by and says, "My father said no!" But a small smile plays across her face, and she continues, "But I say yes, so we will have to sneak to go to the theater."

It's a warm evening here in Philadelphia. Typical August evenings have lots of humidity in the air. Romania tells me she would like to go to the Boyd's Theater, it's located at 1908 Chestnut Street, Center City Philly. She says, "There is a special movie playing there, and it's called *Frankenstein*. This movie is a horror film and quite scary from what my friends at work have told me." There is a lot of excitement in her voice.

After we have dinner at my favorite restaurant, Ralph's, here in south Philly, we catch the trolley, and we go downtown to the theater. She seems very nervous but excited to see this movie. I tell Romania that I too have heard a lot about this film and if what I hear is true, this movie should be great to watch.

As we walk into the Boyd Theater, I realize that I have been here many times since it opened back on December 25, 1918. This time is special. I am with Romania. It has almost 2,400 seats to entertain people, and tonight, many of those seats are taken. The grand lobby is lined with huge etched glass mirrors and has an area carpet imported from Czechoslovakia. It is a movie theater palace. When walking in the front doors, I feel like royalty with its three-level foyer and dazzling colorful mirrors that are two stories high. Just walking into the foyer of the theater is breath taking. We take our seats in the balcony section. Sitting high in our seats, and looking at all the wonders of workmanship is fascinating for Romania and me.

A few times during the movie, Romania grabs my arm or hand, whichever is the quickest for her to squeeze onto tightly. She does make me laugh with her child-like behavior. I am teasing her and telling her to watch out because Frankenstein is coming to her house tonight. We have so much fun and pleasure being with each other. I forget all my worries when I am with her. To spend the rest of my life with her would be a pleasure for me. Being with Romania would be my answer from God to my prayer to live a good life with someone who I love, and I feel loves me also.

After the movie is over, we walk to the trolley stop. Romania hasn't stopped talking about Frankenstein and how big and ugly he is. As she keeps on talking, I just nod my head in approval of whatever she is saying. She gets so excited about the smallest things. To her, life is such a wonderment.

She looks at me and is laughing so hard that whatever she is trying to tell me, she can't get the words out. She even has me laughing—at what? I don't know, other than it's funny to her. Once she settles down and can speak, she tells me that the girls at work have given me a nickname, but I may not be happy to hear what it is. She's back to laughing again. I sit patiently till she can tell me what they call me. *Maybe,* I am thinking, *I might not want to know.*

Romania clears her throat and sits straight up in her seat. Without hesitation, she says loudly, "Mike, they call you Frankenstein," and off she is laughing again. This time I join in with her laughing. She continues to tell me, when it's lunchtime at work, she volunteers to go get their lunch, so she can walk by my produce cart. When she returns to the factory, all her co-workers asked if she walked by Frankenstein's cart. She moves very close to me and puts her hands into my hands.

"Because, Michael, all my co-workers know I have fallen madly in love with you. They can call you Frankenstein if they want, they are all jealous anyway. All I know is that when I am around you, I am very happy to be with you. You are 'My Frankenstein.'"

We had our Wednesday night date, every week for three months. One night, on our ride on the trolley car going down Broad Street, I lean in for a kiss from Romania. I can't wait to kiss her. She has beautiful lips. I've been waiting a very long time to do this, but she is bashful, and I don't want to frighten her in any way. I know I am abrasive when dealing with the opposite sex, but Romania is different to me. I can't wait for our next date every time we say good night to each other, and I think to myself, *I have to wait a whole week to talk to her...*

She gently pushes me away. She tells me, "If you are serious about me, and want to hold and kiss me, then you would have to marry me," because she has never been with a man and wants only to be with her husband when the time comes. Well, for me, that was all I needed to hear. I am 30 years old and never felt so in love with the many girls I dated. But she is different. I have to marry Romania. She is the love of my life.

She tells me she will go home and ask her father if she could marry me. The next day, she comes to my cart. Her eyes are swollen, and she is really nervous. I put my arms around her, and she buries her head into my chest. I ask her, "What is bothering you? Has someone hurt you?"

She lifts her head up as tears are streaming down her face, looks me right in the eyes, and says, "My father says I can't marry you. That if I do, he will never speak to me again. Michael, please, I can't go against my father. My mother is in the hospital now for almost four years. I have no siblings, and I have no one but my father."

I look down into her swollen eyes, wipe a tear off her face and tell her, "This will all turn out. Don't worry. I will go and speak to him, and he will understand how we feel for each other."

That night, I go to talk with Pasquale Pescatori. He is a small man but has a strong, handsome face. He is dressed in his suit that Romania told me he wears every day. He is neat in his appearance and has a beautiful gold chain hanging from the pocket in his trousers. This chain is attached to a pocket watch. He is quite dapper.

Romania doesn't come out of her bedroom. She stays in there while I am talking to her father. But when I asked for his daughter's hand in marriage, well, he stood up from his chair, walked over to the front door and says, "Over my dead body. Now, please leave and don't come back here ever again." His face is red, and his eyes are glaring at me. "I will never give my consent for you to marry my daughter. When I wanted to marry Romania's mother in Italia, my mother would not give her consent for me to marry for the same reason I won't give mine. My father stepped in and gave his consent."

I don't understand his instant anger or what he is talking about, "Mr. Pescatori why won't you allow us to marry? We are both in love!"

Mr. Pescatori's face is getting redder by the minute. His breathing is heavy, and I am afraid the old man is going to have a heart attack.

I can hear Romania running down the stairs. She is yelling, "Michael, don't leave... Wait for me."

Mr. Pescatori slams the door in my face. I can hear her saying to her father, "What have you done to me? I want to spend my life with Michael. I love him."

All night, I can't rationalize why Mr. Pescatori wouldn't want us to marry. I walk the streets of South Philly that night for hours. The next day, I see Romania walking down 9th Street by herself. It's early in the morning. She runs toward me and we both embrace. She tells me she will marry me, and one day, her father will forgive us.

On Monday, November 7, 1932, we married in room 415 at City Hall. She only had a suitcase of clothes because that's all she could get out of the house without her father becoming suspicious of her. The only sad moment at the ceremony was when the judge asked if anyone objected to us getting married. At the time, we were holding hands, and her grip got so tight as if she would never let me go. I told her not to worry. The judge completed the ceremony and pronounced us man and wife. I turned towards my wife, knowing I could finally kiss her, and I knew she would kiss me back. Jokingly, I whisper to her, "When I get you home, I then will kiss you passionately as I have wanted to do for months."

She puts her hands over her eyes and giggles.

As time goes by, her father would pass by her on the street and not a word was spoken between the two of them. I know this had to hurt her; my sister Rose couldn't understand this behavior, and neither could I. One day, Rose saw him and informed him that Romania was six months pregnant. Yes, we became pregnant quickly, and our first child Ralph, named after my father, was born nine months later. I have to say, we made a healthy and handsome baby. He has olive skin and lots of dark, curly hair. I can't be prouder to become a father. I hope I will be as good a father to my son, as my father was to me.

Pasquale Pescatori stops at the house one day unannounced. When I open the door and ask him to come in, I can hear Romania asking who is there. When she walks into the living room carrying Ralph in her arms and sees her father, her face shows all the love she has for him. They embrace, and she puts Ralph in his arms. He is a proud man, but I can see tears forming in his eyes. Instead of wiping them away, he decides to let them fall for all to see, so he doesn't have to put his grandson down. Oh, how a baby can melt anyone's heart and take their troubles away. I witnessed this today with my wife and son.

Mr. Pescatore tells me years later, the reason he didn't want me to marry his daughter was because when he was asking for his wife's hand in marriage, his own mother refused to sign the marriage certificate because she felt that Romania's mother's skin was too dark.

"Strange as it may sound, because of this happening to me, I did the same to you. Even before I met you, Romania told me that everyone called you 'Brownie' because your skin is so dark. I am sorry for feeling that way about you because now, I love you as a son."

CHAPTER 50

CHRISTINA'S POV

It's July 1934. The doctors just informed me that I am dying of breast cancer. They have done all they can for me. My husband died in 1930. I went into the Home for the Incurables for Cancer because I will die soon and don't want to burden my nieces and nephews, my sister's children, though I love them as my own. It's located at 4200 Old York Road in Philadelphia.

I hear my oldest niece, Rose, tell Michael that my death will sadden her even more knowing that I never knew true love. She feels I gave up any opportunity to love someone else because I was taking care of my sister and all of her children. I feel it's wrong for her to be burdened with something that is not true, so I will not die before I can tell her of my love story; I know she will share it with the rest of her siblings. I did have a true love, Giovanni in Italia. He was the only man I ever loved. He is my true love who I will take in my heart through eternity. Giovanni had the same feelings towards me. He always told me that he would never let me go. We are meant to be one. Oh, how I loved when he spoke to me about our love. He would tell me I was and would always be, his everything, always.

But as it would be, Giovanni and I would not be together. I would leave him on three occasions. Each time my heart hurt more than the last time. This time, I will take Giovanni in my heart forever. There will be no farewell and no tears. This time, I know he will be with me. I will be able to rest my head on his shoulder and hold onto him without ever letting him go again. He, after all, is my sweet love.

Today, I am going to tell my niece Rose my love story. She is coming to see me and spend time with me today. Rose walks into my room. She has a big smile on her face. She rushes over to me and kisses me on my cheek, then kisses my other cheek. She says to me, "Now, that's Italian. I have some chocolates for you, Aunt Christina, because you told me that chocolates make you feel better."

I reach up, smile, and hold her hand for a second, "Rose, come get a chair and pull it close to me. I want to talk with you today. I want you to hear every word I have to tell you about my life. I have never told anyone my story until now. And who better than you to carry on my story to our family?" I see Rose's eyes open wide with curiosity and excitement. I point to the box of chocolates she brought and say, "Open the box, any good story needs good chocolates! Rose opens the box and puts it on the side of the bed between us, as I reach for one, I say, "You, are the one with the eyes and ears to absorb everything in your brain. So, you can tell the next generation about your Aunt Christina."

I have Rose's full attention now. Her eyes have lit up like stars in the night.

"Please, Aunt Christina, tell me everything! I want to know all about you. You're very special to me and our family."

I turn to Rose, "I want you to protect my story as if it was yours. I want this love to carry on, and I choose you because I have no daughter to pass this on to." I gather my thoughts and begin my story.

"I will start with when I was in Italia as a little girl. My romance with Giovanni started when we were just kids, playing in the hills of Ateleta, running through the hills, chasing each other; laughing and not wanting our happiness to ever end. We would meet every Sunday after church. I would take your mother, Geltrude, with me, and Giovanni would bring his younger brother, Franco with him. We would meet every Sunday at the church. We never stayed for the entire Mass. As soon as no one was watching, out the four of us would go."

I saw Rose take another chocolate; I can see she is already absorbed in the story.

"We had so much fun, running and chasing each other all over the hills. I still can feel the wind and sun when I close my eyes. I haven't felt this since I was a child. Oh, how I wish I was there just one more time with him. We all were so full of life and had many questions and wonderment about it. We did this for six years without any problem."

I sigh and drink some water.

"When I turned 14 years old, my parents wouldn't allow me to play with Giovanni. They told me Giovanni was becoming a man, and I was becoming a woman. And we should not be running and chasing each other anymore. Now, how they knew about us in the hills on Sundays, I never found out. But it was the end of our childhood as we knew it to be."

Rose says, "My parents always seemed to know what we were doing, even when we thought we were being clever."

I nod and continue, "My parents told me I had to be home to take care of my mother and our house. My mother was sickly, and she could no longer cook, clean, and take care of the vegetable garden. It was all on me because Geltrude was still too young to take on the responsibility of the chores alone."

I reach for another chocolate just as Rose does, and we share a smile.

"I just got to see Giovanni one more time behind my parents' backs. I needed to tell him I couldn't see him anymore, and I no longer would be at Mass or go into the hills with him. I would cry every night before I would fall asleep. All I wanted was to see and hear Giovanni's voice. My heart ached each and every minute of every day. I went to church the next Sunday to see him. I ran up the steps and inside the church. He and Franco were sitting in the same pew as always. I sat next to Giovanni, and he turned and smiled at me. But I couldn't hold my tears in any longer. He took my arm and got me out of the pew and down the steps outside. He was trying to calm me down and was asking what is wrong, he wanted to know why I was crying."

Rose's hand goes to her mouth. I can see she is sad for me. I love this child so much! I pat her arm and continue, "I looked at him, and I could see he had no idea about what I was going to say to him. I remember my exact words, I said, 'Giovanni, I am trying to say I can't see you anymore. My parents told me I no longer can see you. I must say goodbye to you.' I quickly gave him a fast hug. I turned around and ran as fast as I could, because if I didn't, I would turn back to him. I was so sick and shaking badly. I couldn't keep my composure. I could hear Giovanni's shoes hitting the stones in the road, but I kept running till I was at the bottom of the hill."

I remember this as if it was yesterday. I have to wipe a tear from my eye. I continue, "I caught my breath and started walking home when all of a sudden, someone grabbed me from behind. As I turned, I knew in my heart it was Giovanni. He had a hold on both of my shoulders. With his voice quivering, he said, 'Christina, what are you saying? You don't want to see me? You don't care for me?' Now he hits me with the hardest blow of all. 'You do realize you are my best friend, and I can't wait every day for Sunday because of you.'

"As he was still talking, I said to him, 'I can't see you. My parents won't allow me. They don't even know I am with you now. Giovanni, please let me go. I must get home before they know I am missing.' I kissed his cheek as I was turning away from him. I heard him say to me, 'Christina, I will come and get you one day!'"

I look at Rose and gave her a small smile.

"I was so heartbroken. How would I ever get over the love I had for Giovanni?"

"Oh, Aunt Christina, I am so sorry! That is so sad!"

I hold my hand up and say, "The story doesn't end there. A few years later, I heard that Giovanni's family had a store at the market selling the cheeses they made. Giovanni worked there every day. I thought Geltrude and I could take a walk over to the market, and we could stop at his store, so that's exactly what we did. I was so thrilled, thinking I was going to see Giovanni on Saturday. When we got there and I saw him in the store, I froze, I couldn't walk in there. I was pushed inside by Geltrude; until this day, I don't know if I ever would have walked inside. I was standing at the entrance of his shop and saw him staring at me. He walked over to me because I was paralyzed. I couldn't move a muscle or get my mouth to speak. He said, 'Can we go outside to talk?' He took my hand and we walked outside. I told Geltrude, 'Stay inside, and I will come in when it's time to go.' I didn't want her to hear our conversation. I turned towards Giovanni to tell him how much I had missed him, and he said, 'Before you say anything to me, I have something to tell you. So, please allow me to talk first. Come, Christina. Let's sit under this big tree here.'

"I had butterflies in my stomach. We hadn't seen each other for so long, yet I felt the same excitement I did before. I smiled at him as his leg brushed my leg as he sat next to me. He took a deep breath and continued, 'I know I am 18 years old now, I am a man. My parents believe it's time I should think about marriage. At first Christina, I thought they were talking about you. But no, they had someone else in mind. You know the family Rizzo? They have a daughter, Angela, who is also 18 years old. Well, my father told me that we are to get married in one month. My family and her family arranged the marriage. My father tells me this will help our family to prosper in life. I must do this for my family. Please understand that there is no one I want to be with other than you. But my parents need help with their cow farm, and you know the Rizzo family has money. Their farm is much larger than ours. Without them, my family will lose everything. I have to help them now. I must put aside my feelings for you.'"

I hear Rose say, "Oh no! That's horrible! He didn't go through with it, did he, Aunt Christina?" I can see that Rose was deciding to hate Giovanni, so I remind her that things were different in Italia. Before I can say anything more, she says, "I know, I know, please continue."

I take a deep breath and say, "I heard myself yelling at him. I jumped up from under the tree just about ready to run, then I changed my mind. Now I was ready to fight him. I had so much sadness and anger inside of me that I just wanted to hit him. I don't know who I was right then. I think maybe I was acting crazy because Geltrude came out of the shop and stood in between us. She looked at me and said, 'Calm down! Someone else will hear you. You are so loud.' She put her arms around me to calm me down. I was so broken hearted.

"Giovanni said to Geltrude. 'Please take her home. Tell her I am truly sorry about this marriage, but I can't stop it.' We walked home together. Geltrude and I held hands the entire way, never saying one word. When we got inside our house, I turned to Geltrude and told her we are never to speak about Giovanni. EVER."

I take another breath, and Rose hands me another chocolate and takes one herself. She motions for me to continue the story.

"Then things got quite confusing in my life because shortly after that, Geltrude went to America, leaving me there to take care of everything with our parents. So, I was really lonely and heartbroken to lose both of my loves. The two people I loved more than myself."

I stop and look at Rose, "These chocolates are delicious! Where did you get them?"

Rose rolls her eyes and says, "Who cares! Get back to the story, I know there has to be more!"

"Whenever I had a chance to encounter Giovanni, I went after it like there was nothing else in my life. Which happened to be the truth. I did miss him more than words could say. But I knew we could never be together.

"Giovanni did marry as he said he was going to do. In his first five years of marriage, they had three children. I didn't see him or his family in those years. But one day, I was at the fabric store, and in walks a lady with her children. The shopkeeper says, 'Hello Mrs. Vito.' She was picking up her fabric for her daughters' dresses. Her name was Angela Vito, the wife of Giovanni Vito. I could have fainted, but I didn't. I had to look her over and her children because she had the life I wanted with Giovanni." I stop talking because I realize how crazy I must sound to Rose. "Please, Rose, I don't want you to think I am crazy. It was just a life and love with a man I couldn't have in my lifetime."

Rose looks at me with complete understanding and nods her head.

"As Angela was walking out, her youngest daughter ran right into me. I let out a small yell because she had also jumped on my feet. When her mother heard me, she came over to me and apologized for the bad behavior of her daughter. I smiled at her and said, 'Please, your daughter didn't mean to hurt me. She's just a little girl.' She turned towards her daughter and said, 'Christina, tell her you're sorry.' And little Christina did. I couldn't help thinking, did Giovanni name her after me? I believe he did.

"As I was leaving the shop with my fabric, Giovanni and his family were standing there. Our eyes locked, and his wife said, 'Giovanni, this is the lady that our little Christina jumped on her feet.' I smiled at him and said, 'Please, your daughter Christina didn't hurt me.' His wife looked at me and asked me what my name is. Without hesitation, I said, 'Christina DiLullo.' She said, 'I have heard that name before, but I can't remember where.' I looked at her and wished her a good day."

Rose grabs my hand and says, "Oh Aunt Christina, your heart had to be broken when seeing them. Is that when you came to America? You know we all feel blessed to have you in our lives." I hold her hand and smile a secret smile, the kind of smile that girlfriends share when telling secrets. Rose notices it and breaths in a sharp breath, "Oh, that wasn't the end, was it? Oh, please continue!"

"The next day Giovanni came to my house. He walked right in, grabbed me, and kissed me with such force that I almost fell to the floor. We both were laughing at how clumsy he was with me, but I didn't really mind his clumsiness and was overwhelmed at his presence. We talked for four hours, and I didn't want him to leave me again. But he had a family, and I knew that's where he belonged. He was not in love with his wife but did love his three girls. We saw each other for about six months. But by now, my parents were both dead. And he would never leave his wife, and I would not ask him to do that because of his daughters.

"So Rose, I realized there was no future in Italia for me. I decided to pack my belongings and to travel to be with my sister in America."

CHAPTER 51

MICHAEL'S POV

Here I am again at Baldi Funeral Home, this time to bury my beloved Aunt Christina. I feel exhausted and emotionally drained. Aunt Christina and my mother will be together now.

My heart is as heavy today for my aunt as it was nine years ago for my mother. The two most important mother figures in my life are gone now. What does a man do without the love of all of the protectors who watched over him? I will never feel love like that again. Even in death, you couldn't separate the two of them. I am sure they are holding onto each other's hands and smiling with their eyes sparkling like stars. Oh, they both were so beautiful. They definitely looked, acted, and spoke Italian. With their dark brown hair, eyes shaped like large almonds and the color of black olives. Their eyes watched every move everyone took. They both never missed a trick; it was so funny to watch them.

As I look around the room, I never realized Aunt Christina knew so many people. They are all here to pay their respect to her. There were many people who attended my mother's funeral, but I didn't know Aunt Christina was loved as much.

As I am greeting and thanking the people for attending the funeral service, I notice an older lady at the coffin. She is kneeling and holding her black rosary beads in her hands. She is dressed from head to toe in black. Her lips are moving, and you can hear her saying prayers. She now is touching Aunt Christina's hands. She stands up and bends over Aunt Christina and kisses her forehead.

I walk over to her because I have never seen this woman before. Why would she show such respect for Aunt Christina? She's certainly not family. At least I don't think so, but at times I wonder, what do I know? I gently take her arm and escort her to a chair. We both sit down. I introduce myself and ask, "How do you know my aunt?"

She smiles at me and says, "You're Michael Pasquarello, Christina's nephew. She spoke of you often to me! I was hoping we would get to say hello to one another. My name is Maria Palumbo and I too am from the village where your mother and aunt are from. Our beautiful Ateleta."

I nod and ask, "Is that where you knew them or when you came here to America?"

"I knew them in Ateleta, and I came here about 10 years ago, in October 1924, to live with my daughter here in South Philadelphia. I knew your aunt when she was a young girl. She and my nephew were in love." Maria smiles and continues, "Giovanni and Christina would come to my house and visit with me. Giovanni was like a son to me. So, when the two of them would visit, it was like my having two young lovers in my home. It was very warming to my heart. I loved Christina. She was very gentle and loving towards Giovanni. She would have made him a good wife, and they would have had a beautiful life together..." her smile fades as she speaks, "If his father, my brother, didn't forbid him to see her again. His father made him marry someone else. His father felt that Giovanni's life would be easier if they had money. The girl he married came from a well-to-do family. But he didn't love her. What his father didn't realize was that if they would have allowed Giovanni and Christina to marry, marrying Christina and having her love would have made him rich in love and life."

She sighs and shakes her head, "Poor Giovanni was never happy after Christina refused to ever speak to him again. When he writes to me, he always, always asks if your aunt is still warm and beautiful.

It's been over 30 years, and he still loves her. I will get my daughter to write Giovanni a letter this evening and tell him of Christina's passing. I know his heart will break again because she was his love, his one and only love in this life. His heart will be broken all over again."

She looks up at me with soulful eyes, and her voice becomes softer, "Christina didn't marry till she was 39 years old and never had children. They both suffered for the life they never had together. He is still married and his children are grown, but never has had happiness with his wife as he did with Christina." She shakes her head as if clearing out a bad memory, looks up and smiles at me. "Michael, I have talked your head off. I hope you don't mind. I know you didn't know about Giovanni and her because she only talked with me and your mother about Giovanni and her pain. So you see, Michael, your Aunt Christina had a very, very hard life and still remained loving towards everyone.

"I look forward to seeing you again so we can talk about life and how it can affect us in one way or another. Don't wait too long, Michael. I am 95 years old and don't have much time on this Earth."

"Mrs. Palumbo, thank you for all the family history. It's interesting to hear something about Aunt Christina that I didn't know."

"Michael, you're welcome and would you please take me outside? My son-in-law is waiting for me in his car." When I take Mrs. Palumbo to her son-in-law's car, she turns to me and kisses me on both my cheeks. Her son-in-law puts her into the front seat. He shakes my hand and expresses his condolences for the passing of Aunt Christina. I thank him and stand on the sidewalk, watching as he pulls out of the parking spot. I am frozen in time thinking about Aunt Christina and Giovanni's love story.

As I walk up the steps into Baldi's Funeral Home, I tell myself that I am lucky because the woman I married is the woman I want to spend the rest of my life with. Then I whisper to the sky, "I love you, Aunt Christina!"

CHAPTER 52

We are all saddened by Aunt Christina's death. I will never forget my Aunt Christina and her kindness. She left me papers for me to read after her death. She wanted to be buried with my mother, her sister, which, of course, is where we laid her to rest. There also is a letter enclosed inside a sealed envelope with "Michael" written on it. Aunt Christina wanted me to know why my mother, in her delirious state, was apologizing to her father over and over again. It read:

> Dear Michael,
>
> As I promised you, here is some family history about your grandfather and mother. It started with a big trip to Naples. Your grandfather and some of his friends would go once a year, and they would be gone for three to four days on their journey. They went to get household items and fabrics. The men would have a good time being together. And there was always wine tasting going on. So, lots of time spent in Naples was drinking wine.
>
> When your grandfather that summer went, he met an older gentleman who wanted a young wife who would give him many babies. He was wealthy and owned a pottery business; others would use his pottery to ship wine to faraway places.
>
> He wasn't a good-looking man, and he also didn't like to get washed. But anyway, he asked my father if he had a young, beautiful daughter. And your grandfather replied, "Yes, I do. Her name is Geltrude Carmela, and she

is 16 years old. Beautiful, smart and a hard worker. She can run the goats and garden just like a man, maybe even better." Well, this man (and I don't remember his name) asked if he could come home and meet Geltrude, and your grandfather agreed.

This man came to our house and stayed with us for five days and four nights. He was foul, not only his body smell; but he was disagreeable with everything your grandfather said. And your grandmother hated him deeply. She wanted to throw him back to Naples herself. When your mother told your grandfather how unhappy she was, he told her it was too late. That he had already taken some money, and "Geltrude, you must go to Naples and marry this summer."

Your mother cried and cried because she wasn't having any of this. She told your grandfather that if she had to marry this man, she would hang herself from a tree. That she wouldn't marry that old man if he was the last man on Earth.

Your grandfather didn't know what to do. How could this happen and how would he be able to pay back the money he already took from him? He had spent it on getting materials to add more rooms to our house. On his last day at our house, he went to your mother and told her she would come back with him to Naples. They would live there. That he had a large house and had many servants to wait on them.

Your mother did what she does best. That is, she isn't going to do something that she doesn't want to. So, she told him she was already pregnant and would give birth in seven months. So, she couldn't go to Naples until after she gave birth. Sometime in the spring.

Well, that man went crazy calling her all sorts of

names and demanded his money back. And he wanted
all of his money before he went back to Naples by him-
self. Your grandfather had to borrow the money to pay
him back. Everyone in our village knew what your
mother had said. She was the talk of the village. My
father was angry with her for a long time but did come to
understand that the marriage would have been an un-
happy one for Geltrude. So, two years later when your
mother had the opportunity to come to America, your
grandfather told her: "No matter what you say or do, you
are going to marry someone there and be as happy as
you can be."

I cried and laughed a little when I read this story about my
mother. I am very happy it turned out to be this way. Now I understand why my mother continued to keep saying how sorry she was
to her father. She wanted his forgiveness for something she chose
to do, or not do with her life.

As many of our family members are no longer here with us,
another cycle begins. I am married with a child now. I hope my
grandparents and parents are proud of me, just like I am of them!
They came from Italia and built a life in a New Land. They had a
family, worked hard, and showed their children how to do the same.
Without them, we wouldn't have had the opportunities given to us,
to work hard to get what we had chosen for our lives. I couldn't be
happier being married to my beautiful Romania. She makes me
happy but can also drive me crazy. But secretly, building a family
with my beautiful wife is the joy of my life. Maybe that's the secret
to life, to make the next generation better than mine, with children
made from love.

EPILOGUE

It's May, and the sun is shining! My wife along with rest of my family and many neighbors are all here together at 9th and Washington. It's Sunday, and at first, I was annoyed with all of the noise and activity in my house and out in the street. I'm holding my son; my wife and other siblings are all watching for the Procession of the Saints. I can see the statues coming down the street. They are slowing down now for the Blessing of the Market. My only thoughts are about heading home and smelling my supper cooking on the stove. I have another full week of work coming up and was hoping to enjoy a quiet day.

As I look around, I notice an elderly couple with tears streaming down their faces as they watch the blessing and get ready to pin money to a ribbon that is dangling down from the statue of the Blessed Mother. This statue is being carried by members of the Saint Mary Magdalen de' Pazzi Church; this is the first Italian church built in Philadelphia.

I'm not sure what happens, but I go from being my normal grumpy, disagreeable self to an emotional mess in seconds! It hits me like lightning the moment I watched the older couple bless themselves after pinning their money to the ribbon. They both have tears coming down their faces as they look around at the crowd. They look to be the same age as my parents would have been, if they were still alive. My parents would have loved this parade, an Italian parade! When my mother came here from Italia, Italians weren't allowed in the Mummers Parade, and now, we have our own parade! And even better, this parade stops to bless our own marketplace. Back when my parents got married, my mother had to stay in the Italian section and shop in this marketplace. Now, other people from other sections of Philadelphia travel here to purchase goods from the Italian market.

I have been so busy and lost, working constantly, enjoying the little things and the love of my family, that I haven't stepped back to see how far we have come because of the hard work and dedication of people like my parents and grandparents.

I close my eyes and quietly thank my parents; I can feel them here with me. How far we have all come because of their strength, sacrifices, and the values they have ingrained in us! I feel my son's chubby hand touch my face. I open my eyes and look at him. I find myself looking into my own eyes and those of my father's. I always thought my parents' story was a sad one, a story of suffering, disease, and finally death. How wrong I have been this whole time! Looking in my son's eyes, I now see life, happiness, and love.

Looking around at my wife and family laughing and enjoying themselves, I realize now, this is what life is all about. It's about appreciating all of the love our parents have given us, continuing to love our families the same way, and never taking anything life gives us for granted; especially time. I wish my parents had more time with us. I wish they could see how all of their children grew up and how we all value our memories of them and will instill their values into our own children.